The Life Boat

Charlotte Rogan

W F HOWES LTD

This large print edition published in 2012 by
W F Howes Ltd
Unit 4, Rearsby Business Park, Gaddesby Lane,
Rearsby, Leicester LE7 4YH

1 3 5 7 9 10 8 6 4 2

First published in the United Kingdom in 2012
by Virago Press

A CIP catalogue record for this book is available
from the British Library

ISBN 978 1 40749 965 9

Typeset by Palimpsest Book Production Limited,
Falkirk, Stirlingshire
Printed and bound in Great Britain
by MPG Books Ltd, Bodmin, Cornwall

For Kevin
And for Olivia, Stephanie, and Nick
With love

I shall sing of the flood to all people. Listen!

The Myth of Atrahasis, last lines

PROLOGUE

Today I shocked the lawyers, and it surprised me, the effect I could have on them. A thunderstorm arose as we were leaving the court for lunch. They dashed for cover under the awning of a nearby shop to save their suits from getting wet, while I stood in the street and opened my mouth to it, transported back and seeing again that other rain as it came at us in gray sheets. I had lived through that downpour, but the moment in the street was my first notion that I could live it again, that I could be immersed in it, that it could again be the tenth day in the lifeboat, when it began to rain.

The rain had been cold, but we welcomed it. At first it had been no more than a teasing mist, but as the day progressed, it began to come down in earnest. We held our faces up to it, mouths open, drenching our swollen tongues. Mary Ann could not or would not part her lips, either to drink or to speak. She was a woman of my age. Hannah, who was only a little older, slapped her hard and said, 'Open your mouth, or I'll open it for you!' Then she grabbed Mary Ann and pinched her nostrils until she was forced to gasp for air. The two of them sat for a long time in a sort of violent embrace while Hannah held Mary Ann's jaws open, allowing the gray and saving rain to enter her, drop by drop.

'Come, come!' said Mr Reichmann, who is the head of the little band of lawyers hired by my mother-in-law, not because she cares one jot about what happens to me, but because she thinks it will reflect badly on the family if I am convicted. Mr Reichmann and his associates were calling to me from the sidewalk, but I pretended not to hear them. It made them very angry not to be heard or, rather, not to be heeded, which is a different and far more insulting thing, I imagine, to those used to speaking from podiums, to those who regularly have the attention of judges and juries and people sworn to truth or silence and whose freedom hangs on the particular truths they choose to tell. When I finally wrenched myself away and joined them, shivering and drenched to the bone but smiling to myself, glad to have rediscovered the small freedom of my imagination, they asked, 'What kind of trick was that? Whatever were you doing, Grace? Have you gone mad?'

Mr Glover, who is the nicest of the three, put his coat around my dripping shoulders, but soon the fine silk lining was soaked through and probably ruined, and while I was touched Mr Glover had offered his coat, I would much rather it had been the coat of the handsome, heavy-set William Reichmann that had been ruined in the rain.

‘I was thirsty,’ I said, and I was thirsty still.

‘But the restaurant is just there. It’s less than a block away. You can have any sort of drink you like in a minute or two,’ said Mr Glover while the others pointed and made encouraging noises. But I was thirsty for rain and salt water, for the whole boundless ocean of it.

‘That’s very funny,’ I said, laughing to think that I was free to choose my drink, when a drink of any sort wasn’t something I wanted. I had spent the previous two weeks in prison, and I was only free pending the outcome of a proceeding that was now in progress. Unable to restrain my laughter, which kept lapping at my insides and bursting out of me like gigantic waves, I was not allowed to accompany the lawyers into the dining room, but had to have my meal brought to me in the cloakroom, where a wary clerk perched vigilantly on a stool in the corner as I pecked at my sandwich. We sat there like two birds, and I giggled to myself until my sides ached and I thought I might be sick.

‘Well,’ said Mr Reichmann when the lawyers rejoined me after the meal, ‘we’ve been discussing this thing, and an insanity defense doesn’t seem so far-fetched after all.’ The idea that I had a mental disorder filled them with happy optimism. Where before lunch they had been nervous and pessimistic, now they lit cigarettes and congratulated one another on cases I knew nothing about. They had apparently put their heads together, considered my mental state and found it lacking on some score, and, now that the initial shock of my behavior had worn off and they had discovered that it could perhaps be explained scientifically and might even be exploited in the conduct of our case, they took turns patting me on the arm and saying, 'Don't you worry, my dear girl. After all, you've been through quite enough. Leave it to us, we've done this sort of thing a thousand times before.' They talked about a Dr Cole and said, 'I'm sure you will find him very sympathetic,' then rattled off a list of credentials that meant less than nothing to me.

I don't know who had the idea, whether it was Glover or Reichmann or even that mousy Ligget, that I should try to recreate the events of those twenty-one days and that the resulting 'diary' might be entered as some kind of exonerating exhibit.

'In that case, we'd better present her as sane, or the whole thing will be discounted,' said Mr Ligget tentatively, as if he were speaking out of turn.

'I suppose you're right,' agreed Mr Reichmann, stroking his long chin. 'Let's see what she comes up with before we decide.' They laughed and poked the air with their cigarettes and talked about me as if I weren't there as we walked back to the courthouse where, along with two other women named Hannah West and Ursula Grant, I was to stand trial for my life. I was twenty-two years old. I had been married for ten weeks and a widow for over six.

PART I

DAY ONE

The first day in the lifeboat we were mostly silent, either taking in or refusing to take in the drama playing itself out in the seething waters around us. John Hardie, an able-bodied seaman and the only crew member on board Lifeboat 14, took immediate charge. He assigned seats based on weight distribution, and because the lifeboat was riding low in the water, he forbade anyone to stand up or move without permission. Then he wrested a rudder from where it was stored underneath the seats, fixed it into place at the back of the boat, and commanded anyone who knew how to row a boat to take up one of four long oars, which were quickly appropriated by three of the men and a sturdy woman named Mrs Grant. Hardie gave them orders to gain as much distance from the foundering craft as possible, saying, 'Row yer bloody hearts out, unless ye want to be sucked under to yer doom!'

Mr Hardie stood with his feet planted and his eyes alert, guiding us deftly around anything that blocked our way, while the four rowed in silence, their muscles straining and their knuckles white. Some of the others grabbed on to the ends of the long oars to help with the effort, but they were unpracticed, and the blades were as apt to skip over or slice through the water as they were to push against it broadside, the way they were designed to do. I pressed my feet against the floor of the boat in sympathy, and with every stroke I tensed my shoulders as if this would magically further our cause. Occasionally Mr Hardie would break the shocked silence by saying things like 'Two hundred meters farther out and we'll be safe,' or 'Ten minutes 'til she goes under, twelve at most,' or 'Ninety percent of the women and children have been saved.' I found comfort in his words, even though I had just seen a mother toss her little girl into the water, then jump in after her and disappear. Whether Mr Hardie had witnessed this or not, I did not know, but I suspected he had, for the black eyes darting about beneath his heavy brows seemed to absorb every detail of our situation. In any case, I did not correct him or even consider him to be guilty of a lie. Instead, I saw him as a leader trying to inspire confidence in his troops.

Because ours had been one of the last lifeboats to be launched, the water before us was congested. I saw two boats collide as they tried to avoid a mass of floating debris, and a calm center of my mind was able to understand that Mr Hardie was aiming for a patch of clear water away from the rest. He had lost his cap, and with his wild-looking hair and fiery eyes, he seemed as suited to disaster as we were terrified by it. 'Put yer backs into it, mates!' he shouted, 'show me what yer made of!' and the people with the oars redoubled their efforts. At the same time, there was a series of explosions behind us, and the cries and screams of the people still on board the *Empress Alexandra* or in the water near it sounded as hell must sound, if it exists. I glanced back and saw the large hulk of the ocean liner shudder and roll, and for the first time I noticed orange flames licking at the cabin windows.

We passed jagged splinters of wood and half-submerged barrels and snake-like lengths of twisted rope. I recognized a deck chair and a straw hat and what looked like a child's doll floating together, bleak reminders of the pretty weather we had experienced only that morning and of the holiday mood that had pervaded the ship. When we came upon three smaller casks bobbing in a group, Mr Hardie shouted 'Aha!' and directed the men to take two of them on board, then stored them underneath the triangular seat formed by the pointed aft end of the boat. He assured us they contained fresh water and that once we had been saved from the vortex created by the foundering ship, we might need to be saved from thirst and starvation; but I could not think that far ahead. To my mind, the railing of our little vessel was already perilously close to the surface of the water, and I could only believe that to stop for anything at all would decrease our chances of reaching that critical distance from the sinking ship.

There were bodies floating in the water, too, and living people clung to the wreckage – I saw another mother and child, the white-faced child holding out its hands toward me and screaming. As we came closer, we could see that the mother was dead, her body draped lifelessly over a wooden plank and her blonde hair fanned out around her in the green water. The boy wore a miniature bow tie and suspenders, and it seemed to me ridiculous for the mother to dress him in such an unsuitable way, even though I had always been one to admire fine and proper dress and even though I myself was weighted down by a corset and petticoats and soft calfskin boots, not long ago purchased in London. One of the men yelled, 'A little more this way and we can get to the child!' But Hardie replied, 'Fine, and which one o' ye wants to trade places with 'im?'

Mr Hardie had a rough seaman's voice. I could not always understand the things he said, but this served only to increase my faith in him. He knew about this world of water, he spoke its language, and the less I understood him, the greater the possibility that he was understood by the sea. No one had an answer for him, and we passed the howling child by. A slight man sitting near me grumbled, 'Certainly we can trade those casks for the poor creature!' but this would now have involved turning the boat around, and our passions on behalf of the child, which had flared briefly, were already part of our sinking past, so we held our silence. Only the slight man spoke, but his thin voice was barely audible above the rhythmic groaning of the oarlocks, the roar of the inferno, and the cacophony of human voices issuing instructions or screams of distress: 'It's only a young boy. How much could such a small fellow weigh?' I later learned that the speaker was an Anglican deacon, but at the time I did not know the names or callings of my fellow passengers. No one answered him. Instead, the rowers bent to their tasks and the rest of us bent with them, for it seemed the only thing we could do.

Not long afterwards, we encountered three swimmers making their way toward us with strong strokes. One by one they grabbed on to the lifeline that was fitted around the perimeter of our boat, putting enough weight on it that curls of water began to spill in over the edge. One of the men caught my eye. His face was clean-shaven and livid with cold, but there was no mistaking the clear light of relief that shone out from his ice-blue eyes. On Hardie's orders, the oarsman sitting nearest him beat one set of hands away before beginning on the hands of the blue-eyed man. I heard the crack of wood against bone. Then Hardie raised his heavy boot and shoved it into the man's face, eliciting a cry of anguished surprise. It was impossible to look away, and never have I had more feeling for a human being than I had for that unnamed man.

If I describe what was happening on the starboard side of Lifeboat 14, I of necessity give the impression that one thousand other dramas were not taking place in the turbulent waters to port and astern. Somewhere out there was my husband Henry, either sitting in a boat beating away people as we were doing, or trying to swim to safety and being beaten away himself. It helped to remember that Henry had been forceful in securing me a seat in the boat, and I was sure he would have been just as forceful on his own behalf; but could Henry have acted as Hardie did if his life depended on it? Could I? The idea of Mr Hardie's cruelty was something to which my thoughts continue to return – certainly it was horrendous, certainly none of the rest of us would have had the strength to make the horrific and instantaneous decisions required of a leader at that point, and certainly it is this that saved us. I question whether it can even be called cruelty when any other action would have meant our certain death.

There was no wind, but even in the flat sea, water occasionally splashed in over the side of the overburdened boat. A few days ago, the lawyers conducted an experiment proving that one more adult of average weight in a boat of that size and type would have put us in immediate jeopardy. We could not save everybody and save ourselves. Mr Hardie knew this and had the courage to act on the knowledge, and it was his actions in those first minutes and hours that spelled the difference between continued existence and a watery grave. His actions were also what turned Mrs Grant, who was the strongest and most vocal of the women, against him. Mrs Grant said, 'Brute! Go back and save the child, at least,' but it must have been clear to her that we could not go back and escape with our lives. With those words, however, Mrs Grant was branded a humanitarian and Hardie a fiend.

There were examples of nobility as well. The stronger women tended to the weaker ones, and it is a testament to the oarsmen that we so quickly distanced ourselves from the foundering ship. Mr Hardie, for his part, was staunchly determined to save us, and he immediately distinguished those of us consigned to his care from those outside of it. It took the rest of us longer to make that distinction. For several days, I tended to identify less with Lifeboat 14 than I did with my fellow first-class travelers from the *Empress Alexandra*, and who wouldn't? Despite the difficulties of recent years, I was used to luxury. Henry had paid over five hundred dollars for our first-class passage, and I still saw myself arriving triumphantly in the city of my birth, not as the bedraggled survivor of a shipwreck and not as the daughter of a failed businessman, but as a guest at some welcoming dinner, clothed in dresses and jewelry that were now resting in the weedy murk at the bottom of the sea. I imagined Henry at long last introducing me to his mother, whose resistance to my charms evaporated now that our marriage was a fait accompli. And I imagined the men who had swindled my father elbowing their way through the crowd only to be publicly rebuffed by everyone they met. Hardie, to his credit or damnation, adjusted to our new circumstances immediately, an ability I attribute to his seaman's soul and the fact that he had long ago lost his finer sensibilities, if he had ever had them. He had strapped a knife around his waist and replaced his lost cap with a rag of unknown origin, which made a stark contrast to the gold buttons of his jacket; but these changes to his uniform seemed evidence of his readiness and adaptability and only served to heighten the trust I placed in him. When I finally thought to look around for other lifeboats, they had become distant specks, which seemed to me a good sign, for the open sea was a place of relative safety after the chaos and turbulence surrounding the wreck.

Mr Hardie gave the weakest of the women the choicest seats and called us 'ma'am'. He asked after our well-being as though there were something he could do about it; and at first the women returned the favor and lied that they were fine, even though anyone could see that Mrs Fleming's wrist hung at an odd angle and that a Spanish governess named Maria was badly suffering from shock. It was Mrs Grant who fashioned a sling for Mrs Fleming's arm, and it was Mrs Grant who first wondered aloud how Hardie came to be in our boat. We found out later that while emergency protocols called for a trained seaman in each lifeboat, Captain Sutter and most of the crew had remained with the ship, helping others into the lifeboats and trying to maintain order after panic had set in. We had seen for ourselves across the slowly increasing distance that the frantic haste with which crew and passengers alike tried to dispatch the lifeboats was counterproductive, for the foundering vessel was tilting dramatically, a condition made worse as her contents crashed and shifted within her, so that by the time our lifeboat was being lowered, it was no longer a straight line down from the deck to the water. Not only was the smaller craft in constant danger of hitting the steep incline of the ship's side or catching against it and tipping, but the men working the pulleys had to struggle mightily to lower the fore and aft ends at the same rate. A boat that was launched immediately after ours turned completely upside down and dumped its entire load of women and children into the sea. We saw them screaming and flailing about in the water, but we did nothing to help them, and without Hardie to direct us, it stood to reason that we would have suffered a similar fate. After all that has happened, I can answer my own question in the affirmative: if Mr Hardie hadn't beaten people away from the side of our boat, I would have had to do it myself.

NIGHT

We had been in the lifeboat for perhaps five hours when the sky turned a deep pink, shading to blue, then purple, and the sun seemed to inflate as it dropped toward the darkening line of water to the west. In the distance we could see the black shapes of other lifeboats, bobbing the way we were bobbing, set down in that pink and black vastness with nothing to do but wait, our fortunes in the hands of other crews and other sea captains who must by now have heard of our distress.

I had been anxious for dark to fall because of a pressing need to relieve my bladder. Mr Hardie had explained the mechanism by which this was to be done. It involved, for the ladies, using one of the three wooden bailers, whose primary purpose was to scoop excess water out of the bottom of the boat. He stumbled awkwardly over his words as he suggested that one of the bailers be put in the possession of Mrs Grant and that we were to tell her when we had need of it and were to switch places with someone who was sitting at the railing whenever nature dictated that we need this sort of service. 'Hech!' said Mr Hardie, looking up from under his heavy eyebrows in an almost comical way. 'There, that's that! I'm sure ye'll figure it out.' He who had seemed so sure of himself when, only minutes earlier, he had gone over a list of supplies carried by each of the lifeboats and explained the use of each one was rendered progressively speechless by this task.

When the orange rim of the sun had completely disappeared, I took my turn with the bailer at the rail. To my dismay, I noticed that while the sky had turned dark and night had fully fallen, the black had texture to it, and sources of light, and shadows, and behind the shadows, eyes. I was distressed to find that night-time was not the concealing cover I had been expecting, and also that our quarters were so cramped there was no disguising the action I was performing. I thanked whatever forces had a hand in arranging things that I was surrounded mostly by women and that they were delicate of feeling and pretended not to notice what I was doing. We were in similar circumstances, after all, and an unspoken etiquette was arising where we would not look the beast of physical necessity in the eye. We would ignore it, we would dare it to claw apart our sense of decorum, we would preserve civility even in the face of a disaster that had almost killed us and that might kill us yet.

I was immensely relieved on several counts when the task was finished. I had been so preoccupied with how I would accomplish it that I had scarcely paid attention to Mr Hardie's accounting of our circumstances and inventory of supplies. Now I was able to realize that each of the lifeboats had come stocked with five blankets, a life ring with a long rope attached, the three wooden bailers, two tins of hard biscuits, a cask of fresh water, and two tin drinking cups. In addition to these supplies, Mr Hardie had somehow procured a lump of cheese and some loaves of bread and salvaged two additional casks of water from the wreckage, which he surmised had come from a capsized lifeboat. He told us that there had once been a box of compasses stored on the deck of the *Empress Alexandra*, but it had gone missing on a previous voyage, and because the ship's owner had moved up the departure date on account of the brewing war in Austria, it had never been replaced. 'Ye can say what ye like, but seamen are neither more nor less honest than anybody else.' He also made a point of telling us that it was only through his quick thinking that the canvas cover that had kept rainwater out of the boat when it was stored on deck ended up in the boat with us. 'But why do we need it?' asked Mr Hoffman. 'It's exceedingly heavy, and it takes up a lot of room.' But all Mr Hardie would say was 'It can get wet in a lifeboat. Ye'll see that for yerselves if we're here long enough.' Most of us wore life vests, but they had been stored in our cabins, and during the confusion of the disaster, not everyone had had the time or forethought to retrieve them. Mr Hardie, two sisters who sat huddled together and rarely spoke, and an older gentleman named Michael Turner were among those without.

Soon after I had returned to my seat, Mr Hardie opened one of the tins and introduced us to hard-tack, which were rock-hard wafers approximately two inches square that could not be swallowed unless first softened with saliva or water. I held the biscuit between my lips until pieces of it began to dissolve and looked off into the not-quite-dark sky at the myriad stars that pricked the heavens, at the endlessness of the atmosphere that was the only thing vaster than the sea, and sent a prayer to whatever force of nature had arranged events thus far and asked it to preserve my Henry.

I felt hopeful, but all around me women had started to break down and cry. Mr Hardie stood up in the rocking boat and said, 'Yer loved ones might be dead or they might not be. There's a good chance they're in one of the other lifeboats bobbing about out there, so ye'd do well not to waste yer body's water in tears.' Despite his words, little wails and whimpers burst from the darkness throughout the night. I could feel the young woman sitting next to me shudder now and then, and once, she let out a throaty, animal sob. I lightly touched her shoulder, but the gesture only seemed to upset her further, so I took my hand away and listened to the soothing music of the water against the sides of the boat. Mrs Grant made her way between the thwarts, trying as best she could to console the most stricken until Mr Hardie cautioned her to sit still and told us we would be wise to make ourselves comfortable and get some rest, which we did as well as we could, leaning against each other and offering or asking for reassurance according to our needs and abilities. Against all odds, most of us managed to sleep.

DAY TWO

By the time we awoke on the morning of the second day, Mr Hardie had worked out a duty roster, which included turns at the oars for the strongest. Mrs Grant and all of the men except the frail Mr Turner were seated by the boat's eight oarlocks and took turns passing the four oars back and forth whenever Mr Hardie called on them to row. He took some time gauging the breeze and the current, and I heard him remark to one of the men sitting near him that use of the oars would compensate for drift, for our best bet was to stay in the vicinity of the wreck. The rest of us took turns with the bailers. We were floating very low in the water, and even though there was little wind to speak of, every so often a swell splashed over the railing, which Mr Hardie called a gunwale, so that our clothing and the blankets that were part of the boat's little store of emergency supplies were in constant danger of getting wet. It was worst for those who sat in the ends of the boat or on the two long seats that ran lengthwise on either side. They formed a wall of protection for the rest of us who were lucky enough to occupy the thwarts that spanned the breadth of the boat between them.

After passing out a ration of hardtack and water, Mr Hardie bade us arrange the canvas boat cover and blankets in the crease formed by the forward part of the boat in such a way that the canvas protected the blankets from any water that might pool in the bottom of the boat as well as from spray that splashed in over the rail. He declared that the women could take turns resting there, three at a time, for a period not to exceed two hours. Because there were thirty-one women – if you counted little Charles – it worked out that we each were entitled to one turn per day in what was immediately dubbed the dormitory. The extra time would be given over to any of the men who desired it.

Once this was accomplished, Mr Hardie charged the oarsmen with keeping the other lifeboats in sight as far as was possible. I gave myself the task of helping them, so I spent the day squinting into the distance, using my hands to shield my eyes against the blinding sparkle of the sun on the sea. In this way I felt I was contributing to the welfare of the people in our boat. Mr Nilsson, who said he had worked for a shipping company and who seemed a stickler on points of organization, asked Mr Hardie how long our supply of food would last, but Mr Hardie put him off, saying food would not be an issue unless we were not rescued, which he fully expected we would be. For the most part, there was little conversation, and I could tell by the blank stares and enlarged pupils of many of the women that they were suffering from shock. At that point I knew only two of my fellow passengers by name. Colonel Marsh, a large, distinguished gentleman whose wife had died some years before, had sat at the captain's table with Henry and me, and I had often seen Mrs Forester, a silent woman with wary eyes, trailing about the *Empress Alexandra* with a book or knitting in her hands. The Colonel nodded efficiently in my direction, but when I aimed a smile of recognition at Mrs Forester, she looked away.

For the rest of the morning and into the afternoon, we gazed out over the water for signs of a passing ship, while Mr Hardie alternated between stoic silence and eruptions filled with geographical facts and lore of the sea. I found his short monologue on the effect of the sun on the water at the equator versus its effect on the curving surface at the poles bewildering, but I recall very clearly some of the other things he said. He called Lifeboat 14 a cutter and said it had been designed both to row and to sail; and indeed, there was a round hole in one of the forward thwarts where a mast could be inserted, but we had neither mast nor sail. He told us that because the speed of the earth's rotation is much greater at the equator than it is at the poles, there were, over the surface of the earth, various wind belts. We had been traveling due west at approximately forty-three degrees north latitude when the ship went down, a position that put us, Hardie said, right in a belt of prevailing westerly winds. He explained that westerly winds blew from the west rather than to the west and that we were situated in the middle of well-traveled shipping lanes, which had been plotted in the era of sailing vessels to take advantage of these winds. He told us that typically both winds and current were against a ship going from east to west as we had been, but the advent of steamships had made it possible to take the shorter northern route, even if it meant heading into the wind. He raised visions of overbooked steamers to the point where we expected at any moment to have our choice of the vessels rushing to rescue us. Only Mr Nilsson interjected a sour note by saying, 'Who'd be coming to Europe now? There's a war on!' The mention of war caused the Colonel to throw his shoulders back and say, 'Quite so,' but Mr Hardie gave them both a black look as he said, 'There's ships that's going both ways. Keep yer eyes peeled so one of 'em doesn't run us over.' While we watched together for some sort of vessel to arrive, the slight man, who now identified himself as a deacon, led us in a prayer.

The deacon had a beautiful voice, and although he was not someone who would attract notice in most situations, I found it hard to take my eyes off him when he spoke. I noticed later that this effect deserted him when he was confronted with an unfamiliar subject, but with the prayer he was sure of his ground, and his voice rang out over the water and unified us with its words. He had clearly found his calling, and I wondered, not for the first time, if some of life's tragedy arose when people put themselves in situations they were not by nature suited for. I was later to revise my opinion of the deacon, and eventually his tenor seemed evidence of his general weakness; but at the time, I was content to watch the way his faith animated his features and to listen as his voice brought life to the ancient words of the prayer.

Despite our common purpose, petty jealousies arose. Those who sat along the railing were far more likely to be splashed by dripping oars than those who sat amidships, and when Mr Hardie determined the order in which we would take turns in the dormitory, a brusque woman named Mrs McCain insisted that the older women should by rights go first. She would have it no other way, but she lasted only a few minutes on the blankets before declaring that it was beastly and hot under the canvas and that she would take her turn at night. Because of the crowded conditions, movement in the boat was difficult, and when Mrs McCain lost her balance on her way back to her seat, a curl of water slid over the railing, causing Mr Hardie to bark, 'Keep to yer seats unless I tell ye otherwise!'

Mr Hoffman was the first to mention what we all were thinking: the boat had not been designed for so many. A few minutes later, Colonel Marsh pointed out a brass plaque that was nailed next to the second starboard oarlock and engraved with the words CAPACITY 40 PERSONS. But even with thirty-nine of us, it was obvious to everyone that the boat rode far too low in the water and that it was only because the day was still that this did not present a greater danger. The plaque perplexed all of us, but it perplexed Colonel Marsh most of all, for he was a man of order who expected not only a certain regimentation to the universe, but also a gentleman's agreement about meaning among users of the English language. 'The spoken word is one thing,' he said, 'but someone took the trouble to engrave this number into a plaque.' He kept rubbing his fingers over the letters and counting the thirty-nine heads in the boat, then shaking his own heavy head with the mystery of it. Once he tried to engage Mr Hardie in a discussion about it, but Mr Hardie only replied, 'And what do you propose we do? Write to the people who made the bloody boat and lodge a formal complaint?'

We found out later that the craft was twenty-three feet long, seven feet, two inches wide at her widest point, and just under three feet deep in the center and that the first owners of the *Empress Alexandra* had saved money by reducing the specifications for the lifeboats, which had been built to hold only about eighty percent of the stated capacity of forty people each. Apparently the order for the plaques had never been changed. It must have been because we were mostly women and smaller in stature than the average man that the boat didn't sink early on the first day.

Mr Hoffman and Mr Nilsson often sat with their heads together, which gave me the impression they were colleagues of some sort, but since they were seated in the back of the boat and I was two-thirds of the way up toward the bow, I had little chance to talk to them and couldn't hear what they were saying. Now and then they included Mr Hardie in their discussions, though Hardie mostly remained aloof. We were unused to moving about the boat, and the next time a group of women were careless in making their way to the dormitory, water again splashed over the rail. Mr Nilsson made a joke about someone volunteering to take a swim, maybe even two people, and Colonel Marsh replied, 'Good idea, that. Why don't you jump overboard yourself?'

'I'm the only one here besides Hardie who knows a thing about boats,' said Mr Nilsson, who went on to tell us he had grown up in Stockholm, where boats were as common as motorcars. 'Throw me over at your own peril,' he added, looking more defiant than seemed appropriate for a man who had merely been making a joke.

'We're not talking about throwing anyone over,' said Mr Hoffman reasonably, 'we're talking about volunteers,' but we had been in the boat for less than forty-eight hours. The sea was mostly calm and we were certain, still, of being rescued. Over the course of the afternoon, Mr Hardie went from being dismissive of Mr Hoffman's arguments to seeming to consider them. That morning, when someone had asked if we should make contact with the other lifeboats, he had proclaimed, 'There's no need for drastic action. We're sure to see a steamer or a fishing trawler,' but now and then the three men could be seen talking in low voices among themselves, and in the afternoon, when Mr Hoffman again broached the topic of an emergency plan, Hardie nodded and then looked off into the distance as if gauging something I couldn't see.

'If the wind comes up, we won't have time for arguments and discussion,' I heard Mr Nilsson say to Colonel Marsh. 'Making a plan doesn't mean we will ever put it into effect.' Mr Hardie was not the type to take orders from anyone, and I had the feeling we were being manipulated in some way; but my mind was numb with fear and perhaps it is only in retrospect, now that I am facing a different sort of authority, that it seems there might have been webs of influence and deceit in the lifeboat from the very start.

Oddly, I became more clear-headed with the passage of time. In the first hours I was too frightened to think critically about my situation: either too hot or too cold, too hungry or too thirsty, too apt to imagine things and say to the young woman who sat beside me, 'What's that over there, Mary Ann? At two o'clock. Isn't something glinting in the sun?' Or 'What is that dark shape, Mary Ann? Does it look like a boat to you?' Toward evening on the second day, as the huge orange sun sank like a heavy ball and people seemed to wake from their stupor enough to grumble about their aching muscles or wet feet, Mr Hoffman said, 'If we don't get any volunteers, we'll have to decide by drawing lots.'

At that point Anya Robeson, a woman who spoke very little but whom Mary Ann had described as 'someone from steerage,' gave Mr Hoffman a stern look and hugged her son Charles in under her coat. She didn't want him to hear any of it. 'Watch how you talk,' she would invariably say when one of the men spoke of death or used crude language. 'There's a child present.' I don't know why she worried about that – perhaps so she wouldn't have to worry about the sea, which went on and on, changing from blue to gray when a cloud passed over the sun and from gray to crimson when the sun flamed toward the horizon. A German girl named Greta Witkoppen burst into tears, and at first I thought she was crying because it would soon be dark or because she had lost a loved one, but then I realized that the talk of the men had frightened her.

Mrs Grant leaned over to where she was sitting and patted her shoulder. 'Don't worry,' she told her. 'You know how men are.' Greta then showed a bit of gumption by saying quite loudly, 'You're scaring people. You shouldn't say such things.' Another time she said directly to Mr Hardie, 'I'd think you would care more about how you look to the world.'

'The world!' scoffed Hardie. 'The world doesn't know I exist.'

'Someday it will,' she ventured. 'And someday it will judge you.'

'Leave that to the historians,' Hoffman shouted, and Hardie laughed into the rising wind and shouted, 'We're not history yet, by God! We're not history yet!'

Greta was, I think, Mrs Grant's first disciple. I heard Greta say to her, 'If they don't care about the world, you'd think they'd care about God. God is omniscient. God sees everything.' Mrs Grant responded by saying, 'He's a man. Most men think they are God,' and later I saw her pat Greta on the arm and whisper, 'You just leave Mr Hardie to me.'

Three Italian women and the governess named Maria were the only ones who didn't speak any English. The Italian women were dressed in identical black cloaks and huddled together in the front of the boat, alternating between complete silence and rapid, incomprehensible bursts of speech as if something only they could see were about to boil over. Maria had been traveling to America to work for a family on Beacon Hill. She was nearly always hysterical, but I could not pity her. Even the most sympathetic of the women could see that her utter lack of self-control presented a danger to us all. At first I tried to calm her with the few words of Spanish I knew, but each time I attempted to communicate with her, she would claw at my clothing, then stand up and wave her arms in the air, so the rest of us, once we got tired of pulling her back into her seat, would do our best to ignore her.

I will confess that it crossed my mind how easy it would have been to rise to my feet and, in the act of trying to restrain her, fall against her and knock her out of the boat. She was sitting right next to the rail, and it was clear to me that we would be far better off without her and her histrionics. I hasten to add that I did nothing of the sort and only mention it to illustrate how the bounds of a person's thinking quickly expand in such a situation and how part of me could understand the train of thought that had led Mr Hoffman to suggest a way to lighten the load and also how such a suggestion, once made, was difficult to forget. What I did instead was to switch places with Maria, so that if she were to lose her balance and fall, she would fall on top of Mary Ann or me and not out of the boat and into the brine.

I was now one of the ones sitting along the rail being splashed by the oars as the oarsmen tried to hold our position against the current. After thinking about it for a long time, I put my hand down to touch the water. It was very cold and seemed to pull seductively at my fingers, though this effect was not really due to anything about the water and was more a product of the motion of our little boat through it and maybe partly the work of my imagination as well.

DAY THREE

By the third day, some of the shock had worn off. The pupils of Maria's eyes shrank back to normal size, and once she even made a clown face at little Charles when he poked his head out from beneath his mother's skirt. We had traveled far enough that we no longer encountered pieces of the wreckage, or perhaps we had kept our place and it was the debris that had moved. In any case, there was nothing left of the *Empress Alexandra*. She might never have been, but how then to account for our plight? I thought of her as I have often thought of God – responsible for everything, but out of sight and maybe annihilated, splintered on the rocks of his own creation.

The deacon said the experience renewed his faith in God – or if it hadn't yet, it was bound to; Mrs Grant said it renewed her conviction that there was no God; and little Mary Ann said, 'Hush, hush, it doesn't matter,' and led everyone in a hymn about those in peril on the sea. We felt uplifted, both tragic and chosen. It touched my heart to see that even Mrs Grant joined in the singing, so great was our sense of unity and joy at being alive.

If Mary Ann was childlike in her faith in the Bible's literal truth, I was a practical Anglican. I deemed anything that encouraged people to be moral a good thing, but I never parsed the tenets I believed in from those that I didn't. I thought reverentially of the Bible as the sturdy book with closed covers that sat in my mother's reading room, where we gathered for our bedtime story. I had a Bible of my own from which I was assigned passages to memorize by the Sunday school mistress, but my book was small and unimpressive, and after my confirmation at the age of eleven, I put it in a drawer and never looked at it again.

Mr Hardie remained confident, even grimly cheerful. 'We're lucky about the weather,' he said. 'The wind is from the southwest and very light. The higher the clouds, the drier the air. The weather will hold.' I'd never wondered about it before and I never wondered about it again, but out there that day I wanted to know why the clouds were white, when they were supposedly made up of water, which is colorless. I asked Mr Hardie, thinking that he, of all people, would know the answer, but all he said was 'The sea is blue or black or all manner of color, and the spray of the breaking waves is white, and they're made up of water, too.' Mr Sinclair, whom I had observed rolling about the deck in his wheelchair but had never spoken to, said he wasn't a scientist, but he had read that the color had to do with the refractive properties of light and the fact that the cold temperatures of the upper atmosphere turned the suspended water droplets into crystals of ice.

Mr Hardie was on firmer ground with a different sort of fact. He told us that the *Empress Alexandra* had been equipped with twenty lifeboats, that at least ten or eleven of them had been successfully launched, which meant that at least half of the nearly eight hundred people on board had been saved. We could see two of them in the distance, but what had become of the others, we did not know. At first, Mr Hardie ordered the oarsmen not to go up alongside the other craft, but Colonel Marsh spoke up in favor of approaching close enough to talk to their occupants and to find out if they might contain our loved ones or other people we knew, and my heart leapt at the prospect of seeing my Henry alive and well in one of the other boats. But Hardie said, 'What would be the point o' that, since they can do nothing for us and we can do nothing for them?'

'There is strength in numbers,' said Mr Preston, which made me laugh despite his earnest demeanor, for he had been an accountant and I thought he was making a joke.

'Shouldn't we at least see if they're all right?' argued the Colonel, and Mr Nilsson agreed, though he was one of those who had helped Mr Hardie beat the swimmers away from our boat and didn't strike me as someone too full of concern for his fellow man.

'And what if they're not?' barked Hardie. 'What

then? Are we to try to solve their problems as well as our own?' He then muttered that he could tell from this distance that the first boat was as crowded as ours and that the second one wasn't sitting too well in the water.

'What do you mean by that?' asked Mr Hoffman.

'Something is off, that's all.'

While it was natural that Mr Hardie would seek the counsel of the men sitting nearest him, it began to seem as if theirs were the only opinions that mattered. Mr Sinclair, who had lost the use of his legs but not of his mind, and the deacon, whose moral authority could not be ignored, were sitting toward the fore and so did not have Hardie's ear, but at that point they spoke up on behalf of the women. Mr Sinclair said, 'Some people would like to know if their husbands or companions are in those boats.' His voice had a pleasing resonance, which amplified his tone of conviction. The deacon added, 'Just yesterday, you were talking about overcrowding. If you are right about the situation in the second boat, it might be possible to transfer some of our people to it.' But his voice lacked force, which had the effect of making the idea he was presenting seem weak and questioning, and even before he finished speaking, Mr Hardie was shaking his head. 'If it were possible for her to take more passengers, don't you think that some of the people in the overcrowded boat would have moved over to it by now? They're a lot closer to each other than they are to us.'

‘We should at least talk to them,’ insisted the Colonel.

‘Aye,’ said Mr Hardie after a long pause. ‘We’ll go within hailing distance, but what we do after that is up to me.’

The oarsmen took up their oars, and I held my breath as we approached the closer of the boats. I was praying to see Henry, yet I didn’t quite dare to hope. Mary Ann whispered to me that she would throw her engagement ring into the sea as an offering if only her mother were in one of the other boats, and I know that all around me similar bargains were being struck. We were squinting into the sun, so it was difficult to make out faces against the brightness. As we got closer, I recognized Penelope Cumberland, who was someone I had met on the *Empress Alexandra*, but I counted only four men aboard and none of them was Henry. I heard sighs of disappointment as Mr Hardie shouted out, ‘That’s far enough. Ship yer oars.’

A man with a full beard called across the water to inquire if we were all right, and he and Mr Hardie exchanged a few words. ‘Have ye made contact with the other boat?’ Hardie asked him.

‘Yes,’ said the bearded man, who appeared to be in charge. ‘The boat’s not half-full, but there’s a crazy ship’s officer on board who says there’s a hole been punched in its bottom. He tried to send some of his people with me, and when I said we couldn’t take them, he threw two of them overboard, so of course we picked them up. You can see our situation for yourself.' And indeed the lifeboat looked as crowded as our own.

'You have no seamen with you, then?' asked Hardie.

'Nay.'

'Have ye found the boxes of supplies that are stowed under the seats?' The man said they had. Then Mr Hardie went on to say that distress signals and wireless messages had been sent before the ship had gone down and that help in the form of another ship was likely within the next twenty-four hours, forty-eight at most, that he was somewhat surprised it had taken this long, and that it was to our mutual advantage to keep each other in sight for the moment when someone arrived to rescue us.

I did not think to wonder why he had not told us about the wireless messages before, and the men in both boats excitedly asked questions concerning the content of the communications and whether or not any reply had been received. 'The ship was on fire – there was hardly time to wait for replies,' barked Hardie. Then he asked if the bearded man knew the name of the officer in the other boat.

'Blake,' said the man, 'Mr Blake is the name of the officer!' and he pointed toward the lifeboat that still bobbed a quarter mile to the east.

'Blake, is it?' said Hardie, more to himself than to the other man, and I thought I saw a shadow cross his eyes, as if this news surprised him more than he let on. Then he said, 'Keep us in sight if ye can, and if the weather gets rough, use yer oars to point the nose of the boat into the wind. That's the best way to ride out a storm.' And with that he ordered our oarsmen to put some distance between us and the other boat.

'Aren't we going to see who's in the second boat?' asked the Colonel, and Mr Hardie said no, he'd seen quite enough.

The Colonel grumbled, but he didn't argue, and if the others were tempted to side with him against Mr Hardie in this matter, they remained silent. It now seems to me that failing to band together with the half-empty boat was our biggest mistake. I thought it unlikely that Mr Blake would throw more people into the water, and the fact that Mr Hardie knew him seemed like it would work to our advantage. I have since wondered why Mrs Grant said nothing. Perhaps she was about to but was forestalled when, in the next moment, the Colonel took up a different line of inquiry. 'How do you know so much about what was happening in the radio room of the *Empress Alexandra*?' he asked Mr Hardie.

'Blake told me about it. When the fire spread, those of us who were belowdecks came topsides to help load people into the boats. That's when I saw Blake. It was Blake who said, "Better go with this lot, mate. They'll need a seaman aboard if they're to survive."' It was then that I had a fleeting memory of seeing Mr Hardie on the day of the disaster exchanging words with another man. In normal circumstances, I would have said they were arguing, but all around us people were shouting orders and clamoring to be heard. The two men had been similarly dressed, but where Mr Hardie's coat had plain sleeves, the sleeves of the other man were festooned with gold brocade. It seemed to me now that it was the man in the gold brocade whom Henry had approached when we first arrived on deck after the explosion. Then Mr Hardie appeared and I lost track of the officer, who seemed glad to hand us over to Mr Hardie so he could rush off on other business. I confess that my senses were overwhelmed by the chaos that engulfed us, for the next thing I knew, I was being lifted by strong arms. I caught one last glimpse of Henry's anxious face as the lifeboat was lowered, and then I never saw him again.

Mr Hardie said other encouraging things. He told us again that besides being within well-traveled shipping lanes, we were headed toward the Grand Banks, which sounded reassuringly solid to me – like the cliffs of Dover or the marble structure where Henry had worked. 'It's not as if we're in uncharted water,' said Hardie. But how could it be charted? I thought as I looked around in dismay. There was nothing to distinguish one patch of ocean from another, no landmarks or terrain, only a blue expanse stretching endlessly on all sides of the flimsy speck that was our boat.

I admired Hardie from the start. He had a square

jaw and a jutting chin and might have been handsome if not for the toll a life at sea had taken on his features and bearing. His sharp eyes didn't look shifty or dishonest as one might expect the eyes of a seaman to look. Even within the confines of the boat, he was rarely still. He did not seem frightened by the sea: he respected it, and he alone among us accepted our position. Everyone else fought against it. Mary Ann kept imploring anyone who would listen, 'Why us? Why us, dear God? Why us?' while Maria wondered the same thing in her Castilian dialect. The deacon attempted earnest answers to their questions, but Mr Hardie had little patience with that sort of conversation. 'Ye're born, ye suffer, and ye die. What made ye think ye deserved different?' he wondered aloud when the deacon's gentle answers failed to quiet them. Colonel Marsh was apt to mutter after each of Hardie's harsh pronouncements: 'He'd never get away with that in the regiment,' as if we might as easily be somewhere else – on land, perhaps, or on horseback, with the Colonel himself leading the charge.

Hardie's assertions tended to be filled with specifics, whereas those of the Colonel and the deacon and especially of Mrs Grant were more general and philosophical. Hardie said, 'If we're careful, we have enough food for five days, maybe six,' and I can see now that it was his willingness to quantify our situation, to pin us exactly between the forty-third and forty-fourth parallels, along with the fact that he was absolutely incapable of introspection, that was the source of his power. By contrast, Mrs Grant uttered vague and meaningless words of comfort. Even so, I liked it when she turned to one or the other of the women and said, 'How is your shoulder coming on?' or 'Close your eyes for a bit and think nice thoughts.' The deacon had taken it upon himself to search his store of instructive Bible verses and share them with the rest of us. I found it irritating, but Isabelle Harris, a serious woman who had been traveling with her ailing mother, kept turning to him and saying things like 'Isn't there something in Deuteronomy?' and the deacon would oblige by quoting: 'Every place whereon the soles of your feet shall tread shall be yours: from the wilderness even unto the uttermost sea shall your coast be.'

That morning, a feeling of camaraderie pervaded the boat. We had seen what a boat without Mr Hardie in it was like, and we counted our blessings that we had been vouchsafed a leader who knew about wind direction and weather patterns. He wore a knife in a greasy sheath that hung down from his belt. He had salvaged the floating barrels, which I had considered such an extravagance at the time. Who else of us had thought of anything on that first disastrous day but saving ourselves for the next ten minutes? Only the deacon and Anya Robeson had any matching claim to selflessness. The deacon had spoken up on behalf of the child, and Anya's little Charlie was hidden under her coat, and we all knew she would willingly die a thousand deaths for him. Perhaps Mrs Grant was selfless too, for she was always stretching a hand out for someone to hold or turning her unsmiling face, with its fixed look of deep compassion and concern, toward one or another of the women.

As I said, the shock had worn off, or was, more accurately, suppressed. We used up precious breath singing and laughing and talking about whatever came into our heads. Mr Hardie started off a round of stories by saying, 'Do any of ye know how the *Empress Alexandra* came to be named?' He proceeded to tell us that the ship had been christened on the day Nicholas and Alexandra were crowned as emperor and empress of all of Russia. Mr Sinclair added that the match had been forbidden by Nicholas's father, but the father died and the couple quickly wed. 'The coronation, however, was delayed for more than a year. When it finally took place, thousands of peasants were trampled to death during the celebrations in a panic over food. Nicholas assumed the grand ball being thrown in his honor would be canceled out of respect for the victims of the tragedy, but it wasn't, and he was counseled to attend in order not to offend his French hosts. The incident was variously used to prove the ill-fated nature of Nicholas's reign and the heartlessness of autocratic rule.'

'In any case,' said Mr Hardie, 'the ship isn't as big as some, and the owners wanted to give it a grand name in order to make up for the size. Still, she was well fitted out and should have turned a handsome profit . . .' Here Hardie's voice petered out and he lost the thread. He began to grumble about working for nothing and shipowners who thought fancy titles would do the work of sense, but then he must have caught himself being overly loquacious, for he abruptly told us that eventually the vessel was 'sold to an American chappie who knew how to make the bleedin' bucket pay.'

Mary Ann liked to hear about anything to do with marriage, so she asked Mr Sinclair if Nicholas's marriage to Alexandra had been grand. 'I only know that it took place in the Winter Palace in St Petersburg,' Mr Sinclair replied, 'and the Winter Palace is grand enough.' On hearing this, Mary Ann nudged me, and whispered, 'The ship was made for you, Grace. Your name is Winter, and you were just married!' Even though Henry had been in London on business and had only decided to take me with him at the last minute – because, he said, he couldn't bear to leave me and because he wanted to get married beyond the clutches of a mother who sounded more and more to me like a giant hawk – it made me feel both chosen and doomed to think that the *Empress Alexandra* had been created especially for Henry and me. In the days to come, I would fabricate for myself a fantastic imaginary place called the Winter Palace, where Henry and I would live. It had cool rooms that led onto sunny verandas and arched windows that overlooked sweeping emerald lawns. It inhabited the architecture of my mind, and I spent hours exploring its corridors, changing the details of its malleable design as I went.

For the trip out, Henry had chosen a small packet steamer. We were as yet unmarried, and although we told the captain we were husband and wife, Henry wanted to avoid meeting anyone he knew until the knot had been tied, which we did not have time to do before we sailed. Henry thought it would be fun to pretend we were of modest means and said that we would replenish our wardrobes in London. I didn't tell him that I had no wardrobe to replenish, and I laughed to think that I was now only pretending to be poor!

There were seven other passengers on the packet boat, but only one other woman. We all ate with the captain, family style, and served ourselves from big platters that were passed from one end of the table to the other. On one occasion, the talk turned to women's suffrage, and the other woman was asked what she thought. 'It's not something I dwell on,' she said, flustered to be the center of the conversation, which usually excluded the two of us. I found myself saying, 'Of course women should vote!' with an air of great conviction, not so much because I had any strongly held opinion on the matter as because I believed the other men were callously using the other woman to prove some point of their own. Later, Henry said proudly, 'I guess you set them straight.' But for the most part, Henry and I said little, saving our voices for the times we were alone.

When Mr Hardie had finished speaking, other people started telling their particular stories about the explosion and making guesses about what had caused it. There was a difference of opinion about whether the explosion had caused the boat to start sinking or whether it had been a secondary effect. 'A secondary effect of what?' asked the Colonel, and no one could answer him.

Nearly everybody had a story to tell about the *Titanic*, which had sunk in a spectacular fashion just over two years before. Mrs McCain's younger sister had been one of the survivors, so we listened spellbound to everything she had to say on the subject and pestered her for details about her sister's experience. In the case of the *Titanic*, the problem was the lack of lifeboats, but those who made it into a boat were rescued very quickly. 'The ship sank at night, so many people were not properly dressed,' said Mrs McCain. 'Whenever my sister tells the story, she laughs and says that her biggest worry was the fact that she was wearing on her feet only a pair of jeweled Arabian slippers and that her ankles showed beneath her robe when she was getting in and out of the boat.' The other female passengers and I simultaneously looked down at our feet and blushed, which was a nice reminder that somewhere a world existed where this might be our primary concern. Mr Nilsson drew on his knowledge of the shipping business to say that the sister ship of the *Titanic* was to have been named the *Gigantic*, but that after the disaster, the White Star Line renamed it the *Britannic*. 'I suppose they didn't want to tempt fate again by using such an arrogant name.'

'It wasn't the name that sank the *Titanic*,' said Mrs McCain. 'It was an iceberg. Do you think the same thing happened to us?'

'We didn't hit an iceberg,' said Mr Hardie. 'After the *Titanic* sank, the transatlantic routes were shifted to the southern track to prevent that very thing.'

Mr Sinclair added that many of the *Titanic* lifeboats had been rescued within four hours, and it was these stories as much as anything Mr Hardie had told us that encouraged us to believe that our rescue was imminent, even overdue.

Mr Hardie assured us that the experience of the *Titanic* had translated into revised safety protocols, but clearly mistakes had been made putting those protocols into effect. Because of the fire and the listing of the *Empress Alexandra*, it became more and more difficult to operate the lifeboat-lowering mechanisms, and there was understandable confusion throughout the ship as people tried to make sense of what was happening and decide what to do.

'I was knocked clean out of my bed,' said Mrs Forester, the silent older woman I recognized from the ship. 'I had retired after lunch for a nap, while Collin had gone somewhere to play cards. My first thought was that he had come in drunk again and knocked into me. I do worry about him, but Collin is such a survivor.' Because we had all done so, surviving seemed an easy thing, though just beneath the surface of our own stories lurked the stories of the people we had seen throwing babies into the water to save them from the flames.

Isabelle said, 'Why did they start to lower our boat and then raise it back up again?' Then she turned directly to Mr Hardie and said, 'You must know why they did it. Weren't you helping with the boats?'

Mr Hardie, who had been particularly talkative that day, suddenly became quiet and only replied, 'Nay. I don't.'

Then Isabelle asked, 'Do you think the little girl who hit her head on the side of our boat when it was being raised back up got into the next one?'

'What little girl?' asked Mrs Fleming, who was in deep despair over the unknown fate of her family and was untouched by the illusions that buoyed the rest of us.

'The one who was knocked out of the way when our boat was launched.'

'Was someone knocked out of the way? Was it Emmy? You're not talking about Emmy, are you?' Mrs Fleming added that her husband and daughter had fallen behind in the mad dash for the lifeboats and that she hadn't noticed until it was too late. 'They were right behind me! I had injured my wrist somehow, and Gordon pushed me ahead. I thought they were right behind me!'

Hannah gave Isabelle a stern look and said, 'She's completely mistaken. No one was hit in the head,' then launched into a fabricated story about seeing a nearly empty lifeboat rescuing people from the water. Mrs Grant insisted that she had seen it too and wouldn't let anyone say a thing to the contrary. She abruptly changed the subject to report that Mr and Mrs Worthington Smith were last seen sitting in deck chairs and smoking cigarettes: 'He said, "Save the women and children first," and she replied, "I've never gone off in a boat without Worthy, and I'm certainly not about to start now." Later I heard a similar story about a couple from the *Titanic*, and I wondered if this had really happened or if Mrs Grant had merely appropriated the story to distract Mrs Fleming from her woes.

'That's true love,' said Mary Ann dreamily. It made the death and horror of the wreck seem romantic and purposeful. Henry, after all, had done something similar for me, if without the noble words or the cigarette. I tried to forget the look of panic on his face as he hustled me into Mr Hardie's arms and implored him to put me on the boat. I wanted to kiss Henry's cheek and make him promise to follow me, but he was intent on whatever he was saying to Mr Hardie, some last instruction that I was too terrified to absorb, so I didn't say goodbye to him. I preferred to envision him waving at me from a deck chair rather than floundering around in the cold black water and grasping at sticks from the wreckage. But most of all, I liked to picture him dressed in the suit he had worn at our wedding and waiting for me when I got to New York. Henry could always get a table in a crowded restaurant or tickets to the opera. It's ironic to think that he worked the same sort of magic when he booked our passage on the *Empress Alexandra*. With war on the horizon, many people were eager to return to America, and first-class tickets were scarce; but when I asked Henry how he did it, he simply said, 'It's a little miracle. The same sort of miracle that brought you to me just when I thought I was going to have to marry Felicity Close.'

Now Mr Hardie said, 'There were more than enough lifeboats for everyone, twenty boats built for forty persons each,' but even with our untrained eyes we could see that the boats had not been designed for forty. Still, it was a useful fiction, enabling me to convince myself that Henry had survived, in spite of the fact that I had seen the chaos of the *Empress Alexandra*'s last minutes with my own eyes. Afterwards, we learned that most of the lifeboats on the starboard side of the ship had burned in the fire and that others had pushed away from the burning wreck half-full.

At four o'clock, we ate our crust of bread and cheese. Colonel Marsh possessed a large pocket watch and Mr Hardie charged him with keeping track of the hour. Every so often he would call out, 'Time, sir!' and the Colonel would pull his watch out of his pocket and announce the hour. He looked very important as he did it, but also as if he were modestly trying to downplay what he saw as a crucial role in the workings of the boat. Earlier, Mr Hardie had said something about using the watch to gauge our longitude, and they had had a long discussion about how that might be done. Perhaps it was that interchange that gave the Colonel confidence to ask, 'Don't you think you could give us a little more to eat and drink than this? It seems that we have an awful lot, seeing as those ships in the trading route are bound to show up any minute,' and indeed, the biscuit tins and water casks were taking up their share of room in the back of the boat. But Mr Hardie would not change his plan for rationing the food and water they contained. At first we laughed about it. 'Hardie's a tough master,' we said almost fondly. Though we hardly knew one another, a sense of ourselves in the lifeboat was beginning to form, with Hardie at the center the way a grain of rough sand lies at the very center of a pearl.

The high clouds turned pink and gold, like a painted ceiling that was pierced at intervals by bands of silver light. 'Look!' called Mrs Hewitt, who had been a hotel proprietress; and everyone became silent, for one of the sunbeams had sought out our boat and we floated, awestruck and illuminated, in silence, until Mary Ann raised up her voice with the strain of 'O God Our Help in Ages Past.' Predictably, a French maid named

Lisette began to cry, and not until the final note did the heavens shift and the lifeboat move into the shadow of a cloud.

There was much talk of what the meaning of that natural or supernatural occurrence had been. The deacon said, 'I think we can draw a parallel between the ray of light and the fact that we have all been chosen to be rescued in this boat.'

'We're hardly rescued yet,' said Hannah. I started to say, 'God helps those who help themselves,' but I stopped after the first three words when I saw Mrs Grant looking at me in an appraising and maybe calculating way. This time she had refrained from singing and seemed to retreat inside herself, aloof from the general feeling of camaraderie conferred upon us by the glorious evening and our sense of gratitude that so far we had been spared. Even after Mr Hardie made a detailed inventory of supplies and amended his estimate of how long our food and water would last – three to four days, he said now – we did not despair, for it was plenty long enough.

NIGHT

There were more songs as night fell. Hannah, who seemed to have made fast friends with Mrs Grant or perhaps had known her from before, was gazing at me in an odd way, and I reflexively put my hand to my hair and started to worry about how I looked. Hannah had gray eyes and long hair that twisted into thick locks when it blew in the wind. She had put a filmy piece of cloth around her shoulders, and it flapped lightly in the breeze the way the wings of a bird might flap if it were really a goddess disguised as a bird. When it came Hannah's turn to bail, she made a point of switching places with the person beside me, then she put her arm around my shoulders and whispered in my ear that even here, she found me very beautiful. I was as near to happy as I have ever been – happy in a profound way, I mean. Glad to be alive, but also glad to be the object of another being's undivided attention. Her breath was warm on my cheek, and when she pulled away from me, our gaze held for a long moment. I reached across and lifted a strand of hair that had blown across her lips and placed it back over her shoulder. I meant to smile to convey to her something of what I felt, but I don't think I did. Mr Hardie had looked at me earlier in the day, and I had felt stone cold, both heavy and weightless at once, and while he seemed to see right through me as if I were no more substantial than air, he also seemed to comprehend my very essence, which filled me with the kind of terror the Virgin Mary must have felt when the angel Gabriel came down. Hannah intimidated me, but not nearly as much as Mr Hardie did, and I was happy to think that Hannah and I might be friends. A matronly woman named Mrs Cook broke the silence that had come over us by saying, 'Wasn't that Penelope Cumberland in the other lifeboat?' No one answered her, and after a moment I replied that I had recognized her, too.

'Do you remember how she and her husband wormed their way into places at the captain's table? Now there was a high-and-mighty one for you. Mrs Cumberland thought the rest of us were beneath her notice, but what people like that don't think about is that the noticing goes both ways. I overheard the husband and wife quarreling one day, and it seems Mr Cumberland's fortune wasn't quite as secure as the two of them liked us all to believe. The missus said to him, "But we can't sit there – I won't have the right sort of dresses!" to which he replied, "No one will notice what you wear." "As if you would know a thing about what other people notice!" she said sharply, and then she huffed off.'

A few minutes later, Mrs Cook whispered to me, 'Of course, she acted all charming whenever I came face-to-face with her, but I know what she was thinking. She was thinking that I wasn't at the captain's table. She was thinking that a companion is the same thing as a servant and that if it weren't for Mrs McCain, I wouldn't have been in first class at all. She was thinking that Mrs McCain needed a companion only because she wasn't married and that a woman without a husband occupies a lower social level than a married woman like herself. And the way the captain looked at her! There was something unsavory going on there, you mark my words.'

It seemed hardly fair that all of Mrs Cook's hostility toward the Cumberlands was laid on the milky shoulders of Penelope Cumberland and that, for some reason, Mr Cumberland got off scot-free. I had found Penelope quite delightful and her husband a bore, but I also knew that wives made easier targets. I tried to point out that people sat at the captain's table by personal invitation only and that, as I understood it, those invitations were predicated upon social standing, which contradicted both the notion that the Cumberlands had fallen on hard times and the idea that there was something underhanded about their actions.

'That's my point exactly!' said Mrs Cook, either impervious to reason or unwilling to be talked out of her animosity. 'They had no social standing, nor money either! I heard the mister talking to Captain

Sutter one day. I can't say I heard what was said exactly, but the gist of it was clear, and after that they didn't miss a day, always sweeping into the dining room ahead of everyone and demanding to be seated first. You were at the captain's table, weren't you, Grace? Did the Cumberlands ever explain why they started sitting there?'

'Not to me, they didn't, and I would never have asked. It's my experience that we can come up with five reasons why something might have happened, and the truth will always be the sixth.' I did happen to know something about the Cumberlands, but I had been sworn to secrecy, and I didn't see any reason to enlighten a busybody like Mrs Cook.

Of course, trying to stop Mrs Cook from speculating was like trying to stop an ocean wave mid-swell, and she went on with her usual categorizing and generalizations. She considered herself a grand storyteller, and the people sitting near her would listen with rapt attention. When they asked questions, she would make up details and theories to please them. Now she said, 'People who are used to having money are mortified by the idea that someday their circumstances might change. You and Mr Winter were very comfortable, weren't you Grace? Wasn't the idea of not being so something you would be horrified to consider?'

I had been taught that money was not a fit subject for conversation, so I replied firmly that Henry handled the financial matters in our family and that I rarely thought about them, if I ever did.

Mrs Cook's stories were intimate, often told in a conspiratorial whisper to interested parties, who had to be sitting near her, and even then we sometimes had to lean toward her in order to hear. Mr Sinclair, on the other hand, was something of a scholar and would tell us stories about things he had read. He had a booming voice and often claimed the entire boat as his audience, particularly at night, when sounds seemed to travel farther than they did during the day. I don't know how the subject of memory arose, but Mr Sinclair informed us that as far back as the fourth century BC, Aristotle was writing about it in a scientific way. 'Aristotle determined that memory has only to do with the past, not with the present or the future,' he began, only to be interrupted by Mr Hoffman, who scoffed, 'I could have told you that!' But I asked Mr Hoffman to be quiet, and Mr Sinclair went on.

'Aristotle distinguished between "memory," which he said even slow people are good at, and "recollection," at which clever people excel.' I don't remember what he said next, but I understood him to mean that there could be no memory of the present, which involves only the perception of our senses, and that memory is the recoverable impression of a past event. Recollecting, however, is the recovery itself – the investigation or mnemonic process that leads one to a memory that is not instantly retrievable. I think about this now, since writing this account has involved much recollecting. Sometimes I remember one occurrence, and only later does another thing that happened come to mind, which leads to yet another and so on, in a long chain.

Another time Mr Sinclair told us about Sigmund Freud, who was revolutionizing the science of the mind and had written not so much about remembering as about forgetting and how forgetting always relates to the life drives, the greatest of which are to reproduce and to avoid death. In any case, I considered Mr Sinclair the better storyteller, but most of the other women preferred Mrs Cook.

The night was moonless, and the air became increasingly oppressive and damp. My good feelings of the evening were gradually extinguished, though nothing particularly bad had happened except that Mr Hardie remarked to Mr Hoffman that before morning it would rain. A kind of unhinged laughter rippled through the boat when we imagined what new wretchedness rain would bring.

After that, the talk stopped and we were left alone with our thoughts and the musical sound of the water against the bottom of the boat. Remarkably, we all slept those first nights, either taking our turn in the dormitory or leaning against each other or putting our heads in willing laps. We explained this by saying that we were exhausted, shocked – not knowing the depths our shock and exhaustion would eventually reach – but optimistic, practicing in our heads the language with which we would present our experiences when we got home.

Sometime around midnight I was awakened by shouts. A man's voice called out that he had seen lights in the distance. The sighting was unconfirmed, and though my eyes strained to pierce the obscurity of the night, I could see nothing. I slept again, and when I awoke just before dawn, I rose, intending to make my way to the little lavatory Henry and I had used on the ship before I remembered where I was and stuck one of the bailers up under my dress and urinated into it, making fussy little adjustments to my clothing and trying not to attract attention to myself. I mildly resented the men, who made no bones about unbuttoning their trousers and sending frothy streams out over the side of the boat. As time went on, this became less of a problem, for we were taking in so little water that our need to relieve ourselves became more and more infrequent. Even so, our resentments didn't disappear. They only found new differences on which to light.

DAY FOUR

The episode in the night – the false or at least unconfirmed sighting of lights – had an adverse effect on us. There were new renditions of the stories of the ship's last moments, but the romance that had been washed over everything by the haunting beauty of the sunbeams and the singing of the previous afternoon was unequal to the task of dispelling disappointment, and we were overcome by a creeping gloom. This was exacerbated by the overcast day. All around us, the gray of the sky met the gray of the sea at an indistinct horizon. Hardie said, 'The clouds aren't white now, are they, Mrs Winter?' and Maria began once again to stand up and pull at her clothes. 'Sit down,' growled Hardie, 'or I'll have to tie ye.'

Mrs Grant called out, 'Who was it that saw the lights?'

'Preston over there,' said Mr Sinclair. 'It was Preston.'

'I did. I'm not making anything up.' Mr Preston was an earnest, round-faced man who seemed perpetually out of breath.

'Which direction were they?' asked Mrs Grant in

a voice one might use to ask the way to a hotel. 'See if you can remember.' Mr Preston looked immensely relieved and said, 'Five points off the wind.' Mr Hardie had told us how to apply the degrees of a circle or the hands of a clock to locate objects with relation to the wind or to the nose of the boat, so when Mr Preston said this, we all craned our necks toward the starboard bow as if something might be seen there now. There was an air of unrelenting gravity about Mrs Grant, a solemnity she conferred on whomever she addressed, and I could see at once that this sort of respect for his viewpoint was all Mr Preston wanted.

Hardie said, 'In the last hour the wind's shifted forty-five degrees,' and he pointed off in a different direction.

'Oh,' said Preston, clearly discouraged and afraid of losing credibility. 'I'm an accountant, after all, not a seaman, but accountants are noted for their accuracy. I have an eye for detail and the memory of an elephant. Just ask anyone who knows me. If I say I saw lights, then lights are what I saw.'

'Give me your attention, everyone! Listen to me!' Mrs Grant called out in a voice everyone could hear. I was surprised to find her capable of producing such volume, for up until then she had been forceful in a quiet way. 'Mr Preston saw lights coming from there.' She nodded in the direction Mr Hardie had indicated. 'We need to keep our eyes open. I suggest you set up a watch, Mr Hardie. It seems to me we should divide ourselves into shifts of four people, with each of the four responsible for a ninety-degree sector for one hour.' She proceeded to divide people up into nine shifts, exempting Mr Hardie, of course, but also exempting Hannah and herself, saying they would take on more general duties and fill in where needed. It occurred to me that Hardie did not relish taking orders from a woman, for as he listened, his features were set in a wooden stare.

Several times during the morning, Mr Hardie was asked for his opinion of the lights, but he was saving his breath. Perhaps he had been offended by Mrs Grant's failure to consult him before assigning new tasks. 'Won't be long now' was all he would say, but he left it to our imaginations what it was that wouldn't be long in coming. At first I assumed he was talking about the arrival of the ship that would carry us to safety, but then I was hit with a burst of sea spray and I thought perhaps he was talking about the rain that threatened but did not fall. Only in the last couple of weeks have I decided that he was talking about something altogether different, about some rivalry that was emerging between himself and Mrs Grant, some crisis of leadership or some approaching moment when people would see clearly what was what and would unalterably commit themselves to his command; but at the time I had no real basis for thinking anything of the sort.

Mr Hardie passed out the breakfast biscuits and the tin cup full of water, warning us to take no more than the third of a cup allotted to us. I took only my share, but I was one of the few who did. Hardie watched grimly as people fought over the cup and some of the precious water slopped onto the floor. 'Look at ye, acting like children,' he said. From then on, he measured out the exact allotment and passed the cup to us one by one.

When Mrs Fleming again wondered aloud what might have become of her daughter, Isabelle burst out, 'She has a right to know! I wouldn't want to be protected from the truth,' and despite Mrs Grant's stern warning that Isabelle didn't know what she was talking about, Mr Preston said, 'I saw it, too.' This caused Mrs Fleming to spring to her feet and clamber over our legs to cower in the bottom of the boat next to where Isabelle and Mr Preston sat. She clutched at their sleeves and said, 'Saw what? What did you see? Which lifeboat did she get into? She didn't get into the very next one, did she, the one that dumped all of those people into the water?' Mr Preston looked nervously from Mrs Fleming to Mrs Grant and held his tongue.

'Tell me, damn you! You can't stop there!' screeched Mrs Fleming, her injured hand flapping unnaturally at the end of her arm. 'The next boat is the one that turned upside down. I saw it with my own eyes. Were Emmy and Gordon in that boat or weren't they?'

'It wasn't—' began Mr Preston.

'Go ahead and tell her,' said Mr Hoffman. 'I hear you're famous for your accuracy.'

'Yes, tell me!' she screeched again, rising from the damp bottom of the boat, where water continued to pool and slosh no matter how industriously we bailed. I grabbed at her, trying to assist her, but it was Hannah who ended up helping her to squeeze in between Mary Ann and me, and it was Mrs Grant who reattached her sling and wrapped a blanket around her shoulders, for she was shivering and her dress had gotten wet.

'The harm is already done,' said Mr Hoffman. 'You may as well tell her the rest.'

'You saw her too?' Mrs Fleming's lunatic eyes now seized on Mr Hoffman, who said, 'Yes, as a matter of fact I did.' Nobody said a word. Even the deacon seemed to shrink inside his loose coat from the scene of desperation before us.

Mr Hoffman spoke without a trace of emotion. 'She was hit by this boat when they raised it back up. She was knocked off the deck. I saw her fall into the water. She probably drowned.'

'We don't know that,' said Hannah. 'We don't know that at all.'

'Maybe she was rescued,' the deacon suggested gently, and I knew we were all thinking of the child with the bow tie and how Hardie and Nilsson had beaten the men away from the side of the boat with their oars. Mrs Fleming was trembling uncontrollably and kept repeating, 'Thank you, it's best to know,' but I wondered how, in the confusion, Mr Hoffman's word could be taken on faith.

Inexplicably, just before dark, two of the Italian women, who had until then remained mostly silent, shrieked and repeatedly crossed themselves as well as they could while still clutching on to each other. It was Mr Sinclair, the cripple, who translated and told us that they had prayed and received a revelation that half of us would not survive. 'That means half of us will,' pronounced Mrs Grant, making it clear with a look that this was the last word on the subject.

Mrs Fleming seemed to have recovered her composure somewhat, and I prided myself that it had something to do with my attempts to calm her by holding her hand and saying, 'It's just a story they're telling you. It might not even be the truth.' Then I told her of my short but happy married life with Henry and how we were planning a wedding celebration when we got home, so it greatly surprised me when she announced, 'Since we're all being honest, it really should be mentioned that Grace shouldn't be in this lifeboat at all.'

'Nonsense,' said Mary Ann in the soothing tone of voice she had been using with Mrs Fleming all along.

'Perhaps you didn't see it, Mary Ann, but I did. Grace is the reason this boat is overcrowded. Did you hear what Mr Hoffman said? How they lowered the boat and then raised it back up a fraction before continuing to let it down? Mr Hardie was helping people into the boat and had already started lowering it into the water when Grace and her husband appeared and said something to him. What was the conversation about, Grace? We'd all like to know. I saw it because I was expecting to see my Emmy get into the boat. She was right behind me. They told me to get in first because of my hand, but I never would have done it if I wasn't sure my daughter was coming too. What was it your husband promised Mr Hardie? They raised the boat up and that's when Mr Hardie and Grace got into it. And that's when Mr Hoffman says Emmy was hit. If Grace won't tell us, maybe Mr Hardie will!'

'If they raised the boat up, it was to keep it level,' barked Hardie. 'The ship was tilted nearly twenty degrees, the decks were slick with oil, and people were clawing at anyone in a uniform. I'd like to see the lot of you try to work the pulleys under those conditions!'

'They raised the boat for you and Grace – that's the only reason. I saw it with my own eyes!'

'There, there,' I said, for I remembered nothing about getting into the boat except how I had seen smoke billowing from the bridge and how, amid the terror and confusion I had clutched Henry's hand and followed him blindly, putting one foot in front of the other and doing what I was told until I was swept off my feet and deposited in the boat. I could think of nothing else but to murmur meaningless phrases and pull Mrs Fleming in against my chest, but she persisted: 'Is it or is it not your fault that this boat is overcrowded? Is it or is it not your fault that my little Emmy is dead?' Her voice had become cracked and low, and the others had gone on to talk about other things and so probably didn't hear us. Only Mary Ann heard, for she was helping me with Mrs Fleming, and once again she tried to ease her mind, saying, 'Now, now, dear. One person more or less isn't going to make a difference.'

'It wasn't one,' hissed Mrs Fleming, as if she were imparting some terrible secret. 'It was her and Hardie. That's two, isn't it? I count two.'

'And thank goodness for that, then,' said Mary Ann. 'Without Mr Hardie, we'd be lost.'

'And we'll be lost with him!' croaked Mrs Fleming. 'You mark my words.'

Mary Ann and I exchanged a look, but Mrs Fleming sank into an exhausted silence. I continued through the afternoon with my arms around her shoulders, whispering encouraging things to her the way one would to a child. She seemed to sleep for a while, but immediately upon waking she said, 'It should have been you. Emmy should be here beside me, but your husband bought you a ticket, didn't he? That has to be the explanation. If it weren't for your money, the boat wouldn't have been so overloaded in the first place. If it weren't for your money, little Emmy wouldn't be dead.'

I remained calm, for of course she was upset and talking nonsense. I replied that no one was allowed on the *Empress Alexandra* without a ticket. 'You can misunderstand me if you want to,' she began evenly, but then her temporary calm evaporated and she started to scream: 'It should have been her! It should have been her!' It took three of the men to subdue her. Finally, she became quiet and slumped down between Hannah and me, either asleep again or in a trance. Mary Ann took my turn at the bailer so as not to wake her up.

Because of the clouds, the sun faded away rather than set, but in the diminishing light, I could see that Mrs Fleming had regained a kind of peace. When she asked for the bailer, I supposed she wanted it for private reasons. I had no idea she intended to drink seawater. I didn't see her do it, but in the night I felt her shivering, so I adjusted the blanket, which had fallen from her shoulders, and Hannah and I took turns holding her tightly against our bodies. Once in the night she mumbled something incoherent, and in the morning she was dead. Later, after Mr Hoffman had allied himself with Hardie, Mrs Grant used this as an example of Hoffman's treachery, of how he had killed Mrs Fleming with the truth.

THE *EMPRESS ALEXANDRA*

The others in the lifeboat talked about how they had seen Mr Hardie on the *Empress Alexandra*, going about his duties with black looks and evil already evident in his heart, but I never saw him before the day of the disaster. My experience of the deckhands and servants was as uniformed furniture, usefully located for the convenience of the passengers, and by passengers I mostly mean Henry and me. I was newly dazzled, not only by the ship's grandeur, but by Henry, who was proving as substantial in personality as he was in breeding and means. In London, Henry had arranged for me to purchase a new wardrobe, and I glided up and down the decks like a fairy princess, intensely but selectively aware of my surroundings, so that I noticed the chandeliers and fluted champagne glasses and the sunsets that spilled buckets of color across the sky, but not the intricate mechanics that allowed the meals to be served on time or the ship to keep to her course. I have mentioned seeing the Colonel and Mrs Forester on board; eventually, I also remembered Mrs McCain, for she could often be found playing bridge or solidly ensconced with a book of fiction in the reading room on the first deck, but I can't say I remember her companion, Mrs Cook, or her servant, Lisette.

Later, I had a lot of time to think about the ship – about what I remembered and what I didn't – and I tried to apply what Mr Sinclair had told us about the science of remembering and forgetting. Dr Cole told me that the mind can work to suppress traumatic experiences, and I suppose that is true, but sometimes I think the failure to remember is not so much a pathological tendency as a natural consequence of necessity, for at any one moment there are hundreds of things that could take a person's attention, but room for the senses to notice and process only one or two.

I do remember one incident to do with the *Empress Alexandra*'s crew, however. As the ship prepared to set out from Liverpool, I was standing at the rail and gazing with astonishment at the crowds of well-wishers who had come to wave us on our way, when Captain Sutter came striding along the deck as if he were restraining himself from breaking into a run. His boots made a great clatter, and he was followed by several seamen, who were struggling under the weight of two large wooden chests secured with massive locks. The captain kept glaring back over his shoulder and muttering, 'You fools!' and then he would look ahead again and shout out, 'Pardon me, pardon me,' in order to clear a path through the crowd of passengers trying to spot their loved ones on the dock below.

'Why didn't you take those straight to the safe room?' the captain hissed to the men just as he brushed past me. 'You might as well have posted an advertisement so that any thief will know exactly what to look for!'

I followed along at a distance, pretending to scan the faces in the crowd whenever the captain looked back to chastise his men, but he was preoccupied and took no note of me. When he descended a set of stairs, I held well back, my heart pounding as if I were transgressing some unwritten law, but I had no trouble making out what was said in the echoing stairwell. The group soon stopped at a door next to the purser's office, and the captain called out: 'Mr Blake, did you bring the key?' I stayed in the shadows, then hurried back up the stairs so I wouldn't be discovered when their attention turned from their task, as it was eventually bound to. I supposed the door led to the safekeeping room where they had stored the box containing the necklace Henry had bought me in London, as well as my rings and Henry's heirloom watch. This is how I knew that what Penelope Cumberland later told me about two chests full of gold was the truth.

Henry was more interested in the other passengers than I was, but he was always attentive to me, and he more than filled my need for human companionship, which has always been low. He wouldn't have stayed up late to play cards and talk about politics in the smoking room if I had asked him not to, which I never did. I liked to have time to myself to fix my hair and arrange things alone in our cabin before Henry came to bed. I liked to gaze out of the porthole and watch the moon on the water, and I liked to savor my good fortune at having met Henry just when I thought I might have to become a governess. From the safety and solitude of my stateroom, with its Belgian linen and porcelain washbasin, I could look back on the events of the previous year and try to make sense of them; but in the end, the only sense I could make of my parents was that they were weak.

The business partners who had defrauded my father had also effectively ended his life, for when it became clear that he did not hold the patents on which his business relied and for which he had mortgaged not only his offices but also the house where we lived, he shot himself. What had Papa imagined a wife and two daughters would do without him? What my mother did was throw up her hands and let her hair fall down around her face so that when she made her erratic way to and from the shops, the beggar children scurried into the gutter, pointing and afraid. My sister Miranda immediately rolled her sleeves up and managed to get work as a governess, but when she encouraged me to do the same, I resisted. It might have been a manifestation of my mother's passive streak that tempted me to throw up my own hands and hope to be rescued, but I also had some of Miranda's decisiveness in me – perhaps the same decisiveness that had persuaded my father to shoot himself rather than face the humiliation of poverty, which goes to show that admirable traits are often exactly the same as negative ones, only expressed in a different way. Whatever it was, the trait hadn't taken root in me in the same way as it took root in my sister, and I will admit that my mother often called me stubborn as a child. No sooner had Papa been buried than Miranda went straight to brushing up on her French grammar and arithmetic, and off she went to Chicago, whence she sent frightening letters filled with excruciating details about the children's daily life and academic progress. Or maybe I wasn't decisive at all. Maybe I was a hopeless romantic like my mother, just one who was lucky enough to avoid madness by finding the romance and security her heart desired.

Just as Henry and I were embarking for London, the Archduke and heir to the Austro-Hungarian throne was assassinated by Serbian nationalists while visiting the Bosnian capital, and when Austria-Hungary threatened to declare war on Serbia in retaliation, we were advised to cut short our visit and return to New York as soon as possible. Most of the people traveling on the *Empress Alexandra* had booked their passage at the last minute in order to leave Europe quickly, which added to the sense that some global force had taken us in its grip and that we had been powerless to resist. Even before the shipwreck, the grand strategies that were playing themselves out on the continent lent an urgency and gravity to our homeward journey that only served to heighten the stark contrast between the luxury and purpose of the ocean liner and my precarious circumstances of a few weeks before. Penelope Cumberland and I listened to the serious talk of the men with one ear, but the other ear we turned toward each other as we tried out opinions on things we knew nothing about. The captain was receiving regular wireless dispatches, which he reported on at dinner, prompting much discussion and posturing among the men, who liked to pontificate about the events of the previous month for the benefit of the ladies. When we learned that the Archduke's wife, Sophie, had been shot, too, right through her pregnant belly, Penelope and I felt entitled to proclaim our horror to the table at large, for we were women and this was a rare mention of a woman in political affairs. But the talk soon surged on to the invasions and declarations of war that were happening in quick succession.

'Imagine, all that fuss about one dead duke,' I whispered to Penelope.

'Archduke,' said Penelope, causing us both to laugh. But mostly we talked of our weddings, for she had been recently married as well, and while we both acknowledged that our small talk was far less significant than the conversations seething around us, we also agreed that the world would be a better place if all people had to worry about were weddings and stayed away from war.

After we had become friendly, Penelope leaned closer to my ear than usual and said, 'You've probably wondered why Mr Cumberland and I weren't seated at the captain's table at first, but we are now.' Of course I had wondered, but I didn't admit to it. 'My husband is an employee of a British bank,' she went on, 'and he was appointed to accompany a large shipment of gold to New York.' She told me he wore a special key around his waist at all times, and since he needed to be in close contact with the captain and also with the other bankers on board, it seemed best for them to have a pretext for those relationships to prevent people from asking too many questions. 'Of course, it has to do with the war,' she whispered. Later, Henry told me to take Penelope under my wing, saying his bank hoped to enter into a business relationship with the bank her husband worked for. He had once told me that his banking colleagues were watching the European situation with great interest, as there were always large profits to be made in war.

I think I liked Penelope all the better after that, but where I felt I had finally found my true place in the world, she was timid, and I had all I could do to convince her that she belonged at the captain's table as much as anybody did. We practiced table manners. I lent her two of my new dresses, and I taught her to rustle her skirts and walk with her shoulders back and her eye on a distant goal. I told her to smile and laugh – but not too broadly – when she didn't know what else to do, and the captain did his bit to encourage her by letting her walk in to dinner ahead of everyone else, as if it were the most natural thing in the world. 'Even if you can't feel it in your heart,' I told her, 'you can surely pretend.'

The only time Henry and I ever argued was on the *Empress Alexandra*. He had led me to believe his parents knew the real reason he had broken off his engagement to Felicity Close, and whenever I asked him for details, he said, 'They know everything' or 'I can't marry Felicity because I don't love her. It wouldn't be fair to her, and I told them as much,' but it finally became apparent he had left out the part about me. 'But what will happen when we get to New York?' I wanted to know. 'How will you explain me? Surely it would be best to inform your parents in advance!'

'It will take me a few days to arrange things, but I want to tell them face-to-face,' said Henry. 'And of course I'll need to find us somewhere to live, but don't worry. You will be able to choose the curtains and furniture.' He was trying to distract me with furnishings the way a fisherman drops a glittering lure into the water in hopes of attracting a stupid fish, but I wasn't biting. 'But what will I do in the meantime? Where will I stay?'

'Can't you stay with your mother? I had assumed you could stay there.'

'She's gone to live with her sister in Philadelphia. Besides, I want to be with you!'

Henry put his hand on my shoulder and said 'Darling' three or four times in succession, but I shrugged him off. 'You want to hide me away!' I exclaimed as the full meaning of his words sank in. When he saw that I wasn't going to give in, he reluctantly agreed to go to the ship's radio room that very afternoon and arrange for a wireless message to be sent to his mother informing her that he would be coming home with a wife. Only in retrospect did I fully comprehend the import of this, for if Henry hadn't sent that message – and I came to wonder if he had – it would have been as if we had never been married, for any proof of the event would have been lost with Henry in the sea. Of course, the London magistrate who married us must have a record of it, but he was far away, and his country was at war.

Penelope and I remarked to each other that the world seemed to be getting bigger and more dangerous, with countries we had never heard of dragging the rest of us into their affairs. As I write this, though, I can see that a world that collapses in on itself until it is a mere wooden speck is dangerous, too; and in the lifeboat, I spent many hours wondering if there were an optimal size to the world – some equilibrium set of dimensions where things wouldn't boil over and where I would be safe. As a child, I had thought my family's purchase on the world secure, and then my father lost his money and shot a hole in his head. My mother took one look at the blood congealing on the polished floor before dropping her parcel of newly embroidered linens and going almost instantly mad. I had also thought the *Empress Alexandra* was safe. For one naive moment, I had all that I needed – more than I needed; but that, too, had been only a pleasant illusion. I wondered if all a person could hope for was illusion and luck, for I was forced to conclude that the world was fundamentally and appallingly dangerous. It is a lesson I will never forget.

PART II

DAY FIVE

It wasn't until the deacon had said prayers over Mrs Fleming and her body had been lowered into the water by Mr Hardie and the Colonel that anyone noticed that only one of the lifeboats was still in sight. We had lost the other one during the night. I could tell people were dejected to have more bad news coming directly after Mrs Fleming's death, but Hardie was oddly jovial and announced to everyone that he was going to catch us a fish. He unsheathed the long knife he wore at his waist, leaned out over the side of the boat, and gazed into the water, the knife poised above his head. The clouds had lifted and the sun illuminated the ocean to a brilliant jewel-like translucence, and sure enough, barely an hour had passed before Hardie plunged his knife into the water and pulled a huge fish into the boat. It was about three feet long, rather flat in shape, and of a mottled brown color. It flipped about in the bottom of the boat until Hardie slit it from gills to anus, after which it flipped twice more and then lay still.

'Supper,' said Hardie, holding the fish up to gleam in the sun.

Isabelle asked, 'Are we going to eat it raw?' and Hardie answered, 'No, we're going to sauté it in a garlic and butter sauce.' I found myself wondering how this was possible and believing for a moment that because Hardie had said it, it could be done. Even when he had passed out the pieces of dripping, uncooked fish, his hands still covered in reddish slime, the illusion held, and I was able to eat the raw flesh without retching, though Greta barely made it past Mrs Grant to lean out over the side and vomit, and Mary Ann refused to eat it at all until I told her to imagine we were at her wedding banquet and were just starting the fish course.

I ate my morsel of fish slowly, savoring it and knowing that it was as valuable for its moisture as for the protein our wasting bodies so sorely needed. The taste was slightly salty, which might have been because Mr Hardie had rinsed the fish in the ocean after gutting it, but it was the texture that surprised me the most. It wasn't flaky the way cooked fish is flaky, but firm and muscular – almost living. I had of course visited farms and seen where cows and pigs came from, and even in the city it was possible to buy a live chicken or to see one slaughtered, so I wasn't naive about the realities of turning livestock into food. But with the fish, I felt we had come very close to the thin membrane separating the living from the dead and that no matter what pretty names we had for things – coq au vin or angels on horseback or lobster Newburg – the hard fact of the matter was that life depended on the ability to subjugate other creatures to our use.

The fish brought a kind of holiday mood upon us. When Anya Robeson told Charlie to pretend he was eating a seed cake, it gave us the idea to take turns naming our favorite foods and pretending we were eating those. The Colonel said something facetious about military rations, and Mrs McCain had to be stopped from describing all the dishes at a typical Sunday supper in the McCain household. Mary Ann, of course, merely repeated what I had suggested about her wedding feast, but when it came to my turn, I said, 'Right now I can't think of anything much better than raw fish. I am developing quite a taste for it!'

'Good, because ye'll get some more tomorrow,' said Mr Hardie. As he said it, his eyes found mine and we shared a long look. He dipped his chin in a faint nod, as if I had pleased him in some way. I nodded back, and for the rest of the evening I savored that brief exchange. It was something I had been waiting for but had long since stopped expecting. Later, I tried to catch his eye again, but he either failed to notice me or pretended not to, and I wished I had been satisfied with that first small crumb of acknowledgement and hadn't asked for more.

Catching the fish went a long way toward restoring the confidence we had lost during the episode with the lights. It seemed too easy

– one minute Hardie was unsheathing his knife and peering over the side and the next he was drawing forth sustenance from the water; and when he repeated the performance later in the day, Maria and Lisette began to turn their worshipful eyes on him at regular intervals.

The deacon had uttered some kind of verbal incantation over the fish, and even though we had each eaten only a few small chunks of it, we felt a certain bodily satisfaction, because we were reminded of a merciful God and because we now knew Hardie had only to plunge his knife into the back of the sea for it to cough up the elements of our survival. But after those two, we caught no more fish. Every day we expected the ocean to yield more of its bounty, and when Hardie failed to make this happen, we saw it as a wilful withholding on his part rather than bad luck or the fact that soon after, the wind came up and it became impossible to visually pierce the choppy cobalt surface of the sea. The idea of a flat ocean, which we had enjoyed for five full days, took its place with the future and the past beyond our myopic imaginations.

The fish became a symbol of what Hardie could do if he wanted, of what he might do if we would only behave and stop questioning his plan for us. His eventual failure to provide was not the only reason for a growing undercurrent of anger. He continued to predict a change in the weather. He said, 'When it comes, ye'll see for yerselves that there are too many people in the boat,' but we didn't want to hear it. It made us angry because we didn't know what we were supposed to do about it, even when what he said was true. Were we supposed to simply fade away like Mrs Fleming? But these feelings of anger and doubt accumulated gradually. On the evening of the fifth day, we were still grateful to Hardie for the miracle of the fish.

The deacon liked to recount Bible stories, and he used this occasion to tell us about the fishes and the loaves. The moment he launched into a parable or psalm, Mary Ann and Isabelle stopped whatever they were doing, and Anya Robeson let little Charles sit on her lap without his ears covered whenever the deacon held forth. I have to admit that I, too, could be lulled by the familiarity of the stories, despite the fact that some of them were quite grim. People like repetition. They like to know how a story ends, even when it ends with everyone but Noah dying in the flood. The deacon would tell a story that was known to all of us and then find parallels between it and our situation on the boat, and certainly the story of the ark came in handy for that. But the deacon was creative, and he adapted the trials of Moses in the desert and the parting of the Red Sea to our situation, too. He taught us the 'Song of the Sea' – which was all about how God would save the chosen ones even as he sank the enemy like a stone – so that we would be able to recite it when we were finally saved.

Mr Sinclair told everyone that the story of Noah's Ark had been adapted to the Christian tradition from something ancient and heathen. 'Babylonian flood stories included not only the deluge, but other familiar elements as well – the raven and the dove, for instance. That can't be a coincidence,' he said, but the deacon was quick to dismiss the idea as heresy. Mary Ann looked concerned – not so much about possible heresy as about whose side to take in the debate, the deacon's or Mr Sinclair's, which I told her was also mine. Fortunately, Mr Sinclair was not only a scholar but a peacemaker, and he assuaged everyone's feelings by quoting Boccaccio, who apparently talked about how people like to believe the bad rather than the good and how there can be no poetry without myths.

As the days passed, I wondered if Hardie had really caught a fish at all or if we had suffered a mass hallucination. The present seemed fixed and immovable, the past compressed and distant, as subject to interpretation as a passage of dense theological text. It seemed just as likely that we had been born in the boat as that we all had histories and ancestors and a blood connection to the past. As for the future, it was impenetrable, even to thought. Where was the proof that it even existed? Or that it ever would? Like the fish, it had to be taken on faith.

NIGHT

It was remarkable what a little food in our stomachs did for our frame of mind. While we huddled together against the evening chill, Mrs Cook launched into another of her gossipy accounts, filled with personal details about the royal family that she couldn't possibly have known. Still, she entertained us, and I found myself hanging on every word just the way all of the women in our section of the boat were doing. When she ran out of things to say on the subject, Mary Ann told us about the people in her social circle, but her stories lacked cohesion and were as full of sighs and exclamations as they were of words.

There was another sort of story that proliferated on the boat, particularly in the evenings, when we would seek to pass the time in any way we could. These were secret stories, stories that were told in whispers, shreds of stories that might consist of a mere impression or a snatch of dialogue or a look someone had caught in someone else's eye. Isabelle was an expert at diagnosing expressions: 'Did you see the look Mr Hardie just gave me?' she might say with a shudder, and then she would add, 'Only someone completely uncivilized would leer at a person like that.' A single look opened up whole biographies of speculation, and it was this sort of speculation that so interested the prosecutors and that they took as fact. Isabelle credited Hannah and Mrs Grant with having invented a code of communication that didn't include any words, only nods and glances, and these Isabelle would decipher for whoever was sitting near her. She told me once that a particularly dark scowl Hannah gave to Mr Hoffman was a wordless witch's curse; and later, when Hoffman stumbled and almost fell out of the boat, she looked meaningfully over at me and mouthed, 'You see?'

Sometimes a person who had been given a story in confidence would appropriate it and pass it on as his or her own, and of course the stories changed as a result. A story I had told to Mary Ann about how I was planning to win over Henry's mother came back to me as a story about how Henry's mother had refused to receive me. There is nothing a person can do to combat false rumors without making the situation worse, so I did not try to set the record straight, only resolved to keep my own counsel regarding personal matters from then on.

I overheard Mrs Cook telling Mrs McCain that she had witnessed an altercation between Mr Hardie and Captain Sutter on the day we set sail. She hadn't then known who Mr Hardie was and only put it together afterwards, she said, but Mr Hardie seemed to be on the verge of being sacked.

The incident ended with Mr Hardie apparently agreeing to some condition the captain had laid down and the captain calling after him, 'And if you don't abide by that, I'll throw you overboard myself.' The two women spent an entire afternoon speculating on the significance of the incident, as if it had some great meaning, as if it would explain anything about Hardie that could not be fully accounted for by the events we all witnessed in the boat. Days later, when I was resting on the blankets near Mrs Cook, she told the same story to me, but by then she had added details to it. It was after Mr Hardie had told us more about the man named Blake, and she now determined that Mr Blake was the person Hardie and the captain were arguing about. She also added the usual retrospective judgment, saying, 'There was no doubt in my mind even then that our paths would cross again.'

Colonel Marsh whispered to various people that he had once seen Mr Hardie give up a bottle of whisky to one of the officers without so much as a snarl. Could it have been Blake? Did Blake hold some sort of power over Hardie? Were the two men in cahoots regarding some underhanded enterprise? Were they bitter rivals? The stories went round and round the boat, prompting others to come up with their own recollections, all of which, taken together, proved to them that Mr Hardie had a black and mysterious past. The stories about Hardie were the most prized and worried-over stories of all, but they had to be treated carefully as it wouldn't do for him to know he was being talked about. Each whispered revelation or fabrication was put together with the other story fragments and obsessively discussed and interpreted, as if the resulting narrative would finally explain why we found ourselves adrift on that vast and lonely sea.

On the very first day, Mr Preston, who was a stickler for numerical details, told Mr Sinclair that he had befriended the ship's purser and found out that the owner of the ship had fallen deeply into debt. This caused Mr Preston to wonder if the ship had been in ill repair as a result of the owner's financial state and if the hasty departure had left some necessary item of maintenance undone. Eventually this story was transformed into one where the owner of the *Empress Alexandra* had arranged for the destruction of his ship in order to profit through insurance. After Mr Hardie told the story of how the ship had been sold to someone who was able to turn a better profit, Mr Preston brought up the purser's remarks again. Of all the people on the boat, Mr Preston was the least subtle. It never occurred to him that there were nuances and layers of discourse, and I never saw him bending his head discreetly or talking in low tones. If he wanted to say something, he said it straight out, and that night he remarked loudly to the Colonel, 'I thought the *Empress Alexandra* had been sold to an owner who was able to turn a profit! Do you think Mr Hardie might have made the part about a new owner up?' Mr Hardie, who of course overheard him, threw the bailer he was using straight at Mr Preston and snapped, 'You wouldn't find the likes o' me workin' for the tight-fisted weasel who used to own 'er. I gave that bastard enough o' my blood!' If this were not proof enough for Mr Preston, he didn't dare say.

I can't be too critical of the way others used stories to pass the time, regardless of the accuracy of what they were saying, for sometimes Mary Ann and I did the same thing. I would tell her about the day I had first seen Henry, and I would embellish the details for hours: what he had been wearing, how he had drawn up to the establishment where he worked in a sleek motorcar, how he had emerged one inch at a time, slowly revealing himself like a portrait taking shape on a canvas. I could make that part of the story take ten minutes – or longer if Mary Ann was in a mood to ask me questions about details I left out, which she often was. I had lost the heel of my shoe and was hobbling along the pavement, and Henry gallantly searched up and down the gutter and across the street; and when he couldn't find it, he escorted me home in his motorcar. 'Just like Cinderella!' cried Mary Ann. It was one of the few times I ever laughed in the lifeboat, for the image was more apt than she knew. I didn't tell her that the day on the sidewalk beneath the marble steps of the bank was not really the first time I had ever seen Henry, any more than the ball was the first time Cinderella or her stepsisters had heard of the handsome prince, but I liked to think of it that way. For one thing, it was the first time Henry had set his blue eyes on me, and for another, it made a nicer story. I didn't like to think about the week I had spent watching him and figuring out his daily itinerary or the day I had waited for him until evening, lopsided in my broken shoe, and he had failed to appear.

For her part, Mary Ann would tell me about shopping for her trousseau in Paris and about her fiancé, Robert, and how she had allowed him to take her virginity in a lovely wooded glade filled with singing birds and the scent of honeysuckle. It was the weekend before she and her mother had set sail for Europe, and Robert had come to their country house in order to say goodbye.

'He didn't *take* your virginity!' I cried, only at the last second remembering to keep my voice low to protect her privacy. 'You gave it to him as a gift.' After a bit of thought I added that in my experience, people who gave gifts were very likely to get something of equal or greater value in return, but Mary Ann was terrified she might be pregnant and also that she might not have a chance to make her sin right before God if she perished at sea, although maybe she deserved to die, she didn't know. She asked my opinion about it, and I was surprised how fervent she was in her desire to know the exact boundaries between what constituted sin and what didn't, as if there were some watertight membrane a person could step across and through which the sinfulness could not pass. She confessed that her worry was more of a practical nature than of a spiritual one, and in her mind, that fact compounded the original sin several-fold and sent her into a spiral of remorse. 'Shouldn't I be sorry for God's sake alone?' she asked me. 'But I think I am the most worried for my own account, for how it will look if I am pregnant at the wedding and unable to fit into my dress, or how it will look if Robert leaves me and then I give birth to an illegitimate child.'

As I listened, I became convinced that Mary Ann didn't know very much about how a person might become pregnant and how she would know if she were not, but I tried to reassure her. 'The wedding dress is lost, isn't it? So you can console yourself on the first concern right away. When you marry Robert, you will have to buy a new one. Alternatively, you can do what Henry and I did – a quick legality, no frills, no fuss. Not that I wouldn't have liked a pretty dress and a big ceremony, but sometimes expediency prevails over romance. And as for your second concern, there are people who can help you with that sort of thing should the need arise.' I told her that she must cross that bridge when she came to it and not before. 'There is nothing else to be done.' But Mary Ann would not let herself off the hook so easily and went on to suggest that the ordeal in the lifeboat was God's way of punishing her.

'That makes no sense at all! Why would God be punishing the rest of us for something you have done?' She looked at me in a way that suggested that I would be able to answer that question better than she, while I tried to tell her it was my view that she hadn't committed a sin at all, that I myself had had relations with Henry before our trip to the magistrate and that the idea of transgressing had added spice to the adventure; but my words were hardly a match for millennia of Christian teaching. The moon was bathing the boat in silver light when Mary Ann crept over to the little deacon and put her face next to his ear and poured out the entire wrenching story. I watched as the deacon put his hands on either side of her narrow face and used his thumb to make the sign of the cross on her forehead, first dipping his hand over the gunwale as if the ocean were only a basin of holy water, conveniently placed at his elbow for just this moment of need. After that, Mary Ann seemed more peaceful, and a day or two later she had physical proof that she wasn't pregnant after all.

With so many women in the lifeboat, some of them must have had to deal with the problem of bleeding, but if so, they were quiet and said nothing about it. I wondered if the shock of our circumstances and the dehydration that was affecting our salivary glands might also be inhibiting the flow of blood. In any case, when Mary Ann tugged at my elbow and whispered to me that she was bleeding, I was not sure what to tell her. I used the occasion to attract Hannah's attention, and she gave me several pieces of cloth, ripped from an old petticoat, that Mary Ann was able to adapt for her purposes. After Mary Ann was settled, I signaled my thanks to Hannah. For the second time on our journey, our eyes locked for longer than was necessary. Her half smile, which at first seemed to be a friendly welcome to my thanks, faded and turned into a different expression altogether, almost as if she had been startled by something she had seen in my face or over my shoulder, and my first instinct was to turn around and protect myself from whatever was behind me. But I didn't want to break the contact, which was as thrilling as it was disturbing, so in the end, Hannah was the first one to look away when Mrs Grant called her name and asked her to hand over the satchel she carried with her, which had contained the pieces of cloth.

That night, our fifth in the boat, the question the men kept coming back to was whether or not the owner of the *Empress Alexandra* had kept her in good repair. Mr Preston insisted that this was a crucial fact. He couldn't understand the views of a vocal minority that it mattered not at all. Not now. Not when there was nothing that could be done about it. In an attempt to prove this point, Mr Sinclair asked us to engage in what he called a thought experiment. 'Suppose we replace the word "ship" in this discussion with the word "world." What if the world was kept in ill repair, but we could not know this? Furthermore, the idea would never even occur to us. Would it matter?' He paused to give us a chance to consider this before going on to say, 'And now suppose we somehow find out that yes, the world has been shamelessly neglected by whoever is responsible for its upkeep. Does that change things? Does it change how we live our lives on earth? I contend that in the case of the world and also in the case of the *Empress Alexandra*, we are faced with the here and now of our situation and that the irreversible and unknowable events that brought us to this time and place not only cease to be important, they cease to matter at all.'

Isabelle asked who was responsible for the world – if Mr Sinclair was talking about God, he should come right out and say so. But if people were responsible, then of course they could always recognize their mistakes and change their ways. I instinctively looked over at the deacon, certain that he would have something to say about this, but he was staring moodily over the gunwale, and whatever he was thinking, he kept it to himself. Instead, it was Hardie who spoke up. 'It all depends on whether or not ye're to meet the bastard in the future. For my part, if I ever have a chance to meet my maker face-to-face, I'll bloody well have a few things to say about the way things here on earth are run.'

DAY SIX

In those first days we looked at Hardie as a kind of oracle. His sort of encouragement was neither glib nor plentiful, so when his first predictions failed to come true (we were not immediately rescued and the fine weather continued to hold), we were not overly alarmed. What happened, though, was that certain people began to pump him for more particulars: 'Is the wind from the west or the southwest? Is that a good sign or not?' 'What is it they say about a red sky at dawn?' or 'What is the significance of a pinkish-yellow halo around the moon?'

'It means a change in the weather,' replied Hardie, and, indeed, on the sixth day, the blue sky gave way to a layer of ragged clouds, which only now and then parted to show an angry sun. The wind had subsided overnight, but now it stirred the surface of the sea, which changed color dramatically depending on whether or not the sun broke through. It was no longer green and glassy or cobalt and opaque, but a dark and fathomless color that was neither gray nor blue. Little waves crested and broke over the rail of the boat, prompting Mr Hardie to give up the tin cups he kept under his seat and to set two more of us to bailing, despite Mr Nilsson's warning that this would contaminate our drinking water with salt. He made us memorize a detailed roster of duties: in addition to the five bailers and the four people sitting along the rail who were to keep watch for signs of approaching ships, two others were appointed to keep tabs on the lifeboat that still bobbed in the distance, and four people at a time manned the oars and were charged with keeping the prow of the boat headed into the waves to prevent them from breaking over the side. Six women were assigned to scan the water for signs of fish, but its corrugated surface foiled our efforts. At one point, a thin woman named Joan startled everyone by calling out, 'I see one!' but it was only Mr Hardie's fish, which he had secured to the side of the boat in order to preserve its meat in the cool ocean water. Every hour, the Colonel called out 'Time!' and we switched jobs or rested in our seats or went forward in pairs or threes to sleep on the piles of damp blankets that could not be kept dry despite the canvas boat cover that we tucked in over them. Mr Hardie made a great production of mealtime, even though our water ration had been severely reduced and we received only a piece of fish or a bite-sized square of hardtack. Twice a day the deacon was called upon to say grace, and that evening, Hardie held up the second fish for a blessing from the sky.

Hannah was ill-tempered that day. She kicked Mary Ann's foot when it encroached on what she perceived as her territory, causing Mary Ann to weep quietly into her sleeve; and as we were eating breakfast, she said, 'If we're going to get rescued soon, what are you starving us for?' Perhaps it was inevitable that Hardie would be blamed for our hunger and maybe for our plight, but I had the sense Hannah didn't really blame him herself. Instead, she was, in a roundabout way, encouraging this sentiment in others, for she seemed to suppress a grim smile and nod in Mrs Grant's direction when others started to grumble and echo her complaint. I, too, had been eyeing the fish and the barrels of water and wondering what Hardie was saving them for.

Despite his edict that no one change seats without permission, Hannah said in a loud and provocative voice, 'Come now, Mary Ann, stop sniveling. I'm going to change places with you,' and she squeezed herself in beside Mrs Grant, abruptly displacing Mary Ann, who shot Hardie a fleeting look of injury; but Hannah stared right back at him in what seemed to me an open challenge, and he remained silent. I think Hardie might have lost some of his authority that day. He should have commanded Hannah to regain her original position, but he didn't, and then it was too late.

Unaided, Mary Ann was not able to withstand Hannah's determination and eventually moved to a vacant spot on the rail, so that she was sitting on the other side of Mr Preston from me. Then Hannah bent her head close to Mrs Grant's, and by dinnertime, most of the others were grumbling too, but about what, it wasn't entirely clear.

The wind had increased steadily over the course of the day, and just when Hannah and two of the other women left their seats to approach Hardie with a demand that the dinner rations be increased, a large wave crashed over the side of the boat, drenching everyone on the port side and knocking one of the standing women overboard. Hannah only saved herself by clutching on to Mrs Hewitt, a large, silent woman, who screamed and was knocked into the bottom of the boat. I heard someone shout out the name of Rebecca Frost, who had been an employee on the *Empress Alexandra* and who had sat, until now, quietly in her seat at the back of the boat. While I had never spoken to Rebecca, I had seen her glancing admiringly at Hannah and Hannah smiling at her in return; but now Rebecca was flailing about in the water behind the boat before disappearing inside a cresting wave. A second wave broke over her head, but again she rose from the blue-black water, and I remember her pitiful eyes staring, I thought, directly into mine. 'Do something!' I yelled. In her sworn statement, Hannah insisted she and Mrs McCain were the ones who exhorted Hardie to action and that I was only idly looking on, which goes to show that Hannah was not aware of as much as she claims.

Mr Hardie was standing in the aft of the boat. Behind him the clouds were made livid by the half-obscured sun. Dark water had engulfed Rebecca up to her nostrils. Strands of hair streamed over her face like black eels, and her white, beseeching hands clutched the air. 'Sit down!' barked Hardie, and Hannah, after her near miss, sat down and was quiet for once, while I shouted out, 'Isn't anyone going to help her?' Two of the men got up then and made as if to throw the life ring to Rebecca. The boat was rocking to and fro with the redistribution of weight, and each time it rocked, more water slopped in over the side.

'Bailers!' shouted Hardie. 'Who are my bailers? Stop gawking and get to work!' As he said it, he grabbed the life ring away from whoever was holding it. Mrs Grant shouted, 'She's over there,' and pointed to where Rebecca was frantically waving her hands at the sky and gurgling with watery attempts at speech. Her dress billowed around her, her cap was tied tightly over her ears, and while her life vest was serving to keep her head above water, it was not keeping the waves from rolling over her or the current from increasing the distance between her and us. Her expression was more surprised than horrified, and I thought I heard her call, 'Over here, Mr Hardie, over here,' almost politely. She was sure of being rescued, just as we were all, still, sure. The sea was rougher than it had been, and the level of water in the bottom of the boat was rising. Hardie spent precious minutes redirecting the bailers to their task, for everyone was either watching Rebecca or trying to keep from slipping off their seats in the pitching boat, during which time it began to occur to me that Rebecca's rescue was by no means a certain thing.

Only after what seemed like ages did Hardie order the oarsmen to steer the boat toward her, and when at last he fished her out of the water, I did not have the feeling that it was a heroic act. Hardie exuded more strongly than ever that air of omnipotence and the ability to bend nature and events to his will, but it now seemed slightly tinged with malice. In the succeeding days, I tried to think that his hesitation in rescuing Rebecca stemmed from an honest indecision about the manner in which a rescue could safely be accomplished given the choppy surface of the sea, the overcrowded situation in the boat, and the precarious balance of those who had jumped to their feet rather than remaining seated as they had been told. At the same time, it occurred to me – and it must have occurred to Mr Hardie as well – to wonder if Rebecca was the victim of some sort of natural selection and to think that if she had fallen overboard, maybe it was for the best. This thought was followed by the idea that Hardie's dedication was to those of us in the boat, not those outside of it, however they came to be there. Then, underneath everything else came the notion, sneaking into the strongbox of my thinking like water through an uncaulked chink, that Hardie was attempting to teach us a lesson of sorts. Oh, I knew my fate was in his hands already. It was not a lesson I needed to learn.

I don't think I was the only one who felt this way, given the silence that stretched between us, taut and thin as a rope, and the number of times I caught one or the other of the passengers staring fixedly at Hardie after he had finally hauled Rebecca in and the Italian women had stripped off her clothing and sandwiched her in among the blankets. It was fear in their eyes as much as awe and respect, though those words wouldn't describe the way Hannah looked at him, or Mrs Grant. Of course, it could have been the wind, which seemed to press down on us rather than blow, or our hunger, or the fact that now many of us were wet through; and of course we had all watched Rebecca almost die. We sat shivering in our places like bedraggled dogs as Mrs Grant made her way forward one careful step at a time to comfort Rebecca while the boat rocked and Mr Hardie shouted at the bailers and the Italian women emitted a chorus of operatic wailings and turned their tragic faces to the sky. All the while, Mrs Cook, who when she wasn't telling stories was strangely submissive, ineffectually dabbed at Rebecca's hair with a sodden rag and Hardie held the tin of wafers up to the dark afternoon sky and the deacon forced false enthusiasm into his voice at the repeated mention of Jesus Christ and we finally ate our scrap of crust in spiritless dejection.

I don't know what Rebecca was thinking, if she was thinking at all. For a long time she cowered in the dormitory and didn't speak. At one point she said, 'If only little Hans were here.' She shook visibly beneath the damp blanket. Hardie said gruffly, 'Well, we don't have room for 'im.' Hardie was not the only one who seemed angry. Mr Hoffman and his friend Nilsson were talking in low voices and now and then they looked from Rebecca to the rail of the boat, which was riding very low in the water, though probably no lower than it had been before, and I could see they were thinking that Hardie had made the wrong decision about fishing Rebecca out of the sea.

Overnight the wind lessened, but a thick fog had set in. When it lifted a day and a half later, the other lifeboat was nowhere in sight. I can't tell you how I missed it. Knowing other people were out there somewhere was not the same as seeing them floating more or less within reach and occasionally within hailing distance, even if we never got close enough to recognize their faces or to make out what was said.

DAYS SEVEN AND EIGHT

During those two days of fog, we all heard the sounds of a foghorn. There was no mistaking it. Mrs Grant asked if the other lifeboat might have carried such an instrument with it, and Hardie said, 'It's possible, but it sounds to me like the horn of a ship.'

Everyone was excited, but frustrated by the lack of visibility. We shouted out with all our might. We banged on the sides of the boat with the oars and the bailers, with anything that would make noise, but by noon, the sounds of the foghorn had ceased; and when the fog finally lifted and we saw that the second lifeboat was gone, it was as if some protective fog had lifted from our souls as well, leaving us clear-eyed and able to see the profound starkness of our situation. We had all heard the foghorn – there wasn't a question about that as there had been about Mr Preston's lights. After much discussion, during which Hardie was silently measuring the angle of the sun, Mr Preston decided that the occupants of the other lifeboat had been found and that our chances of a similar rescue were gone. This prompted Mr Nilsson to say, 'If we could see the other lifeboat, then surely they could see us. They'd never let a rescue ship leave the area without mounting a search.'

'You don't know Blake,' muttered Hardie. 'There's no telling what Blake would have done.'

'Blake,' said Mr Preston. 'He was the one who came up from the radio room. He was the one who helped to launch our boat.'

'He was the second officer on the *Empress Alexandra*,' added Greta.

'Aye,' said Mr Hardie. 'Meanest mongrel that ever passed for a man.'

Mr Preston turned to me and said, 'You knew Mr Blake, didn't you?' I replied that I didn't think I did. 'Then your husband knew him, for I'm sure I saw you standing together on the deck.'

I gave him a questioning look, and he stole a glance at Mary Ann before he said, 'I must be mistaken,' but he seemed to be holding something back, and I wondered what he was thinking of or if Mary Ann had merely been telling him one of those stories that circulated on the boat and that seemed to change with each telling.

'How do you know it was Blake's boat that stayed with us and not the other one we saw?' the Colonel wanted to know. 'Since the first days, we haven't been close enough to see them clearly.'

'It was Blake all right,' said Hardie. 'The other boat was full and the one we have been seeing wasn't. Besides, you notice how they never approached us.'

'But it was you who told us not to go near them!' exclaimed Hannah.

'Blake is a rabid dog. Didn't you hear that bearded fellow tell us how Blake pushed two people out of his boat? With the captain out of the way, he'd as soon kill me as look at me. It was better to stay away.'

'Or safer,' said Hannah.

'Safer is better. You haven't spent your lives at sea as I have. The men who go to sea are often the ones with something to escape!'

'Are you including yourself?' Hannah asked, but I was willing to believe Hardie had stayed away from Blake's boat in order to protect us. It was Hannah who whispered it around that Hardie had done it to protect himself.

'We don't really know why Blake pushed people out of his boat – maybe they caused some sort of trouble. What if there had been extra places in it after all?' demanded Mrs Grant, finally voicing something that had occurred to me days before and had probably occurred to the others as well. 'Even if the boat was damaged, it seems to me we might have helped fix it and then moved some of our people over. We should have at least tried. We might not be in such danger if we had.' As with many of the things Mrs Grant said, the suggestion of repairing the other boat was vague and without any specifics about how it might have been accomplished without materials or tools, but the idea that Hardie was acting out of pure self-interest had begun to creep into our consciousnesses. He had been so precise with other details; why had he neglected to tell us about his history with Blake back at the beginning? Perhaps he was making it up to cover for his mistakes. Perhaps Mr Hardie was the one with a past he wanted to hide.

The Colonel tried to steer the conversation back onto a more useful track: 'I'd lay a wager that the other lifeboat was hit in the fog by a passing ship and sank without being seen,' he said. 'If its occupants had been rescued, one of them would have mentioned us, regardless of Blake's thoughts on the matter.'

'Wouldn't the ship have felt the collision? Surely they would have known they'd run into something and tried to find out what it was,' said Mrs McCain, while Mrs Cook, who had been so vocal in the beginning, looked on like someone in a trance.

Hardie refused to comment on our interpretation of things. All he would say was 'Maybe' or 'Maybe not' when asked his opinion directly. Eventually Mrs Grant said, 'All this talk of being rescued, as if everything depends on someone else. I say we plot a course and set about trying to rescue ourselves,' which gave me a momentary burst of hilarious hope. It was so simple and obvious that I wondered why no one had mentioned it before. The inescapable fact was that we hadn't been rescued, so there seemed to be no reason now to stay in the vicinity of the wreck.

'Of course!' I exclaimed out loud, and others took

up the cry: 'God helps those who help themselves!' It was a principle I lived by, and while it sometimes might make a person who espoused it seem selfish and theologically uninformed, people who refused to live by it looked, to me, weak and parasitic. When the sun had first broken through the fog, I had been reluctant to face it, having grown accustomed to taking refuge in the night, in limited vision; and those crystal days where we could see forever, at least until the world curved and dropped off into nothingness, haunted me, because there was nothing to see. But now that we had a plan, I was glad to be able to see as far as the horizon because it gave us a destination – west!

God helps those who help themselves, I said over and over to myself, exactly the way I had said it to Felicity Close the time she came to see me. She had followed Henry one day, which is how she knew where I lived. She was well dressed, but she lacked airs, and I thought we might have been friends if we hadn't been rivals. I told her that we were both practical people and that practicality must prevail, but mostly I just listened. One of the things she told me was that Henry was steeped in traditions I couldn't hope to understand and that once he had come to his senses, she feared he would mourn their loss. She also said, 'This is very out of character for him. Henry is not rash or passionate in the least,' and I wondered if we were talking about the same man. She had her say and left, and while I felt sorry for her, I could see that I had freed Henry, both from tradition and from emotional restraint, which was something the upright Felicity would never have been able to do. It was this realization that took away any feelings of guilt I might have had.

Mrs Grant kept a constant vigil. She was dressed entirely in black. Her hair was pulled severely back, and even a week of wind and waves was not enough to loosen it from its fastenings. Her gaze did not waver in the face of nothingness. Her face burned. Then the skin peeled off and she turned a dark brown color; and still she gazed out to sea. I had the idea that if a ship appeared on the horizon after all this time, it would be because she had drawn it to her by her sheer determination and the force of her will. I could see the effect she was having on some of the others, who would make excuses to move near her or touch her shoulder as she went about her duties. I saw this and I think I understood it, but still I looked to Hardie as the foundation of my strength.

Hardie's continued belief was that it was wise to stay in the vicinity of the place where the ship had gone down and from which the distress signals had been sent and also where we had heard the foghorn, but Mrs Grant had made a forceful argument, and when, toward noon, the wind again sprang up, Hardie set to work fashioning the canvas boat cover into a sail by lashing it to two of the oars with strips cut from one of the blankets with his knife. He then cut away part of the safety rope that was attached to the perimeter of the boat and used it as a means of pulling the sail in and letting it out again, depending on the strength and direction of the wind. After inserting the oar-mast into the mast hole, he set a course that made sense, I assume, to him. To the rest of us, the horizon in front could not be distinguished from the horizon behind or to the sides. Still, I took courage from the fact that Mr Hardie seemed to have a plan. His hands were rarely still, and if Mrs Grant was the picture of quiet strength, Hardie was the picture of violent industry.

The oarsmen shipped their oars, and soon we were moving through the water quickly enough that we half expected the shores of America to rise before us at any minute. Using the long, stick-like tiller that was attached to the rudder and controlled its movement, Hardie pointed the boat as close to the wind as he could, which made the air rush at us across the port bow and caused the choppy water to feel a lot rougher than it had before. Because the sail had a tendency to push the boat over in the water, we had to counterbalance the tipping effect with our weight. This required constant alertness on our part, and it became a kind of grim game to keep the railing out of the water and the boat from capsizing altogether.

Rebecca, who had taken a chill and fever ever since her drenching in the ocean, now stared about with glassy eyes. At one point she fixed her gaze on Mr Hardie and shouted out, 'Father, Father! The little dog has run into the road!' Mrs Grant did her best to calm her, and Hannah said, 'There's no dog, Rebecca. You're thinking of something from long ago'; but this made Rebecca angry and upset. Tears oozed from her eyes. She said, 'You never liked him anyway, did you? It was only because of Mother that you bought him for little Hans.'

Even though these comments seemed to be directed at him, Hardie did not reply, concentrating instead on the many tasks he had set himself and which none of the rest of us understood. Finally, Mrs Grant snatched a rag from the satchel she kept at her feet, wrapped it into a bundle, and placed it into Rebecca's hands, saying, 'He's safe now, dear. Your little dog is safe.' Rebecca rocked back and forth in the bottom of the boat, oblivious to the water there, stroking her make-believe dog throughout the afternoon.

The wind continued to pick up, and before long the boat was shooting through the water with great speed. The bailers were steadily bent to their task, but the level of water in the bottom was rising rapidly, and I had the idea that the boat had sprung a leak. When it came my turn to bail, I searched the boards near my feet for anything that looked like a hole. At one point I found myself contemplating the water that swirled around my ankles. It was as if I had suddenly come awake from a deep sleep. I don't know how long I had been staring into nothingness, but when I 'woke up,' I was aware of an encompassing bodily weakness, of the tendency of my eyes to lose focus, of my ears to hear only disjointed snatches of the murmured conversations going on around me. For instance, I heard Hannah very clearly when she said, 'There was something between Hardie and that ship's officer, Blake. We might have been saved by now,' but I only made out the last part of Mrs Grant's reply: '. . . nothing about sailing . . . bide our time.'

When Hardie dropped the sail, saying, 'The wind's too strong' and 'She's far too heavy with water to sail,' and took up a bailer himself, even Mrs Grant didn't protest, for the boat immediately flattened out and the constant stream of water over the railing lessened to an intermittent spray. It was just in time, too, for the water had now reached a height well up on my shins. I redoubled my own efforts with the bailer, but the weakness that clouded my mind suffused my limbs as well. That was when Hardie said it, softly, I think, though I also have the sense that everyone heard him, in which case he must have been shouting to be audible over the wind and the flapping of the makeshift sail, which billowed up in the bow of the boat, where it had been spread to dry: 'Unless we lighten the load, we'll sink like a bloody stone.'

There was no reason to doubt him. I looked at the pile of sodden blankets, the casks of water and the hardtack tins that Hardie kept all but hidden under his thwart, the small accumulation of personal possessions stowed beneath the seats or floating about in the brine: Mrs Grant's sodden satchel, upon which her small feet rested, the Colonel's strongbox, little Charlie's stuffed bear, and thought, 'We can do without those,' not yet making the connection that we needed the food and water and blankets in order to survive and that the other things weighed twenty pounds at most, hardly the difference between salvation and death.

The others must have caught Hardie's drift before I did, for the wave of consternation was as sobering as the cold water that now and then washed in on us. There was a low murmuring. My leg was touching that of the deacon, who had turned in his seat in order to face what he had started to call his flock: it was as if an electric shock passed from his body to mine, and that is when I comprehended that Mr Hardie was finally asking for volunteers.

'Volunteer yourself!' said Hannah angrily, as though the rising water were Hardie's to deal with and had nothing to do with her or anyone else.

'The boat's too heavy to sail. We can't bail fast enough. As yet, the wind is no more than a breeze. Even if we give up on the idea of sailing, if we're hit with a gale it'll be too late.'

All of us looked out at the sea. I had been bailing and peering peevishly at the bottom of the boat for over an hour, so I had a distorted perception of what kind of water we were talking about. I had seen a pool approximately one foot deep, greenish in color, but mostly clear and filled with wet leather shoes of various sorts. Now I realized my mistake. The water he was talking about was bluish-black and rolled past us like an unending herd of whales. The lifeboat alternately rose high on their broad backs and slid down into the deep depressions between them.

Above us, clouds hurtled through the sky before the wind. The deacon had closed his eyes and clasped his hands under his chin and was murmuring, 'Yea, though I walk through the valley of the shadow of death, I will fear no evil.' I shivered, and for the first time since the day of the shipwreck, I felt profoundly afraid. We were doomed. This I knew for a certainty, or close to certainty, but still I looked to Hardie, outlined there in the back of the boat, glaring unwaveringly at us all, waiting patiently for us to make sense of our situation and respond in some way to what he had said.

The deacon was the first to speak, but he was merely buying time by asking, 'What do you mean? You need to explain everything clearly. Once we know what our options are, I'm sure that a rational decision can be made.'

'I think you know,' answered Hardie. 'By tomorrow, if the weather continues to worsen, water will be pouring over the gunwale faster than we can get it out. I'd say she'll take less than a minute to go under after the water reaches this point.' He tapped the wood just a few inches above the height the water had already reached. Of course, this was merely speculation, but whatever Hardie said, I took as fact.

As I write this, I realize that I make it sound as if we were having a conversation the way people converse in parlors over tea and biscuits, when in truth, my companions had to shout to make themselves heard over the sound of the wind and the crash of the water as it caved in on itself. Several people were shouting at once. Their words were jumbled about by the wind, and it was impossible to make complete sense of them.

'If we're not rescued, that is,' said the deacon desperately. 'You yourself said that they'd find us.'

'I know what I said, but they haven't found us yet, have they?' Hardie went on to tell us his interpretation of the foghorns. 'I'm convinced that was a foghorn from a large ship. If it collided with the other lifeboat, and I'm not saying it did, the people aboard would never have noticed, any more than we'd notice if we ran into a twig or a matchstick. And if, by some miracle or chance, the other boat was rescued and they tried to find us, the hard fact is that they didn't.'

There was silence in the boat, followed by angry muttering. My heart sank with disappointment. I felt misled as much as anything, even though part of me realized that Hardie had agreed to put the sail up because his hope of rescue had dwindled and maybe died. At that point I hated Hardie, but I loved him too – I needed him anyway, and I wanted him to know it. In order to please him, or at least to get his attention, I cried out, 'Let's not blame Mr Hardie for telling us the truth!' and to my relief, the grumbling in the boat subsided. I'm sure that Hardie gave me a look of approval, and my spirits soared briefly before settling down at a much higher level than they had been at only seconds before. I caught the poor little deacon's eye and felt a crimson flower of triumph blossom in my breast. 'Thy rod and thy staff, they comfort me,' I said and was rewarded with a wan smile not only from the deacon, but also from Mrs Cook, who briefly came out of her trance and reached across to pat my hand.

Hardie said, 'Even if the wind dies down immediately and we succeed in clearing the boat of water, we have only a little bit of fish left and only a few drops of water. Without water, we won't last six days.'

'Six days! Anything can happen in six days!' said the deacon with some of his old fire. 'Why, the world was created in six days!'

'All I'm saying is to think about it,' shouted Hardie, and with that he called for a shift of duties. He directed Mr Nilsson to use the rudder to keep our nose to the wind, while he himself set to work furiously scooping at the calm green water in the bottom of the boat and throwing it back out over the side to join with its turbulent black brethren. A change of shift was called seven more times. Seven hours passed, during which I was aware of each second, each bite of the wind against my face, each eternal moment of dread, each minute detail of that desolate scene, yet the time in retrospect passed in a heartbeat. Wave after wave crashed over the prow of the boat, undoing in an instant our hours of backbreaking labor, and still Hardie stuck with it, refusing to pass his bailer into less capable hands.

I fell into the grip of a great lassitude, a resignation

so powerful that I felt I could meet any future calmly. I do not know if this is because I trusted Mr Hardie with my life or because I knew that if I died, it would be with him. Whatever's coming to me, let it come, I thought; but around me the others were not so willing to resign themselves. Mrs Grant made her way into the center of the boat and delivered a speech about the human will, which inspired the deacon to remind us of divine will, and even little Mary Ann stopped whining long enough to direct an angry outburst at Mr Hoffman, whom she accused of lacking faith, when faith was the thing we needed most.

At some point that evening I fell asleep, though I thought it would be impossible to do so. It seemed only minutes later that I was shaken awake by Mary Ann, who was shivering uncontrollably. 'It's Rebecca,' she said. I watched as one of the Italian women reached over to brush Rebecca's tangled hair out of her eyes, which was when I saw how her mouth was open and her eyes were rolled up into her head.

The deacon said a prayer over her and the Colonel gave her life vest to one of the two sisters. Then the Colonel and Mr Hardie lifted her over the side and let her go. Her dress, which had been put back on her once it was dry, billowed up around her like wings, keeping her afloat for a minute or two. Then she sank and with her went the last shred of hope I had for myself.

HENRY

I first saw Henry when his photograph appeared in the society pages of the *New York Times*: 'son of . . . employed by . . . betrothed to . . .' et cetera, et cetera, nestled in among a host of details about a lavish engagement party and the bride's impressive family tree. It was intriguing information, and it came at a time when a governess job like the one held by my sister seemed to be the target at which my narrowing expectations were aiming. I had been bred to believe in a fanning out of prospects as I made my way from the wellspring of my birth to join ever-greater rivulets and streams of possibility, until the day I was deposited at a fertile delta where the last of the widening rivers finally met an ocean of opportunity. This seems an ominous metaphor now, but it seemed apt to me then, and that sunny and shimmering destination I was conditioned to think of as the happily ever after of married life. At the time of our parents' misfortune, Miranda was keeping company with a young physician, but their understanding did not survive the tumultuous year of our father's death. Instead of being crushed by the doctor's desertion,

Miranda seemed only momentarily dismayed. She took stock of her options, gathered letters of recommendation, and told me never to put my fortunes in the hands of a man.

'But you're going to be a working girl!' I cried, not believing for a minute that her chosen solution was a happy one for her.

'I will be my own master,' she declared.

'You will be little more than a servant,' I countered, but whether she was following a principle or whether the principle came along afterwards to help her accept the only solution she could think of, she never let on, and off she went to Chicago, leaving me to find affordable lodgings for myself and our mother in the top half of a house owned by someone our solicitor knew. We had sold most of the furniture and packed the rest of our possessions in boxes. I thought of it as a temporary arrangement and only unpacked what we needed for daily living, leaving the rest of the boxes stacked in a corner of a spare room.

That Henry was already engaged seemed only the mildest of impediments. I even viewed it as a good thing, for how would he have come to my notice without the write-up of his engagement party in the *Times*? In the same issue, which I had found when unwrapping a box of crystal goblets that had somehow escaped the sale, I found an article entitled LONDON MARKET CHEERFUL, which talked about gold and short-term bonds and mentioned the very firm I had just read about in the paragraph discussing Henry's employment. The task of unpacking was forgotten as I hastened to scan the paper for a date and realized that the issue I was reading was over three months old.

It was only the third time we met when Henry suggested the theory that each person was destined for one great love and that if he was lucky enough to find it in his lifetime, he ignored it at his own risk. I told him I thought that only some people were fortunate enough to have been born in the same time and place as their one great love, but that others, maybe even most, had been born ahead of or behind their optimal era. I thought of my mother, who had missed the opportunity of being swept off her feet by a dashing horseman by several centuries and at least one continent. Not long after making this declaration, however, Henry failed to appear at a prearranged meeting place, and as much as I tried to concoct alternate explanations, I suspected he was with his fiancée. 'I was worried about you!' I cried, throwing myself into his arms when he appeared the next day. 'I knew it must have been important, or you would have come.'

'It was important,' he said grimly, but for the rest of the evening he was moody and silent, and no matter what sort of things I said to him, he seemed not to hear. He told me he was going out of town for a period and would come to fetch me when he returned, but a mere three days later, he appeared on my doorstep looking haggard and ill.

I was overjoyed to see him. The governess job was beginning to have names and dates attached to it, and I saw the streams of possibilities running backward toward a fetid swamp of menial employment.

'I wasn't truthful with you!' Henry blurted out when I had fetched my shawl and we were outside, alone, or as alone as we could be in the squalid neighborhood where my mother and I now lived. Ragged children played in the yard and dared one another to ask Henry for money, but Henry, usually so cheerful and generous, didn't notice them.

'You had your reasons,' I told him, but the fact that I gave myself over to him completely and didn't care if he had been dishonest with me only made his face more gaunt and tortured. He sank to his knees in the dirt and said he wasn't moving an inch until I promised to marry him. I tugged at his jacket and said, 'Of course I'll marry you!' but that didn't seem to be what he wanted to hear either, and he stayed there, crouched in front of me, until I burst out, 'Henry! What is it?' as forcefully as I could because now I was beginning to be frightened that something was wrong with him, that he was sick or even dying and that he was worried my promise to marry him had been obtained under false pretenses that he was committed to, yet fearful of, making right.

Finally, because I couldn't think what else to do, I sank to my knees too, and we knelt there in the dust with the curious children, now emboldened by our diminished stature, circling round us and scuffing their shoes in the dirt, wanting desperately to pester Henry for the coins they knew he kept in his pocket but held back by the emotion that emanated from us both, strong as the magnetic field pulsing up from the earth's core, and also by astonishment, for I am certain they had never seen adults act like that before.

Henry's eyes had become dark – I'll compare them to the color of the sea when the clouds pile high above it, but of course that comparison did not occur to me at the time. My mind was blank and terrified, unable to fathom what had brought my handsome and worldly lover to his knees in a patch of dirt that was not a rich and earthy loam built up through generations of natural processes, but a combination of horse dung and wash water and boot scrapings and kitchen scraps that were too spoiled for even the ragamuffins to eat. Then I realized with a shock that seemed to leap like primordial fire from Henry's blazing eyes to my own that the thing that had brought Henry to his knees in that filthy courtyard was me.

I reached out with both of my hands, no longer frightened but not yet sure what to do with my power, and declared, 'I have found my one true love.' I grasped his two hot hands in my cool ones and told him that I didn't mind in the least if he lied to me so long as he had a good reason, which I trusted he did. 'I don't think I could bear to be lied to lightly,' I said, trying to elicit a smile, but

Henry was the picture of misery. He looked thin and endearing, not at all the worldly banker I had built him up in my mind to be.

'I lied to you twice,' confessed Henry. 'I didn't go out of town, but that's the least of it. The bigger lie is that I am already engaged and I haven't broken it off. I have meant to, but when I went . . .'

Of course I knew he was engaged, but the news, coming from his bloodless lips, struck me as if I were hearing it for the first time. 'Then how can you ask me . . .,' I started to say. 'Then how can I . . .' I was paralyzed by the conundrum of who should be the subject of the sentence and who the object. Had he done something awful to me or I to him? And now that he had confessed, should I own up to my own charade? I wanted to. I wanted to lie down in the grime and beg his forgiveness, for I realized with a start that whatever it was I had loved about Henry's station in life, I loved Henry himself more, and I didn't stop to consider whether Henry without his station would even be the same person, though the question fleetingly occurred to me – not out of any selfish reasons, but because the same could be asked about me: would I be the same Grace if some aspect of me Henry counted on were suddenly hacked off and discarded?

What I did think about was that Henry needed something from me, and what he needed was for me to be strong. I thought about what had happened to my family when my father and then my mother fell apart, when neither one of them decided to fight for themselves or their home or their children. We had all suffered for it. It had been selfishness on their part to succumb, and I wouldn't do that to either Henry or myself.

I told Henry that I would always love him, that I would talk about marriage with him when he was stronger because I didn't want to take advantage of his illness or whatever it was that explained his weakened state; and I sent him home with a kiss and a promise that I would stand by him in exactly the way I knew he would stand by me. 'Any decision that confronts you is yours to make,' I told him. 'I will help you, but I won't try to influence you.' I was shaking with the effort of it, and while I knew I couldn't afford to dispense with practicality, even in the blistering heat of that moment, I also knew I had no real idea what was going through Henry's tormented mind.

After he left, I went up to my little attic room and drafted a response to my prospective employer saying I could be in Baltimore the following week. I had not yet researched train schedules or thought through other considerations, but where there was a will there was a way, I supposed, all the while thinking of my sister toiling away in Chicago and alternately being sure I could do it and sure that I couldn't. Then I addressed the envelope and placed it with a vague prayer in the back pages of the big Bible that not even my mother cracked open any more, and there I imagine the letter remains to this day.

Henry appeared the next afternoon looking more like his old self. I hesitated when I saw him, not wanting to assume too much, but neither wanting to let him completely off the hook of the promises he had made to me and I to him. At the same time, there went through my mind a tremor of fear that I had misread the situation and that Henry's regard for me was the product of agitation or the jitters some men feel when approaching a critical crossroads in their lives. I also considered the possibility that he had been ill or had suffered a mental disturbance, so instead of giving voice to the questions that filled my head, I remained silent, for I knew that the only way to ascertain the truth was to let him speak.

I had worn a pale dress and outlined my eyes so they looked big in my ashen face. It wasn't a costume or disguise, exactly, but a form of communication. I wanted Henry to see that I wasn't strong enough to lose him. I wanted him to see that for all that I would be a valuable adjunct to his personal and professional lives, I wouldn't be headstrong or difficult to contend with.

'I owe you an apology – several, in fact,' Henry started off in a formal manner and with only the barest glimmer of fever showing in his eyes. 'I acted badly, and it won't happen again.' He paused, and I was filled with terror that that was the end of it, that he would be off to be married on the date that was enshrined in my crumpled copy of the *Times*. The wedding date was less than four weeks away. He would return to his fiancée having sown his wild oats, and I would be on the train to Baltimore with only the memory of what might have been . . . But Henry stared into my eyes and what I saw melted the chill that was clutching my heart, and I dared to imagine. I dared to hope. I wanted to run to him and shake the reluctant words out of him – one way or the other he needed to reveal my fate. I stood like a statue, and though I was a good three feet away from him, I was able to feel the heat radiating from his body as he said, 'Even if I am damned to eternity for what I am doing to Felicity, I will have you as my wife.'

Henry told me he would have to plan his extrication carefully, as the families were old friends. I didn't mind that he had to keep me secret for a while, for it made our time together feel stolen and sweet. I didn't ask anything about the girl he was engaged to, but I might be forgiven – or perhaps not – for suggesting that she, too, might be a captive of expectations and would eventually appreciate freedom as much as he, whether or not she knew it at first. He looked childish and hopeful when I suggested it, as if I were a favorite auntie with a present tucked behind my back. Neither of us believed it for a minute, but it was a useful fiction that allowed Henry to question Felicity's motives just enough to gird him for the task ahead.

PART III

DAY NINE

The next morning Lisette pointed to something floating on the water on the starboard side of the boat. It turned out to be Rebecca's cap, and I closed my eyes against the possibility that the next thing we might see floating by would be Rebecca Frost herself.

Mary Ann began to cry and wail. It was a pitiful sound and would have been heart-rending if I had not gone long past pity and if it weren't for the clearly advantageous fact that the boat was now two people lighter than when we had started out. Besides, there was nothing practical we could do about it. As it was, I felt a profound irritation and an urge to throttle Mary Ann. Mrs Grant, who was sitting two rows ahead of us, made her way back and squeezed in between us and put her arm around Mary Ann's shoulders. It was well over an hour – nearly two shifts of bailers – before she became quiet and fell asleep against Mrs Grant's immovable shoulder, but my resentment persisted. Why should weakness get rewarded like that? I would have liked to lean against Mrs Grant too, but I was also a little afraid of her, and it was not something I would ever ask to do. She showed different sides of herself to different people, and she had not yet made any effort to comfort me.

I am trying to be honest. In memory, I can feel a tug at my heartstrings as I think of Mary Ann. She was frail and beautiful. Her engagement diamond slipped uselessly around on her thin finger. The indigo veins on her wrist looked like delicate calligraphy on the white parchment of her skin. In other circumstances we might have been real friends, but there in the boat, I had no sympathy for her. She was weak, unlikely to survive or to be of use in prolonging the lives of others.

I think Hannah and Mrs Grant had similar thoughts, for later I saw them sitting near the rail with their heads together and serious expressions on their faces, looking now and then at Mary Ann. I had no idea what they were talking about. It would be untrue to say I knew, but I'll put down here that I did catch the phrases 'weakest ones' and 'strategy.' Don't ask me to attribute significance to it. Even now, with all of the benefit of retrospect, I don't have any inkling of what they meant.

This was our first day with nothing to eat. Not a square of hardtack or a scrap of fish remained, and when Hardie passed around our ration of water, there was scarcely a swallow for each of us in the cup. Mrs McCain wondered aloud if the water was finished, and Mr Hardie said it was not. He also assured us that the boat was not leaking, that the rising level of water under the seats was all coming in over the rail. I wanted to believe him, but I didn't. Again I suspected him of saying things to avert panic, and despite the fact that this was a noble end, I did not like to be lied to. The only time Henry and I had ever disagreed was when he led me to believe that his family knew all about me. 'I know you will handle your family as you think best,' I had told him when we first decided to marry, but once his ring was on my finger, I wanted to know the true situation, and eventually we had argued. In the lifeboat, I experienced a similar desire to comprehend exactly where we stood and precisely what we needed to do about it, though it stands to reason that Mr Hardie did not know the true situation or what to do about it any more than I did. He made his best guess, that was all, and it was certainly better than mine. Yet I and others blamed him as if he knew the truth and kept it from us – capriciously, or as a form of punishment for our sins.

Oddly, I liked bailing. It made me feel useful, or maybe it was a feminine desire to order my surroundings. It gave me something to do other than looking out over the terrifyingly black and empty sea. While I bailed, I inspected the bottom of the boat for the leak I knew to be there, but I never found it. Sometimes I imagined I was cleaning the house Henry and I would one day have, which merged in my imagination with the Winter Palace I had designed in my head. I imagined a sun-filled drawing room graced by my grandmother's Louis

Quinze settee, which was to have been given to me as a wedding present if we had not been forced to sell it when we moved. Henry liked blue, so I chose for the walls of the room a robin-egg blue – blue enough to please Henry, but nothing masculine or cold. Henry warned me that we might get nothing from his mother, who didn't approve of our match, but I had every confidence that in time I would win her over.

Anya Robeson refused to bail. She alone was exempt from any sort of duty. She didn't want to leave little Charlie even for a moment, and they huddled in the very middle of the center thwart like the motionless center of a gyroscope. She was terrified of getting her skirt wet, for once something was soaked with salt water, it took days to dry. It was cold enough, but how to measure the effects of fear and wind, of wet cloth next to raw and salty skin, of the chilling knowledge that in some indecipherable way we were responsible for our lot?

Mrs Grant talked about trying the sail again, but we had already learned that the wind-filled canvas would cause the boat to heel over and water to pour in over the side. With that in mind, her suggestion was not taken seriously, but I could see that she was trying to present some sort of solution rather than merely sit and hope. Her suggestion was followed by a long, dispirited silence that was finally broken by Mr Nilsson, who said, 'Then we must row.'

Mr Hardie croaked out what might have been a laugh and said we'd have a hard time merely keeping pace with the current, to which Mr Nilsson replied: 'I don't mean we should row to America, even if that is the continent to which we are closest. I mean we should row back to England.' He went on to tell us about two Norwegian men who had rowed across the Atlantic Ocean in an eighteen-foot open skiff some years before.

'But those were experienced oarsmen!' exclaimed the Colonel; and it was true that of the eight people Mr Hardie had assigned to take turns with the oars, only Mr Nilsson and the Colonel showed any aptitude for rowing.

'And at the top of their form,' added the deacon.

'The alternative seems to be to drift about waiting to die,' said Mr Nilsson, and after some thought, Hardie agreed. 'We might still encounter a passing ship,' he told us, filling my heart with hope until he added, 'But then again, we might not.' He went on to say that perhaps the *Empress Alexandra* had drifted out of the proper shipping lane or that the war had affected the number of boats making the crossing, both of which might explain why we had not yet been picked up.

The Colonel and Mr Nilsson were appointed to school the rest of us in the art of oarsmanship, but many of the women and the older gentleman, Michael Turner, were either too weak or were otherwise unsuited to the task. Once we began rowing, our spirits lifted to see the boat slice through the water with the wind behind it rather than stall as we tried to hold our position against forces for which we were no match. But even those who had been deemed strong enough to row tired easily. After only ten minutes, the Colonel's oar came loose from its oarlock and fell into the water, and we had to spend precious energy retrieving it. He and Mr Nilsson and Mrs Grant were able to last their allotted hour, but most of us lost rhythm after only a few strokes. Our hands blistered despite the cushions Mr Hardie had fashioned out of strips of blanket, and when Mr Preston took the oar from me, I dipped my hand into the ocean, thinking the water would soothe it. But I had not accounted for the salt, and I quickly drew it out again, as near to crying as I had been since the *Empress Alexandra* had disappeared beneath the waves. By evening it was apparent that we had not the strength to continue. Mr Nilsson and Mrs Grant were the last to ship their oars, taking great care that they were nestled properly in under the rail so as not to be lost. Mrs Grant's features did not betray any emotion, but Mr Nilsson bent his head in defeat and didn't reply when Mr Hoffman thumped him on the shoulder and said, 'It was a good idea, anyway. We'll try again tomorrow.'

Mrs Grant said that if we couldn't row to Europe, we would have to sail there, and Mr Hoffman just shrugged his shoulders. He didn't have to remind us that the boat was too full of people for sailing, and what was meant to be a note of optimism ended the day with a sour chord.

NIGHT

The nights were cold, and the more emaciated we became, the less our bodies worked to keep us warm. When I looked at the others, I was shocked to notice their sunken eyes and hollow cheeks. The changes had been gradual, but in the fading light I saw that their lips were chapped to the point of cracking, their eyes seemed glassy and unseeing, and their clothing hung loosely on the unnatural protrusion of their bones. Mr Hoffman had a line of dried blood under his hairline from when the butt of an oar had hit him in the face, but he seemed unaware of it. There is no doubt that similar ravages had been worked on my own features, but in my inner eye I was unaltered from that last morning on the ship when Henry had watched as I used the looking glass to arrange my hair. There were no more stories, only an occasional sigh or Mrs Cook's hacking cough, which had started the day before and gotten progressively worse; and I knew we had all retreated into memory in order to escape the harsh realities of our plight.

I had begun to notice that the closer the *Empress*

Alexandra got to New York, the more agitated Henry seemed. He and Mr Cumberland frequently sought each other out, and I guessed it must have to do with the bank business Henry had told me about, for they often made mention of 'our special responsibilities.' The previous night, he had stayed up drinking and talking with a man he had recognized from his family's social circle, so as I observed his reflection in the glass, I surmised that his vexation might stem from fatigue. It was only later, when he took my hand and drew me into a protected corner of the deck where we could enjoy the sunshine without being exposed to the wind, that I understood the cause of his concern. 'I have been drafting messages to my parents,' he said, which aroused my curiosity and then my suspicion that no telegram had yet been sent to inform them of our married state.

At first I was upset because we had been over the same ground several times and he had assured me that the matter had been taken care of. I also couldn't help but feel that we should not be talking about practicalities on our honeymoon. We should have been laughing over frivolous matters, such as why Mrs Forester always seemed to be on the verge of tears or how serious and ill-at-ease Mr Cumberland looked in his new role as a wealthy banker, or delighting in long silences where we gazed into each other's eyes, or discovering weighty truths about each other, truths we would wonder over and use as a basis for our growing trust. I started to say I thought the matter had been handled, but Henry put a finger to his lips until a high-spirited couple who had come onto the deck to take some air had passed us by.

Once we were alone again, Henry said, 'I received a telegram from my mother this morning, and she says she is bringing Felicity with her to meet the ship.'

'But she can't do that!' I cried, and my heart grew cold when I realized what Henry was really telling me. 'She is thinking that Felicity can win you back!' I said, my voice cracking with something between anger and grief, for the only way his mother could entertain such a misconception was if she thought her son unwed.

We stood for a moment mindful of the ocean stretching on either side of us – in one direction was Europe, where I had been so happy, and in the other lay New York, where who knew what awaited me. 'You have put it off too long,' I said. 'It is unfair to Felicity and your mother, and it is unfair to me.'

Henry looked like a chastened schoolboy and could only agree. He said he would make the matter right directly after lunch, and I said lunch could wait and he should send a telegram right away. Together we came up with suitable wording, then Henry escorted me back to our suite and rushed off looking either purposeful or relieved, I couldn't determine which. When he returned, we had to hurry in order to be seated, so we did not broach the subject until the meal was over. 'I have taken care of it' was all he said to me, for just when I was going to ask for details, somebody slapped him on the shoulder. It was Mr Cumberland, who seemed to have some pressing matter to discuss. Henry appeared glad to see him and asked if I could find my way back to our cabin on my own. I thought it was an odd question, as we had been on the ship for over five days. 'Of course,' I said, not stopping to wonder about those words the way I wonder about them now. Now I think they are evidence that Henry was still anxious about something, but perhaps there was a worrisome business matter that required his attention and that is what he was thinking of. 'I have taken care of it,' he had said, but as I watched the play of moonlight on the water and pulled my life vest more tightly to my body to cut the biting wind, I began to wonder if he had.

I tried to remember what Mr Cumberland had been saying to Henry as they walked away. It was something about the Marconi and how it had stopped working and so had prevented him from accomplishing some item of business, which is what he wanted to talk to Henry about. Henry had replied, 'But I was just there, and it was working just as it should.' Then Henry had glanced over his shoulder at me and nodded before walking away to discuss whatever it was out of my presence.

As I proceeded toward the staircase that would

lead to our cabin, my heart leapt a little because these words, if I had heard them correctly, seemed confirmation that Henry had indeed sent the wire to his mother – and just in time, for it was later that afternoon that the *Empress Alexandra* sank. But now, as I sat in the lifeboat, I wondered if Henry's pronouncement had not been for Mr Cumberland's benefit at all, but for mine. Then I racked my brain for Mr Cumberland's exact words, for if they were as I remembered them, they held another meaning with significance far beyond whether or not Henry had informed his family of our marriage. And that was that the Marconi might not have been working at the time of the shipwreck, and if it had not been working, then no wires or signals of any kind had been sent. And if there had been no distress signals, our position all along had been far more precarious than Mr Hardie had led us to believe.

I sat for a long time with my eyes closed against the darkness, numb with fear and cold. Now and then I dipped my torn hands into the water at my feet for the very purpose of feeling the sting of salt in the wounds. I wanted to feel something besides the fear that enveloped me. Mary Ann was stretched out across my lap, and I shifted my weight not only to find a more comfortable position, but to wake her if she was only sleeping lightly. She breathed deeply but otherwise didn't stir. 'Mary Ann,' I said, leaning down over her ear. 'Are you sleeping?'

'What is it?' she said, only half hearing me, and

then, when she came more fully awake: 'Is something wrong?' But by then I had lost the urge to tell her what I had been thinking so I said, 'It's nothing. Go back to sleep.'

I tried to think nice thoughts about Henry and our time in London, but I couldn't, and it was nearly dawn before I finally fell asleep.

DAY TEN, MORNING

The tenth day dawned gusty and cold. The sea rolled under us in giant swells. Despite the size of the waves, they didn't break, and we somehow managed to keep the level of water in the bottom of the boat to a matter of inches. Mrs Grant continued her quiet reassurance, and once or twice she voiced her regret that, for fear of swamping the boat, Mr Hardie would not allow us to put up the sail, for she was sure that our salvation lay in making progress toward some far-off shore.

Mr Hardie refused to look me in the eye, but every now and then I smiled in his direction, trying to impart encouragement. I didn't know if he needed it or not. I had come to think of him as something either more or less than human, so little did he resemble any of the rest of us. Mostly, though, I directed my attention inward, trying to make one moment turn into the next with whatever that would bring, evil or good. I noticed little of what went on in the boat that morning beyond the enormous discomfort of sitting in damp clothing in the middle of a nothingness that was everything, or everything that mattered. I measured the intervals of time between the spasms of shivering that shook my body or between the ticks of my shrunken heart. I examined the chill of my breast and compared it to that of my feet. I tried to decide whether it helped at all to press my hands between my legs or if it was better to pull them inside my life vest and hug them tightly around my chest.

I remembered my worries about the distress signals from the evening before, and twice I opened my mouth to speak of it. Once I started to tell Mary Ann, and later I turned to the deacon, who had caught my eye when Mr Hardie failed to pass around the water cup. But no words presented themselves, and I also wondered what good it would do to sow seeds of distrust against the only man who could save us. Besides, I had no firm proof that the Marconi had been in anything less than perfect condition. It was as I was trying to assemble my tumultuous thoughts that my mind descended to yet another layer of thinking.

Mr Hardie had indicated that Mr Blake was in the radio room until the fire forced everyone to come up on deck and that Blake had confirmed that distress signals had been sent. Indeed, I recalled seeing Mr Hardie with a ship's officer who might have been Blake when Henry and I came up on deck that afternoon, so it would seem reasonable that Blake would have told Hardie about the distress signals at that time. But if the

Marconi had been broken, then either Mr Blake had been lying to Mr Hardie or Mr Hardie was now lying to us; and if Mr Hardie was lying, I could only assume the reason was to reassure us. Still, it seemed to me that Mr Hardie must believe that signals had been sent, for why else would he have been so insistent that we hold our position in the vicinity of the shipwreck if he knew that no vessels were likely to be searching that location? Now I wondered if Mr Blake, and perhaps Mr Hardie, had been somewhere else after the explosion and Mr Hardie was merely assuming that signals had been sent by whoever was in the radio room, since that would be the logical course of action in a disaster. If that was the case, he was lying not about the distress signals, but about what he – and maybe Blake – had really been doing in the first minutes of the disaster. But despite the intensity of my concentration on the matter, there was no way I could know what that was.

Instead, I practiced speeches I would give to Henry's family, speeches about love and inevitability and about how all my life I had wanted aunts and cousins and how I fervently hoped the Winter family would provide them for me. I tried saying I loved them already from what Henry had told me, but I couldn't say it sincerely, so I decided not to say it at all. During our argument, Henry had told me how his parents had adored Felicity Close, how they had known Felicity since she was a child, how Felicity's mother was his own mother's dearest friend. 'Henry,' I whispered to the water that stretched around us in all directions, 'don't you dare desert me now.' In all of my imaginings, Henry was standing sturdily by my side; I didn't know how on earth I would be able to face his mother alone. I worried that she would blame me for his death, that she would somehow decide that I had taken Henry off to Europe, not the other way around, and that I had caused us to return on the *Empress Alexandra*, not a war between nations over which I had no control.

That morning, it finally began to rain. At first, the drops were small and fine as mist, and the amount anyone was able to catch and drink would hardly have filled a thimble, but the drops grew steadily larger and soon we were all soaked to the bone. It was this rain I was reminded of the day in Boston when Mr Reichmann called me insane. Around me, people turned their faces up to catch the water. Mary Ann continued to prove herself troublesome by refusing to open her mouth, so Hannah had to slap her and hold her nose until she did. Mr Hardie pointed into the distance to something that no one else could see and said that the weather was about to go to hell and that we would too if we didn't face our situation squarely. We were already so wet and cold that it was hard for us to have any clear sense of what he meant.

Mrs Cook came back from where she had been sleeping in the dormitory and tapped my shoulder. 'Be sure to pull the canvas cover over you so the blankets don't get soaked through,' she said. I didn't think it was my turn again already, but no one protested, so I made my way forward and burrowed into the musty blankets, where I experienced something that wasn't sleep so much as a sort of natural drifting even further into my inward-turned state. Inside were pockets of warmth – not memories, exactly, but places where the parameters of life were less stark and unyielding. Perhaps this thinking only of myself was wilful, but I could not think of myself, then, as possessing a will. I had only a body. I did what I was told almost automatically, as if I had entered the trance-like state I had observed in Mrs Cook. My smallest sensation was apparent to me, a matter of intense interest; but what was going on with the others made very little impression on me at all. When Mary Ann came to shake me out of my stupor and take my place on the blankets, I returned to my place to find that while I was sleeping, Mrs Cook had sacrificed herself to the sea. I felt nothing, only a mild curiosity about why she had done it. 'Orders from Hardie,' whispered Hannah, and Greta said, 'You know how Mrs Cook would do whatever she was told.' It frightened me to think that the same could be said of me.

I can neither confirm nor deny Hardie's involvement in Mrs Cook's death. My lawyers questioned me over and over on this point, but I could only say that I had been asleep. Apparently Hannah said in her statement that my turn to sleep had come earlier in the day, that no one was allowed to take extra turns on the blankets unless they were sick, and that I had not been in the dormitory during the incident at all. Mrs Cook, who could have testified to tapping my shoulder and sending me forward, and Mary Ann, who later took my place in the forward crease, are both dead, and apparently no one else remembers my small part in the incident. I don't know what it would have proved even if I had been awake, which I wasn't. Mr Reichmann said the lawyers for Hannah and Mrs Grant were trying to establish that we had a reason to fear Mr Hardie, that the incident with Mrs Cook had given us a valid motive for what happened later; but no matter how Mr Reichmann peppered me with questions, I said that when it came my turn to testify, I would state truthfully that I harbored no such motive in my heart and that I had not been present to hear anything Mr Hardie might have said to Mrs Cook.

In any case, when I emerged from under the dripping canvas cover, Mrs Hewitt, the hotel proprietress, was wringing her hands and shuddering in great dry heaves. She said she been the last to speak to Mrs Cook, and I had no reason to doubt her until some of the others whispered it about that Mr Hardie had talked to her after that. Mr Hardie did not make a habit of talking individually to the women, so I thought that maybe the story had changed in the telling or that Hannah and Greta had exaggerated or even lied. But since

I had witnessed none of it, I did not offer an opinion on what had transpired. Although Mrs McCain had been Mrs Cook's traveling companion, she refused to show any emotion at all. 'There's naught I can do about it now, is there?' she said.

The rain abated and the morning passed. I have little memory of it, except that sometime before noon, Mr Hardie pointed to a distant line where the texture and color of the water abruptly changed and said, 'Squall.' A minute passed before he added, 'We have until it reaches us to decide what we want to do.' I looked around me at the remaining thirty-six of us, then blinked at the water sloshing around my ankles before turning to watch the far-off line of wind-whipped water with a kind of detached trepidation, as if I were remembering it rather than living it for the first time. When Mr Hardie spoke up to inform us it was fifteen minutes away, his bottomless eyes finally met mine. 'We're in your hands,' I tried to tell him with a look. 'Just tell us what to do.' His gaze rested on me for a long roll of the boat. I was thrilled by it, buoyed up. For the first time in days I felt warm. I knew Mr Hardie would save us if he could.

So many waves were now breaking over the gunwale that such occurrences were unremarkable, but the sky had turned a greenish-yellow color that we had never seen before. Hardie said, 'Say your prayers, mates,' and my hopes of the moment before were immediately dashed. Around me the bailers worked with furious and futile activity. 'Oh, give it up!' I cried, for the level of the water was clearly rising in the boat despite their best efforts to stop it. 'We're going to drown!' I could see no possible alternative. I squeezed my arms about the airless room of my chest. 'There's no way out,' I shouted to the others or maybe only to Mary Ann. 'Don't you see that we're going to die?'

'Why, of course there's a way,' said Mr Hoffman reasonably. 'We've talked about it before. Some of us can go over the side to lighten the load.' He paused to let the words sink in, then added, 'It's our only option.' I looked at Hardie to gauge his reaction, but he was glaring at the squall line with a fixed expression. Colonel Marsh shouted, 'Is it true, Mr Hardie?' and the beam of Hardie's gaze swept across our upturned faces like a searchlight. 'Aye, it's true enough, unless ye all prefer to drown.' His words were like opening the door to a caged beast, and once it was loose among us, I could breathe again. 'Of course,' I said, coldly calm. My fear had disappeared completely. I felt like a man rationally assessing his investment options based on a ledger full of numbers and probabilities.

Mary Ann looked horror-stricken. 'Jump over?' she asked. 'On purpose?'

'Of course on purpose!' I hadn't meant to shout at her, but suddenly, it did not seem to me that this course of action involved death, but life. It did not occur to me that I might have to sacrifice myself. Until my father's misfortunes, doors had been opened for me, dinners served to me by pretty young women like Mary Ann. She must have sensed this, and it caused her face to stretch out over her bones with fear and loathing.

It seemed to me that someone weak like Mary Ann or Maria would be the obvious choice, but when one of the men – was it Mr Nilsson? – pointed out that men were more useful than women in these circumstances and that if anyone should be sacrificed, it should be a woman, I was horrified; yet on some level, I agreed with him. Maybe we fought so hard against this idea because it was true. When Mary Ann cowered against me in a near-faint, I pushed her hair away from her ear and whispered, 'Why not, Mary Ann? You'd save yourself a lot of suffering by flinging yourself into the sea. You're going to die anyway, and I've heard drowning is far more pleasant than dying of starvation or thirst.'

Am I to be blamed for this? We do not ask certain ideas to enter our heads and demand that others stay away. I believe that a person is accountable for his actions but not for the contents of his mind, so perhaps I am culpable for occasionally letting those thoughts turn themselves into words. I can only say that I had to sit next to Mary Ann. I was the first one to whom she turned with her whining and complaints. In any case, when she came to her senses, she said she had had a vivid dream where she had saved us all by throwing herself into the sea.

'Ten minutes!' shouted Mr Hardie. I counted out sixty seconds and said, 'Nine,' more to myself than to Mary Ann. Mr Preston became highly agitated. 'The men!' he screamed. 'All of the men should gather back here.'

'What for?' asked Mr Nilsson, and Mrs Grant said, 'I'm sure there's another way.' But then she fell silent and busied herself with a bailer she wrested away from someone else.

'Hardie's right! We men must draw lots to see who goes over,' said Mr Preston, his voice high-pitched and quivering, just as Hardie said, 'Eight.' A sudden terror seethed through my entire being, but it only remotely belonged to me. I was able to examine it the way I had examined my chattering teeth, the barrage of raindrops that hit my face, the steady trickle of water that found its way inside my collar and down my neck, the arrhythmic flutter of my heart.

Nilsson said, 'Why the men? Why only the men?'

Mary Ann asked, 'What about the women? Are they still thinking of sending one of us?'

'Of course not,' I said, 'what do you think? But I doubt they would stop a woman if she volunteered.' I did not notice then how we both believed in the concept of 'they,' of omniscient decision-makers who occupied a place in the power structure above us – a 'they' who made the decisions and took the spoils or suffered the consequences of being wrong. I did notice, however, that Mary Ann was greatly relieved to hear that no one would call on her to be heroic, and she put her useless little hand trustingly inside of mine.

Hardie held up a fistful of tiny splinters of wood that seemed to appear for the purpose by magic. 'Only the men,' he stated. 'Two straws are short, six are long. The short straws lose.' I don't know why we thought two people fewer would make the difference between life and death, but we didn't question it. If Hardie said two was the magic number, then it was two. We assumed that Hardie knew.

A minute or so passed. The black line of rough water was now only about twenty-five or thirty boat lengths away. In the distance forks of lightning ripped through the livid sky.

'I'm not forcing anybody,' Hardie said. Then he himself drew one of the splinters. He looked at it without much interest, but I could tell by the faces of the people sitting near him it was a long one. Mr Nilsson drew next, and from the glazed vacancy of his eyes, I had the sense that he wasn't entirely aware of what he was doing.

Colonel Marsh was stoic and remote as he took his turn, but Michael Turner made a joke of it, saying, 'If I win this lottery, it will be the first thing I've ever won.' He was one of the ones who had never had a life vest, which made him appear even thinner and less substantial than he was. No sooner had he taken his turn than he stood up, laughed crazily, and leapt out of the boat. There were four straws left, and one of them was short. I watched

Mr Preston draw and heave a sigh of relief, but the deacon looked panic-stricken as he crawled aft to take his turn. Only he, Sinclair and Hoffman were left of the men. Hoffman merely shrugged and drew, all the while regarding Hardie through narrowed eyes; again I had the sense that some secret was crossing the air between them. 'God help us,' said the deacon. He knelt in the bottom of the boat facing Hardie, his back toward the rest of us, his clenched hands upraised to the violent sky. 'O Lord,' he wailed, 'I'm willing to sacrifice myself for these dear children of yours, but why is it so hard to do?' He looked wretchedly out at the waves, a quivering incarnation of fear and maybe the dawning realization that 'dear children' was not an apt description of his companions in the boat. I blocked my ears to the sound of him and clung harder than ever to Mary Ann. The bare bones of our natures were showing. None of us were worth a spit. We were stripped of all decency. I couldn't see that there was anything good or noble left once food and shelter were taken away.

The deacon looked with infinite sorrow in Mr Sinclair's direction, then took both of the remaining splinters. 'I wonder if this counts as suicide,' I heard him say. 'I wonder if paradise is forever lost.' He reached around to pat Mr Sinclair on the back and laid the two splinters out in his open hand, where they were immediately caught by the wind and blown into the sea. The deacon rose slowly to his feet, saying, 'The Lord bless you and preserve you.' Then he removed his life vest, which he tossed to Mr Hardie, and dove into the water and immediately vanished. Mr Sinclair shouted after him, 'Come back! That was to have been mine!' but no one paid him any attention; and when Mr Sinclair pulled himself up with his extraordinary arms and hauled himself to the boat's rail, no attempt was made to stop him. The saddest thing about the sacrifice was that it was being made for people such as we. I thought these things imperfectly. Anyway, I was immediately distracted, for it was then that the squall line hit.

DAY TEN, AFTERNOON

Now I knew why Mr Hardie had said that the wind up until that point had been nothing but a breeze, but I think even he was unprepared for its force. The little boat was thrown like a nutshell by waves the size of ocean liners. I thought of the deacon and Mr Sinclair, and how Hardie could have avoided becoming a murderer – yes, that is the word I used – for it seemed to me that the exact number of people in the boat mattered little if at all. We would all die in seconds anyway, and what I regretted most was that I was not to die with my view of human nature intact. I had been allowed to believe in man's innate goodness for the twenty-two years of my life, and I had hoped to carry the belief with me to my grave. I wanted to think that all people could have what they wanted, that there was no inherent conflict between competing interests, and that, if tragedies had to happen, they were not something mere human beings could control.

I thought these things, but not, that afternoon, in any coherent way. The boat pitched and rolled as it alternately climbed the foamy heights of the waves and then descended into hellish troughs so that we were surrounded on four sides by walls of black water. It was terrifying to see. Mr Hardie and Mr Nilsson took up one oar each while the Colonel and Mr Hoffman struggled with a third. Together they made a valiant effort to keep our nose to the wind, for we could only hope to ride it out, and we grasped at one another the way I grasped at the shreds of my beliefs. Mrs Grant and Mr Preston did what they could with the last of the oars, but they were no match for the fury of the storm. Still, I was grateful for their efforts and admired the way they wrestled with the long blades. Despite their lack of effectiveness, neither one of them gave up. With one hand I gripped the seat so as not to be thrown from it like the rider of a wild horse, and with the other I held on to Mary Ann, who was sitting next to me and clutching at me with both hands as though I were the buoyant plank that would save her.

Adding to our distress were the torrential rain that battered us from above and the jagged lightning that split the sky. We could hardly see the length of the boat, so if I were to say that the waves rose to twenty feet or thirty, it would be mere speculation on my part. Hardie later told us that they had reached at least forty feet, but how he knew this I cannot say. Sometimes the boat would crest a wave and hang for an instant before pitching downward from that height like a sled down an icy slope. Our stomachs lurched and heaved when this happened, but sometimes we weren't so lucky, and the wave would slam into our shoulders and fill the boat with even more water, which was now almost to our knees, but still the little cutter did not sink.

In the minutes before the squall hit, Mr Hardie ordered a change of oarsmen and passed the empty hardtack tins to Hannah and Isabelle, who immediately started bailing furiously with them. Then he ripped the tops off two of the casks he had been guarding as jealously as if they still held water, and Colonel Marsh and Mr Hoffman struggled to hold on to the slippery wood as they filled them and emptied them into the ocean. All the while, Hardie made a valiant effort to keep the prow of the boat pointed into the waves while the other oarsmen did their best to help him. The boat was pitching with such fury that only one in five attempts to empty the barrels over the side was successful, but they kept at it, insanely, heroically, and I wondered what we would have done without those five strong men. What if Colonel Marsh had drawn the short straw, or Mr Nilsson or Hardie himself? Michael Turner had been the oldest of the men by far, and the deacon had been thin and weak; and while Mr Sinclair had had impressive muscles in his arms, he could not move about the boat or use his legs at all. With a shudder of horror, I realized that it could not be luck that had arranged it so, even if I had not noticed the sleight of hand by which this result had been accomplished. Hardie had left nothing to chance, but had chosen who would live and who would die. I could not rid my mind of the idea that there was evil in that little boat, that it was the devil himself who was keeping me alive.

Not too much time passed before Mr Hoffman lost hold of his barrel, and it immediately disappeared in the maelstrom. Hardie said not a word, but thrust his oar at Hoffman and tore the covering off the third and last of the containers. This time he kept it for himself, thrusting it into the water and hauling it over the side, but only after I had seen that it contained no rainwater at all, only a small box that Hardie hastily stuffed inside his jacket. This made no impression on me at the time. I thought only that Hardie had done well to make the supply of water last as long as it did.

Only one other event stands out against the background of horror of that terrible storm. The dark day turned into an even darker night. The rain was relentless. It was as if the sea and sky had merged. Still, the boat rose up and either plummeted down or crashed into the crests of the waves as they broke. Despite the sickening feeling of falling into a bottomless void, I thanked God and Mr Hardie every time we were spared a deluge of water upon our heads.

I was giving thanks for another safe slide down when there was a resounding thud against the hull of the boat and a burst of unintelligible shouting from those sitting on the starboard rail. Hardie stopped bailing for a moment to inquire what the fuss was about. 'We've hit something!' came the answer, or 'Something has hit us!' – not that the exact words matter in the least. Whether it was the lost barrel or debris from the *Empress Alexandra* or something placed there by God for our destruction, we couldn't know.

Eventually the wind lessened somewhat and the monstrous waves became merely huge, though the rain continued until well after dark. Mr Hardie propped the two remaining barrels between the side of the boat and the sodden pile of blankets and instructed those sitting nearest to divert the rainwater that collected in the canvas boat cover into the barrels. I wouldn't have thought of it, or if I had, I would not have acted on the thought. I understood what an optimist Hardie must be, or maybe these were just the reflexive actions of a creature determined to survive.

NIGHT

Mrs Forester, who had been so silent and watchful, went mad overnight. She started raving about her husband, who had been drinking the day of the shipwreck and was probably lost. 'If you dare to lay a hand on me this time,' she said, 'I'll kill you in the night with your own knife.' It was only when she started addressing Colonel Marsh, who was sitting directly in front of her, as Collin and making slashing motions at him with her fist that anyone tried to restrain her. The woman named Joan, who had been her attendant for twenty years, clung to her and beseeched her to restrain herself. 'That's not Collin, missus,' she said reasonably. 'Collin isn't here.'

'Poor thing,' said Hannah in a burst of compassion, but any attempts to touch Mrs Forester or soothe her were strongly rebuffed. Finally she fell unconscious, and Joan, with the help of Mr Preston and Mrs Grant, succeeded in dragging her forward and making her as comfortable as possible on the wet blankets, which had the effect of preventing anyone else from going forward to rest or sleep.

Mr Hoffman was all for tossing her over the side, but Hannah and Mrs Grant protected her, saying that it was men who had made her that way and they could damn well live with the results.

I slept fitfully. When I wasn't thinking about the events of that devastating day, I was dreaming about them. I would lurch awake when I imagined I was falling overboard, and sometimes I really was falling, but only onto Mary Ann or Mr Preston, who was sitting beside me, toward the rail.

The thing that preoccupied me that night was the notion that a person's choices are only rarely between right and wrong or between good and evil. I saw very clearly that people were mostly faced with much murkier options and that there were no clear signposts marking the better path to take. Had Mr Hardie been right to arrange the lottery? I could only determine that right and wrong didn't come into it. As I considered this, an incident from the first day kept scratching at my consciousness until I opened the door to it, and that was when we had left the child to die.

I don't know how difficult it would have been to reach him. One minute I was convinced that a rescue might have been accomplished without too much trouble and the next I remembered an ocean full of dangerous obstacles between our boat and the boy. I still wonder if my imagination has magnified or reduced the dangers changing our course to save him would have entailed, but now I think that if I and the others in the lifeboat are to be tried for anything, it should be for that.

Perhaps it was the misery of sitting in soaking clothes or perhaps it was those strange feelings of remorse over the child that kept me awake, but as I brooded over him, I became aware that Mrs Grant, who was sitting on the other side of Mary Ann from me, was looking out over the railing to where a few stars were now shining in the sky. Because Mary Ann was lying across my lap and so was not a solid presence between us, Mrs Grant came to realize that I was awake and for the first and last time, she reached over and took my hand. I told her I was thinking about the child and she said, 'There's no use. What's done is done.' Then I poured out the story of the Marconi and my suspicion that Mr Hardie might have dissembled when he told us about the distress signals. She thanked me for telling her, then said somewhat cryptically, 'If we had known this . . .,' but she didn't follow with whatever corollary she was contemplating. If we had known it, what? Would we have acted differently during those first days? Aside from throwing people out of the boat sooner and putting up the sail or rowing for Europe while we had the strength, I am not sure what we could have done.

Soon after dawn, it was discovered that the two sisters who had sat quietly in the back of the boat had disappeared without a trace. No one had seen them go overboard, and even though Mary Ann had never spoken to them, she was quite affected by their loss. Perhaps because they were near to our age, she took it as a sign of what could happen to us. She turned to me with a wild look in her eyes and asked, 'Do you think we'll die?' At that point I fully expected that we would and I thought of telling her so. I was as devastated by the events of the previous day as Mary Ann had been, and I resented her expectation that I had either answers or strength. I wanted to shout, 'Of course we're going to die! The sisters are the lucky ones – for them it is over!' but I didn't. I put my hand on her shoulder the way I wished for someone to lay hands on me and uttered some kind of invocation. I think I said, 'Lord protect us,' but I might also have said, 'Mr Hardie is doing whatever he can. I wouldn't give up on him yet.'

When we took further stock of our situation, we saw that whatever had hit us had punched a fist-sized hole in the side of the boat just under the starboard rail. A steady stream of water was pouring through it, which Mr Hardie had spent the night trying to stanch; so in this regard, we were no better off than we had been before.

DAY ELEVEN

Counting the two sisters, but not Mrs Forester, who languished on the blankets for another two days, we had lost eight of our original thirty-nine. 'We didn't have to kill Mr Turner or the deacon and Mr Sinclair, then, did we?' screamed Mary Ann. 'We could have waited a day longer!'

'Shut yer mouth, fool!' Mr Hardie shouted back. 'We almost sank last night as it was, or didn't ye notice? Can't ye see that we're still taking on water where we were hit? That means we're still overcrowded and now instead of too little food, we have no food at all.' I noticed then that Hardie seemed smaller. He was extremely gaunt and appeared to have caved in on himself. For the first time, he seemed tired and was sometimes idle. He held his left hand in against his side as if he had sustained an injury during the fury of the day before. I didn't like to see him like this, but it seemed to make Hannah very bold as she moved about the boat setting things in order. Hardie watched her the way an injured dog watches a wild and hungry cat.

I knew we were dying. The only surprising thing was that we were not yet dead. Throughout the day I felt profoundly connected to the countless men and women through the ages who have at some time or other come to this realization about themselves: that life is a relentless sliding down, that eventually everyone finds himself in water up to his neck, and that the ability to have such realizations is what distinguishes men from beasts.

Put differently, it was on day eleven that I began to feel intensely alive. I was finally able to forget my empty stomach and wet feet. I stopped believing that a ship would save us or that Henry would be waiting for me when we got to shore. I looked at my own two hands, raw and scraped as they were, and thought in a new way about how God helped those who helped themselves. Was God a necessary part of that equation? I wondered. Couldn't people be strong or good without always crediting their strength and goodness to God? During the night it had rained hard enough that we were able to replenish the water in the barrels and, thanks to Hardie's foresight, we were all able to get enough to drink.

The day dawned clear, and while there was a good breeze, the waves were modest in size and tended to roll rather than break. Because of our reduced number, we could more easily adjust the weight in the boat to counterbalance the heeling, so Hardie, who had plugged the hole as best he could, fixed the boat cover onto the oars once more, and again we started to make progress through the water. Mr Nilsson worked the rudder, and the rest of us took turns spreading the blankets out across our laps so that they could dry in the sun, which finally warmed us even as it dried our skin to the point of bleeding. My blisters had started to scab over, and I marveled at the capacity of the body to heal itself, to carry on with its life force even in the face of certain death. For once we had had enough to drink, but we had no food, and it wasn't far from our thoughts that we were slowly starving to death. I asked Mr Preston how long a person could live without nourishment, and he told me it was somewhere between four and six weeks. 'That's assuming you have enough water,' he said.

'We're set for a while longer then,' I said, and he replied that he expected we were, but he looked so dejected that I added, 'I think we're going to pull through,' though it stood to reason that we probably weren't.

It was then that Mr Preston told me something he had once heard from a medical doctor he knew. 'Starvation doesn't depend only on the body,' he said. 'It also depends on the mind. People who resist are more likely to survive than those who have lost the force of their will.'

'Then we must resist,' I told him, but I felt my heart fluttering as I said it.

'I think about Doris,' he told me. 'Doris is my source of strength.' I assumed that Doris was his wife even if he didn't explicitly say so. 'I don't care so much for myself, but I must survive for her!'

'But wouldn't you want to live anyway?' I asked, astonished by his vehemence. 'Don't you want to live for yourself?'

His lips were painfully cracked and swollen to twice their normal size, and I saw that his palms were a bloody pulp from struggling with the oars during the storm. He kept them curled into fists, and I only saw them when the boat lurched and he reached out to steady himself. His shoulders heaved once, but his thin voice was steady as he told me about going every day to an unheated warehouse where he sat in a dim pool of light and entered long columns of numbers into a ledger; and if he could do that day after day and year after year so that he and Doris could put food on the table and have a decent place to live, he could do anything. I thought about my own sister Miranda and how I had not imagined her as strong at all. She seemed to me like a combination of Mr Preston and Mary Ann, and I wondered how she would have fared if she had been in the lifeboat instead of me.

After we had sold our big house, Miranda persuaded me to go with her to see it. We stood in a side street and surveyed the back garden with its box bushes and pickets before Miranda became bolder and we strolled past the front of the house, trying to look nonchalant. Suddenly Miranda stopped in the street directly opposite the front door and cried, 'How could they take our house!' I replied that they hadn't taken it, that we had given it up. Miranda's emotion struck a chord deep inside me, but this manifested itself as irritation with my sister, not as anger at people who were more successful at life than my family had been.

While we were standing there like beggars in the street, a young woman opened the door and came out, followed by a man who might have been her father. We had moved down the street and were slightly obscured by the shrubbery so I don't think she saw us, but her presence seemed to knock some sense into Miranda. I was able to convince her to come away, but not before she had given the new owners of the house an evil look. But I felt differently. A large part of me admired them, and the sight of the young woman dressed in a long white gown adorned with blue ribbons gave me a strange kind of hope.

Something about my talk with Mr Preston steadied me. I don't know whether it was the idea that I contained my motivation to live within or whether he had aroused in me a sense of competition, a resolve not to be bested by circumstance. I looked around me at the others in the boat, then snatched the nearest bailer out of the hands of whoever was holding it and started bailing as if my life depended on it, which maybe it did.

We had decided to sail for Europe, even though it was farther away than America. Occasionally Mr Hardie would shout, 'Bearing away' or 'Hard alee,' which meant he was changing the course of the boat in relation to the wind. Then we would be required to shift our seats to compensate for the weight of the wind against the sail. During one such maneuver, I found myself sitting just in front of Mary Ann, who had positioned herself between Hannah and Mrs Grant. Her eyes flickered back and forth between the two older women, and I heard her say, 'He didn't exempt himself. He drew a straw, too.'

Hannah replied cynically, 'Do you think he didn't know which straw was which? He was controlling the entire thing. What would we have done yesterday without Mr Nilsson, Mr Hoffman, and Colonel Marsh? Even Mr Preston is stronger than most of the women. We lost only the weakest of the men. Do you think that is just a coincidence?' In a flash I realized that I had had exactly the same thought the day before but had entirely forgotten it. 'If he arranged it,' I ventured to say, 'it was to save the rest of us.'

'So,' said Hannah coldly, 'you subscribe to murder so long as it saves your skin?'

I did not know how to answer. I did not know why Hannah suddenly seemed to dislike me, but Mrs Grant looked me up and down in that appraising way she had and said, 'Don't worry about Grace, Hannah. Grace will be of use to us yet.'

Mary Ann later went to sit beside Greta, the young German woman who so revered Mrs Grant, and I saw them with their heads together, talking in an earnest way. Thus the seeds of mistrust were spread and nourished. Later that day, Mrs Grant questioned Hardie about his sense of direction.

'We're sailing around in circles,' she said. 'First we go one way and then another.' This caused Hardie to scoff and ask, 'What do you know about it?' Again I realized that he must have injured himself in the storm, for he had removed the life vest the deacon had given him and bound his left arm against his chest. But I was glad to see him holding his knife at the ready and scanning the surface of the water for fish. This was the old Hardie. Perhaps he was not so handicapped after all.

Hannah said, 'I thought we had decided to steer due east in order to take advantage of the wind and the current, but now, for some reason, we are headed south.' Indeed, the sun had started to sink from its zenith, which made the cardinal directions increasingly evident. Mary Ann burst into wails. All of us were upset by this conversation, whether it meant anything or not. Hardie said, 'And I'd like to see ye sail directly into the wind. If ye knew anything, ye'd know it can't be done.'

'But I thought the wind was blowing from America,' said Hannah.

After that, Hardie stubbornly refused to speak, addressing himself to the many little tasks that constantly occupied him; but it was not lost on me that he corrected our course so that we were again headed in what seemed to be an easterly direction. Mrs Grant called us 'dear' in her somber way and assured us that all was not lost, that as long as we kept heading east, sooner or later we were bound to reach England or France. The division between

Mrs Grant and Hardie had been working under the surface for some time, but I now saw how she had played several situations to her advantage since that first day, when she had come out in favor of picking up the child. She had been the first to suggest trying to sail, which had seemed like a good idea to us, even if the boat had been too crowded for it to work. Then, she had loudly criticized the entire notion of drawing lots without objecting to it in a way that would have caused it not to happen. That the men had died had benefited us all, but Mrs Grant had emerged from the incident as the one holding the higher moral ground.

As Hardie searched for fish, his shoulders hunched in on themselves, giving him more and more of an animal look. His eyes sank into their sockets, and every now and then he glared at us with thinly veiled suspicion. I knew instinctively that he was no longer sure of his command. He was also physically weaker – as we all were – and made his pronouncements, which in the beginning had given us such courage, far less forcefully than before. The women as often turned to Mrs Grant for predictions as they did to Mr Hardie, and once, when he had drifted into a deep sleep to make up for his lack of rest the previous night, Mrs Grant brazenly made her way to the storage casks that held our water supply and looked inside. 'There's not as much as I expected,' she answered to our inquiries; then she whispered something to Hannah, whose eyes had narrowed to cat-like slits. 'He thinks we're incapable of understanding a thing,' said Hannah, and when Hardie awoke, she asked him outright how much water was now contained in the barrels. 'Enough for at least four days,' said Hardie, which we now presumed to be a lie, for Mrs Grant had just inspected the barrels for herself.

'Don't lie to us,' shouted Greta. 'We're not children!'

Hardie was surprised, but he stuck to his story.

'Open the barrels and show us, then,' said Hannah.

'This isn't a democracy,' he replied, and he once again set about measuring the angle of the sun. The wind had turned into a steady breeze, and we were skimming along at a fine clip, but the water incident and the mistake in direction of the morning had seriously damaged his authority. And with three fewer men among our number, he had lost important natural allies. Perhaps if he had explained everything to us in a clear manner, he might have helped his position, but he had gruffly gone on about apparent wind versus true wind and missing compasses and chronometers and people who had too much money but too little sense in a way that evidenced disordered thinking. We thought that sailing was something one either did or did not know how to do. We didn't want to hear about atmospheric disturbances or prevailing currents or wind shifts or acts of God.

That evening, Mrs Grant and Hannah, with Mary Ann creeping along behind them, made their way to the back of the boat and again requested that the water barrels be opened so that we could judge for ourselves the gravity of our situation. Again, Mr Hardie refused. I could only see glimpses of Hardie's face because the three women were blocking my view. My hearing and my vision, too, had a way of clicking on and off, whether because of malnutrition or exposure to the elements, making it very hard to understand exactly what was going on, though some of the pieces have fallen into place as I look back on the events of those days. On the one hand, I wanted to believe Hardie's assertion that there was plenty of water for the foreseeable future, a time period that had shrunk to span no more than a day or two, for I was sure that in a day or two we would all be dead. On the other, I had an intellectual interest in the truth. I was aware, however, of being as angry at Mrs Grant and Hannah for filling the boat with a new sort of tension as I was at Hardie for any lies he might have told us or mistakes he might have made. Above all, I did not want to see the fear that flickered briefly in Mr Hardie's eyes. I did not want to see any seam of weakness exposed, for I had put my hopes of survival in him. I sensed the same reluctance on the part of several others for any sort of showdown. Mrs Grant might well have been right in her claims, but we clung to our illusions, or at least to what shreds of them remained.

DAY TWELVE

On our twelfth day in the boat, a flock of birds fell inexplicably from the heavens.

'It means we're going to live!' exulted Mrs Hewitt.

'It means we're going to die,' screamed Mary Ann, who was never far now from a state of panic.

'Of course we're going to die,' said Hardie cheerfully in response to questions from every quarter of the boat. 'It's just a question of when.'

'It's a gift from God,' said Isabelle, who was unfailingly serious and godly, causing Maria to make the sign of the cross. Immediately, Mr Hoffman and Mr Nilsson grabbed up their oars and used them to move the birds close enough so that the rest of us could gather them into the boat.

The prosecutor told Mr Reichmann he planned to use this in the trial as evidence that we did not have to kill each other, for who knew when God would rain birds down on us again? 'How could we expect that,' I asked in amazement, 'when none of us had ever heard of such a thing before?'

We argued all day about what kind of birds they were. Hannah, who had taken over the deacon's duties of blessing the food and making pronouncements about God and providence, insisted they were doves, if only symbolically, in the way that all birds and messengers are either doves or hawks; and since we were all eager to think we were approaching land, we tacitly agreed to call them doves, even as we laughed and ripped their tawny feathers off and gnawed the raw flesh from their fragile bones.

It was Hardie who spoiled the mood by saying, 'It's not because we're near land that these birds fell into our laps, it's because we're *not* near land that they dropped dead. Sheer exhaustion, that's what did them in.'

We heard him. We even understood him, but we already knew that we were in the middle of the ocean, far from land and all that was familiar. We didn't want to be reminded of it in the face of this great blessing. When we had eaten our fill, Mrs Grant suggested that we dry some of the flesh so that we would have something to eat for the next day. 'It's not likely that such a miracle will befall us twice,' she said, so we busied ourselves with the task, and soon we were covered in down and offal, like laborers in some gruesome butchery. Mrs McCain, who had established herself as rigid and devoid of humor from the start, surprised everyone by saying, 'If only my sister could see me now.' We laughed to hear such a serious person say something that could only be construed as a joke.

The bird flesh tasted oily and slightly of fish. I had the fleeting image of myself as a predator, until I looked around me and realized that we were all predators and that we always had been. But what was foremost in my mind was what Mr Preston had told me about how long the human body could last without nourishment. We were being given the opportunity to stave off starvation for another day or two, which seemed to me like the greatest blessing we could hope for; and as I think back on that day, I realize that we had stopped hoping to be rescued and had started thinking that our only salvation lay in rescuing ourselves. I was not alone in feeling a strange sympathy for all that lay around me: the sky, the sea, and the boat full of people, all of whom now had blood dripping down their chins and lips creased with painful fissures that cracked and bled when they chanced to smile.

NIGHT

It might have been a mistake to eat so much, for some of us suffered the pains of indigestion, and throughout the night came the muffled sounds of people addressing their physical needs. I had no such trouble, and as the light faded, the strange ease and sympathy for my fellow man I had felt during the afternoon increased. I don't know what to call the feeling that expanded in my breast except optimism, and when Mary Ann put her little hands around my shoulders and pulled me toward her in a hug, I squeezed her back.

Because Mr Hardie had seated us next to each other that first day, Mary Ann had adopted the habit of looking to me for guidance. I think this instinct also had something to do with Mr Hardie's cold unapproachability – one needed a representative, almost, to get an audience with him – along with the fact that Hannah and Mrs Grant were always in such demand, whereas I was not in demand at all. Earlier in the evening, as the sun burned toward the horizon, everything in the boat had been bathed in a rich glow, which made our blood-caked faces seem to belong to a pack of demons. Hannah had dipped a rag into the sea and gone about the boat wiping the blood off people's faces. Mary Ann suddenly seemed to realize how frightful she must look, if only because all of the others in the boat were caked with feathers and gore and it stood to reason that the same must be true of her. 'Grace,' she whispered, hiding her face in her hands. 'Do you have a bit of cloth?'

'What do you want it for?' I asked.

'I want to wash my face! It looks ghastly, doesn't it?'

I told her I had no cloth, but that Hannah had one and would soon help her the way she was helping everyone else.

'I want to do it myself!' she cried. 'Can you help me get to the railing, then? I can lean over and wash in the sea.' She pointed to an empty space beside Mr Preston, so I let her hold on to me while she moved over, but she didn't let go and insisted, 'No, you must come, too. You don't mind switching with Grace, do you, Mr Preston?'

At that point, Mary Ann had nearly pulled me down on top of him and he had little choice in the matter but to move. When we were settled, Mary Ann said, 'Now we will wash each other. I will be your mirror and you will be mine.' By then, the sun had half disappeared over the horizon, and soon it would be dark. 'In a minute we won't be able to see anything,' I said. 'A mirror is of little use in the dark.'

'That's why we must hurry,' said Mary Ann.

I thought perhaps she was concerned that by the time Hannah got to her, it would be too dark for her to do a proper job of cleaning. It also occurred to me that Mary Ann was suffering from stomach cramps and only wanted an excuse to sit by the railing so she wouldn't have to make a fuss about it later on. It was only when Hannah came to us some thirty minutes later and asked if she could help to wash our faces that I found the real explanation for Mary Ann's urgent insistence that we help each other wash. The reason that arose in my mind when I looked up at Hannah and heard her say, 'Right, then. It looks as if you are all set,' was jealousy. I decided that Mary Ann had noticed the looks Hannah and I had shared, few as they were, and wanted to prevent us from sharing another such opportunity, and for a moment I was filled with resentment at having been manipulated in such a way.

Of course, I might have been wrong. In looking for a rational explanation for one of the things Mary Ann did, I ignore the countless other instances where her actions defied explanation of any sort and could only be accounted for as the behavior of someone in deep emotional distress. I would be hard-pressed to explain all of my own actions there in the lifeboat, so to require explanations of someone who was clearly in a precarious mental state is hardly fair. Still, this is what I thought at the time and so, in the interest of honesty, I have written it down. I also relate this incident to show that during the endless hours when we had little occupation, our minds sought to make sense of things, just the way people have always sought to make sense of their situations.

Later that night the moon rose and bathed the boat in its cold light. I knew that ancient people had worshipped the moon because they couldn't explain it, and without thinking about what I was doing, I sent up a little prayer that we might be saved. I spent some time wondering if my prayer would only be valid during a full moon and not the waning crescent that was present that night. Then I said a prayer for Henry, filled with shame that he had recently been so far from my thoughts.

At that point in the night, I am nearly certain that Mary Ann still sat beside me at the railing, but it wasn't a matter that concerned me at the time so I cannot be sure. In any case, when the sun rose the following morning, she had moved back to her seat on the thwart and so was sitting close beside Mr Preston, who still occupied my usual place. They were both awake and seemed to be sharing some private words, but drew apart when Mary Ann glanced over and saw I was looking at her. I remembered her desire of the evening before to move to the railing and her insistence that I accompany her, and my interpretation of those events began to change. Now I wondered if the entire charade had had more to do with a desire to speak privately with Mr Preston than anything to do with Hannah and me, but I suspected that my imagination was running away with me. People in the boat were beginning to stir, and the events of the next days would drive all thoughts of Mary Ann's petty motivations from my head.

DAY THIRTEEN

The day after the birdfall, one of the other lifeboats reappeared in the distance. Whether it was one of the two we had seen earlier or a different one altogether, there was no way of telling, although Hardie seemed sure it was one of the original pair. Mr Hoffman was responsible for watching the northeast quadrant of the ocean and was the first to see it, but it immediately disappeared from his view, so we had only his word for it until later in the day. By that time, news of this kind was assumed to be the product of a hallucination and did not cause an immediate stir. There was, of course, a kind of wishful interest, but nothing resembling belief.

The hole in the boat had left us in a perilous position, and there was the unspoken fear that if bad weather again hit, we might once more have to lighten our load. 'Can't it be patched, Mr Hardie?' asked Mrs Grant as soon as the sun showed itself above the horizon. 'Surely you can think of something!' But try as he might to stuff the hole with blankets, the flow of water could not be altogether stopped. 'It's not a simple round hole,' he said. 'You can see for yourself how the wood has splintered.' But every now and then Mrs Grant repeated, 'Surely you can think of something, a man of your experience and resolve.' Finally, he lost his temper and shouted, 'Patch it yourself, then! Take charge of the whole bloody mess!'

I was shocked to see him lose his temper at such a slight provocation, especially when we had eaten our fill the day before and had the strips of meat that were drying on top of the canvas boat cover to look forward to for breakfast. I tried to send Hannah a questioning look, but her thoughts were evidently turned inward, and she seemed insensible to her surroundings until Mrs Grant asked her to pass two strips of bird meat to each of us. On most days, Mr Hardie took charge of the water barrel, but he grumbled something to Mr Hoffman, who responded by taking the duty of passing around the tin cup upon himself. With so little moisture in our mouths, it was hard to swallow the lump of meat, and I wondered if we should have taken the pains to dry it. I watched as Isabelle dipped her piece into the ocean and knew that while seawater might make the flesh easier to chew and swallow, the added salt would do nothing but further deplete her body of its precious store of water and add to her thirst.

The waves came at us in a hypnotic pattern of large swells. The up-and-down motion was as regular as clockwork and mostly we were silent and inert, except for the bailers, who scooped at the water and threw it back over the side the best way they could. We were dazed and wishful and lulled, almost, by the strain on our bodies and minds and by the rhythmic rocking, until, miraculously, both boats rose simultaneously on the backs of separate swells, and there it was, silhouetted against the sky at a distance of perhaps a quarter mile before they and then we slid down the glassy green haunch of the ocean and into another trough.

This time, several people saw it. 'Man the oars!' shouted the Colonel, breaking the stunned silence. 'Make for the craft!' There was a flutter of activity as people absorbed this news, as they checked it against the dwindling list of things they knew for certain and against the much longer list of things they only hoped. With much bumping and clattering, the oars were dislodged from where they had been jammed in under the rail and where they had lain mostly dormant since the gale, but Hardie rose, arms outstretched like Christ on the cross, and admonished: 'It's Blake's boat! Damned if it isn't! Ship the oars!'

'I don't care if it's the devil himself,' said the Colonel. 'Prepare to row!'

It was at this point that Hannah began to make her way aft, crouching low and holding on to whatever presented itself in order to keep her balance. Mr Hardie's attention lay elsewhere, and he appeared not to notice her until she had her hands on one of the two water barrels that remained to us now that we had lost one in the gale.

'Back to yer seat, damn ye!' cried Hardie, noticing her too late to stop her from ripping off the lid. He lunged in her direction, shouting, 'Ye will imperil us all!' but Hannah's hand disappeared into the barrel and emerged with a wooden box, which was tied tightly around with a bit of rope.

'You who fear no one act as if you fear Blake,' she cried. 'Is this the reason why?' She seemed to have known the box was there, so Mrs Grant must have seen it when she had checked the barrels for water and passed the information on.

'Put that back,' said Hardie. 'Ye don't know what ye're doing.' But Hannah's hands were scrabbling at the string, trying to undo its knot. For a moment, the other boat was forgotten, out of sight behind the large swells that rhythmically rocked us as if the world's overall pattern would not be disturbed, regardless of the countless little dramas of human life; and it was easy to believe it had never been there at all. 'Get his knife,' called Mrs Grant. 'Mr Hardie,' she commanded, 'produce your knife.'

Hardie looked about at us. His eyes were protruding from his gaunt face. His hand sought the scabbard at his waist and emerged with the knife, but instead of passing it to Hannah or using it to cut the cord, he held it between them in a decidedly threatening way before saying, 'All right then, if you won't take my word for it, pass the box here.'

Before Mrs Grant could object, the boat rose again on the back of a giant swell, began to slip over its steep side, and there, above us and poised to plummet downward on top of us, was the other boat. 'To the oars!' shouted Hardie as the two boats came within inches of each other, causing Hardie and Hannah to fall against each other and the knife, whether by accident or design, to slice deeply into the side of Hannah's face. She cried out, lost hold of the box, and fell into Hardie's embrace. He was somehow able to catch hold of her, and again, whether by accident or design, the knife went over the side and the box must have gone with it, for it was never seen in the boat after that, and it was only by the grace of God that Hannah and Hardie didn't go with them. Hardie swore to us – and it might have been so – that he could not have saved both the box and Hannah, but he had been invested with such powers of control that it was commonly believed he had orchestrated events so that whatever secret or evidence the box held would be lost.

Hannah was shoved to the floor while Hardie seized an oar out of Mr Hoffman's hands and, despite his injured arm, tore at the water in an effort to gain some distance from the other boat. 'Do ye still think we should team up with them?' shouted Hardie, but of course it was a rhetorical question. 'Do ye still think we'd make a cozy couple rafted up together side by side?'

I have an imperfect memory of the people in the

other boat. Many of them were slumped and motionless, and it was hard to know if they were dead or only injured or sick. Only four or five people in the boat showed any life at all, and their mouths were frozen open in horror when it appeared that we would crash. One woman held out her arms to us, and a man called out something, but it was impossible to hear what he said. One thing that was crystal clear to all of us was that there was plenty of room in the other boat.

When Hardie had grabbed Hoffman's oar, Mr Preston had moved next to me to compensate for the changing balance of the boat. Now he leaned in toward me and said in a low voice, 'Whatever was in that box must hold great value.'

'All people hold their personal possessions dear,' I said. 'I'd think that nowhere is that more true than in a setting such as this, where most of us have lost everything.'

'But do we make them into such secrets? I wonder that Mr Hardie doesn't just tell us what is in the box. Perhaps when things calm down, someone should ask him outright rather than trying to wrest his secrets from him.'

'Now is hardly the time for that!' I said. Then I added: 'And the man is used to being around all sorts of people. It's no wonder he doesn't know whom he can trust.'

'True, true,' said Mr Preston, and for the second time I felt he was holding something back, that he knew more about the box than he was letting on.

After we had gained some distance from the other boat, Mr Hardie directed that the oars be put away. 'It's her or me,' he said, pointing with his good arm at Mrs Grant. 'Either ye want her in charge of things or ye want me. Ye'd best decide.' He told us that the box had belonged to him and that it was no one's business what it contained, and after that, he refused to say more. I remembered the box I had seen him slip inside his jacket during the storm and I could only think it was the same one. If so, he was taking great pains to keep it concealed, but I kept this observation to myself.

Mrs Grant looked around the boat and gave us all a chance to speak about whatever was on our minds. She set the tone by speaking first. She said it was her opinion that Mr Hardie had misused his power and kept us from the other boat out of some personal animosity he had for the man named Blake. This might or might not have cost lives, since we had never explored the possibility of moving some of our people when we had the opportunity. Then she charged that with his lottery, Hardie had directly caused the loss of three lives and possibly more, but it was our opinion she was interested in, not her own. The Colonel rose to his full height and said that Mr Hardie had indeed endangered all of us by failing to approach the third boat in the first days and that he had, through his own actions and lack of judgment, lost the confidence of those placed by God or fate in his charge: 'It might be folly to approach the other boat in such heavy seas as we saw today, but we should have done so when we could.' The Colonel came off looking almost heroic because he spared a thought for 'the poor souls we just saw, who no doubt would have benefited from our earlier involvement and aid.'

Only Mr Hoffman spoke in defense of Mr Hardie, pointing out that we ourselves had lost only eight of our number. There were still thirty of us, and except for Mrs Forester, who was to die almost unnoticed later that day, we were in relatively good health; and while there was disagreement about whether the boat we had just seen was Blake's boat or the one skippered by the bearded man, its occupants were clearly sicker and more depleted than we. We knew that one of the boats had started off filled beyond capacity, so if that was the one we had just seen, it seemed the chances of dying in that boat were far higher than they were in our own. It was Mr Hoffman's staunch belief that this was due to Mr Hardie's superior ability to keep his charges alive. Mr Nilsson sat quietly by and said not a word either for or against.

Mr Hardie growled that whichever boat we had just seen, there was now plenty of room in it. 'If some of ye want to take yer chances with it, I am sure it can be arranged,' he said, but Mrs Grant said that if any of us were to be transferred to the other boat, it should be Mr Hardie himself. At this suggestion, Mr Hardie's face took on a twisted look, and I shrank against Mr Preston in horror to think that a person could harbor in himself such opposing personalities. In any event, the boat was now nowhere in sight, so even if there were some practical way to transfer Mr Hardie, the question was now moot.

Lisette spoke up to tell a story that had been whispered about since the third day, when we had learned that Mr Blake had thrown two people out of his boat. I had heard the story several times, and each time it contained new details that were either factual additions from valid observers or pure fabrications based on our increasingly active imaginations. Lisette ventured that Mr Blake's boat was riding strangely in the water because he was carrying something heavy in it, something stolen from the locked room on the *Empress Alexandra*.

Greta, who was completely enthralled with Hannah and Mrs Grant and who had developed an irrational dislike of Mr Hardie, then suggested that Hardie and Blake were co-conspirators and that Hardie was somehow helping Blake by keeping our boat away from his. 'But what evidence do you have?' I cried before I was even aware that I had a desire to speak, but the Colonel interrupted to declare, 'If the charge is false, Mr Hardie will tell us so.' Mrs Grant, who returned Greta's affection, said, 'Greta deserves to be heard just as much as anyone else.' Then she turned to Mr Hardie and asked, 'Do you have anything to say in your defense?'

Hardie replied, 'If Blake and I did steal something, something which would otherwise have sunk to the bottom of the ocean, where it would have remained buried in the muck for all eternity, I would say: What do ye know about doing without, ye who have always had everything? Poverty is a shipwreck! It's very easy to live moral lives when all of yer baser needs are attended to. And if we didn't steal anything, I would say only: I wish we had.'

'You are not only charged with theft, whether it be the box you have concealed from us or something more substantial that is carried in the other boat,' said Mrs Grant. 'What do you say to keeping us away from it and reducing the possibility of our rescue?'

'How has it reduced anything? I don't expect ye to listen to Hoffman there, but the proof of his argument is floundering about out here just like we are.'

When it came her turn to speak, Mary Ann shook her head to indicate that she had nothing to say, but she leaned toward me and whispered, 'I can't help thinking about what Mrs Fleming said. About how your husband paid Mr Hardie to take you on board. Maybe that's what was in the box. Maybe he was given it by your husband and didn't steal it at all. Did the box look at all familiar to you? Did you get a good look at it? Surely you should say something if you did!'

I replied that Mrs Fleming had been delusional and that my husband was not the sort to pay for something when he could get it for free and that when a ship is sinking, only a scoundrel would be concerned with something as frivolous as diamonds and gold.

'But they were already lowering this boat when you got on,' said Mary Ann. 'They stopped it for you. I know that for a fact. And that's when Hardie got on, too. It's possible your husband did pay him and you just failed to notice.'

'I'm impressed you remember it so clearly, Mary Ann. I, for one, was in a complete panic. I ended up in a lifeboat and I'm glad I did, but I can't for the life of me remember how it came about.'

NIGHT

That night I slept not at all, or if I did, it would be more aptly described as a drifting in and out of consciousness, where the border between one state and the other was a wide territory that was more filled with mental activity and physical movement than the periods when I was awake. I think we were all fearful of being thrown overboard while we slept, which had the effect of causing people to start suddenly and to shout out whenever they ventured to cross the frontier into sleep. Mr Preston, who had regained his seat on the rail, was still close enough to hit me with his fist when he started awake, shouting, 'I can explain everything!' and another time he muttered, 'The box couldn't have been mine! I'm only an accountant, after all – what would I be doing with jewels?'

I reached over to shake him fully awake, fearful that he might harm himself in his sleep. 'Mr Preston!' I cried. 'Calm yourself!' But my own brain was experiencing the same sort of disordered thinking. At one moment I would be standing in front of our old house with Miranda, vowing to get it back for her, and at another, I would be holding on to Henry as he sank beneath the waves. At still another moment, after hours of trying to hold myself upright, I felt myself slipping, not off the thwart onto the damp boards that formed the bottom of the boat, but off the deck of the *Empress Alexandra* and into a sea that was teeming with bodies and debris. A child raised his face to me and stretched out his arms, but when I reached for him, his eyes turned red with little flames and he laughed a childish yet demonic laugh.

Our anxiety that night was certainly due to the fact that the tensions that had been lurking beneath the surface had now been made explicit. Mrs Grant had said what many people in the boat were thinking – that Mr Hardie was no longer fit to lead us; that he had made several decisions based on some unstated purpose of his own; and that innocent people had died when, if we had played our hand differently, they might have been saved. Whether Mrs Grant was right in her suspicions that Mr Hardie had acted out of selfish motives or not, once they had been articulated, they could not be unsaid. Whatever the truth, our situation was now more perilous than it had ever been, for we felt ourselves threatened not only by the forces of nature, but by the human beings with whom we shared the boat.

The night stretched on. Clouds obscured the moon, adding a thick cover of darkness that made it impossible to see who was stirring and who was crying out. I suspect Mrs Grant had assigned some of the people sitting closest to Mr Hardie to take turns watching him, and just before dawn, when one of the women near him gave out a blood-curdling scream, I was sure she was being murdered. A moment later, I heard a rustling and felt the balance of the boat shift and then I heard Mrs Grant's soothing voice telling whoever it was that whatever had frightened her had been nothing but a dream. Eventually, the sun cast its gray morning light on us, illuminating our floating world by nearly imperceptible degrees; but any hopes we had harbored during the night that a new dawn would erase the drama of the previous day were about to be shattered.

DAY FOURTEEN

Everyone was strangely calm when, once the day had fully dawned, Mrs Grant called for a vote on whether Mr Hardie should go over the side. I can only explain this equanimity by the trust that had been established between Mrs Grant and the other passengers and that I have described before, or perhaps it was the fact that the day dawned windless, gray and still. Only Anya Robeson displayed a kind of shocked attention, as if she were only now sensible of the events around her. 'What about the other lifeboat?' she asked, making sure that her hands were covering her son's ears. 'If you don't want him in this boat, couldn't he go in that one?'

When I think back, I credit Anya with trying to come up with some kind of middle ground, but at the time, the suggestion seemed highly unrealistic, almost grounded in delusional thinking. For one thing, the other boat was nowhere to be seen, so there was no real possibility of enlisting its aid. And for another, I think we had become so used to thinking of ourselves as separated from any sort of human society that the idea of succor coming from outside our little boat had long since stopped occurring to us. Mrs Grant answered Anya kindly – I remember the tone, but not the exact words. 'A yes vote means he dies,' added Hannah, so there would be no mistake about the purpose of the vote. Mary Ann, however, turned her wild eyes on me and hissed, 'What? What is she asking?'

I was more and more ruthless toward Mary Ann, who seemed to assume that people would take care of her despite her accusations and emotional instability. All along, her timid indecision had given me courage, but I did not credit her with giving me anything, only with taking. If the situation was bleak, I would not shield her from it. It was not in my nature to come up with metaphors she could understand or accept, as Hannah might have done. I found her questions silly and unnecessary, but because she was desperate to think that one of us had answers, she hung on every word I said. Often, after getting my attention, she would have nothing to say, or she would hope for an answer without having first to frame a question. I, too, was hungry for absolutes, and on some days it was only Mary Ann's grasping desperation that lifted me above the compulsion to act in the same childish manner. If Mr Hardie said, 'The wind has shifted to the west,' she would say, 'The west? Did he say west?'

'Yes,' I would answer, or 'No,' as the case might require, and mostly I told her the truth.

'What does that mean?' she would ask, or 'Which way is west?'

I would use what little I knew of our position to tell her the grim facts: 'It means we are being blown back toward England,' I said in those early days when we were desperate to hold our position. 'Look on the bright side,' I added. 'If we're blown back far enough, you can get a brand new dress for your wedding.' Hannah, however, would say something like 'Think of it as a seesaw, Mary Ann. It's bound to shift right back again.'

Now we were being asked to make a difficult choice about Hardie's culpability and about the resulting sentence, but I made it seem as if the problem were with Mary Ann's lack of staunchness. 'Oh, come now,' I said. 'You can't pretend we're playing in the bathtub, Mary Ann. I'm sorry if you don't like the choices, but the hard fact is that Mr Hardie has become dangerous to the rest of us. He has lost his authority and his ability to make sound decisions. Either he goes overboard or we all drown, it's as simple as that.'

Even as I uttered them, I wondered if my words were true. I honestly did not know then and I don't have any better idea now. When I looked at Mr Hardie that morning, I was hard-pressed to recognize the superhuman figure of those first days in the boat. If Mr Hardie was still godlike, he had become god in his human form, and we all know what happens to gods like that. Perhaps he had changed, or perhaps we had, or perhaps it was only the situation that was now calling for something new. But whether Mr Hardie had changed or not, Mrs Grant had only become more of whatever she had been at the first: solid, enduring, endlessly capable. But even more than those two people, it was the prevailing mood in the boat that needed to be assessed; and while I was putting Mary Ann off with whatever words came into my head, a deeper part of my consciousness was scrutinizing the faces of the people around me and trying to decipher their thoughts.

Did I know in advance what the order of voting would be? As it happened, Mary Ann was called upon before I was. To a person sitting at a desk assessing the facts, this was perfectly predictable: in taking turns at Mr Hardie's roster of duties or in passing the cup of water around, we always started clockwise from where Mr Hardie sat in the back of the boat, then proceeding up one thwart and down the next as we came to them, so it would be natural to assume that Mrs Grant would follow a similar pattern, thus occasioning Mary Ann, who was now sitting on my right, to cast her vote before I was called upon to cast mine. Of course, Mr Hardie had been in charge of the duty roster and Mrs Grant was now running things, and there was no real reason to assume that she would adopt the same convention, but it had become a habit with us; and if I had thought it out beyond the first or second round of analysis – which I'm not sure I was capable of doing in my weakened state – I would have come to the conclusion that Mrs Grant would want to keep things as normal as possible in order to convince us that this was just another of many routine duties, what anyone who found himself adrift in a lifeboat would be asked to do.

In any case, Mary Ann voted before I did. After what I had said to her – I also said something like 'Don't think so much of yourself. Think of your Robert. Think of *us*, or think of yourself if you must, floundering around in the black water, struggling to prolong your life for a useless minute or two, not because it will do any good, but because struggling against death is the very nature of the beast' – Mary Ann hid her face and murmured pathetically, 'I am not a beast' before raising her hand and nodding her head to signal assent.

Then came my turn. Mary Ann's eyes remained hidden behind her clenched fists. Her hair fell forward in a knotty tangle. There were already enough votes to pass the resolution, so when Mrs Grant and Hannah turned their eyes on me, I whispered, 'I abstain. You don't need my vote. Do whatever you like.' I'm not sure Hardie could hear my words from where he sat, but I shook my head, hoping he would think I had voted no. I still felt some obligation to the man in charge – to men in general – and, of course, to God, who I had always assumed was a man, albeit now I envisioned him in liquid form, capriciously rising up and threatening to drown us but keeping us alive to endure more of his capriciousness and threats.

Hannah hissed something under her breath. Her

emaciated face narrowed to a grimace. Her wound was a long red gash across her cheek. I could not hear her words, but to this day I can see her lips, which were cracked and bleeding like another wound carved in above the jut of her chin. 'Coward,' she seemed to be saying, but Mrs Grant calmed her with a touch and turned her impenetrable gaze on me for an instant, and I felt consoled, somewhat, for I too was partially under her spell. It was a gift Mrs Grant had, of making a person feel understood. She had an even stronger effect on the other women than she had on me. They exchanged serene looks with her, and some of them were emboldened enough to look fearlessly at Hardie himself.

If you counted the Italian women, who had raised their hands and wailed, though it was anyone's guess whether or not they understood the issue before them, all of the women except Anya and me voted without hesitation to kill Mr Hardie, and all of the men voted to save him. I still do not know how I would have voted if they had forced me to make a choice. I stole a glance at Mr Hardie. He was giving me a fixed and evil stare, and at that moment I might have sent them all to the devil, every man and woman of them, every wretched human speck.

I repeat that we were weak. Even I find that hard to remember now, and I was there. The officials of the court seem absolutely incapable of comprehending our circumstances, and how could they? I only fault them because they failed to comprehend that they could not comprehend. My vision seemed to resonate, to echo. Primary images were confused with after-images, with red and yellow splashes of light, with a watery smearing together of faces and features and the muted glimmer of the sun on the sea. 'Resolution passed,' said Mrs Grant. The Italian women looked eager and blank, as if now the way was cleared for our salvation. Mary Ann whimpered beside me, emitting thin, spasmodic sobs. I hated her then. 'Stop it!' I shouted. 'What good will it do? Isn't it enough that we have to listen to the endless wailing of the wind?' But then the hopelessness of our position burst over me like one of the relentless green waves, and I put my arms around her and we clung to each other, her blonde and tangled locks falling against my cheeks in exactly the same way that my dark and tangled locks fell against hers.

So Mr Hardie was to die. The problem now became one of getting him out of the boat. He was crouched on the aft thwart like the mongrel he was, baring his yellow teeth and snapping at the air. 'Ye 'aven't got me yet, ye 'aven't got me yet,' he barked, and if the vote had been held then, I would have raised my voice and shouted, 'Let the mangy mongrel die!'

Mr Hardie had removed the top of one of the water barrels and was holding it before him like a shield. Hannah had crawled forward and was clawing at it, trying to push it out of the way, but she lacked the strength to do so. As she approached, Mr Hardie pushed the shield outward, ostensibly to hit her with it, but his injured arm was all but useless and he was so weak that he fell backward against the side of the boat.

'Grace! Mary Ann!' shouted Mrs Grant. 'Go to help Hannah!' To this day, I don't know why I was chosen, but she looked at me in that familiar appraising way she had and called my name softly, as if she were certain of my loyalty. I was the only one who had failed to cast a vote, and it has occurred to me that it was her way of implicating me, of making me vote with my actions whether or not I would vote with my words. Her round face and amethyst eyes were aimed at us like beams of purple light as I followed Hannah through the swirling seawater in the bottom of the boat, which was still awash with pieces of bird bones saved for their marrow and stray wing feathers and the last bits of rotting meat. I closed my eyes and tried to bring order to my thoughts. I was cold to the core now that Mary Ann was not pressed in against me. Mr Hardie was saying, 'Ye won't get me, ha! Not if I get ye first!'

Hannah said, 'He's insane! He'll kill us all! We must save ourselves! Grab him!'

I opened my eyes, as much to restore my balance, which had faltered without the aid of sight, as to ward off any threat. I think if Mr Hardie had looked straight at me or called out my name or made any show of recognition, I might have sat down next to Greta and moved no farther toward him. But it was Hannah who was watching me, and it was Mrs Grant who called my name, followed by soft words of encouragement. As I made my way closer, crouching and clutching at the shoulders of the others in order to keep my balance in the rocking boat, my ears pulsed with the sounds of the Italian women, who were moaning and shrieking behind us. I steadied myself against the Colonel, who was shrinking into his seat as if to avoid detection. Something large and black was flapping in my peripheral vision. I thought it must be the angel of death, but it was not at all clear at that point who the angel had in its sights. Only when Hardie lashed out at Hannah did the angel stumble forward and take the shape of one of the Italian women, who was brandishing the wing of a bird and stumbling forward to poke it into Hardie's eyes. I think I called out Mr Hardie's name, giving him one last chance to assert himself. His eyes grazed over me, but they were unseeing marbles and he seemed to be beyond sensible speech.

Mrs Grant was suddenly beside me, her solid presence giving me strength. The moment ballooned and time stopped, allowing me to take in the metallic surface of the water and the dull glint of the sun on it. It seemed to me that anyone forced onto that icy tundra would merely pick himself up and walk away, relieved to be free of the boat and the stinking humanity it contained. I do not know what the others were doing – it was as if I alone controlled the strings of destiny. I know now that it was the height of egotism to think that I held any power at all, but for that moment, I was sure I was standing up for the forces of good. Somewhere I even heard a voice that might have been Mrs Grant's croon, 'Good girl,' but I can't swear she said anything. I only know that for several seconds that seemed to have been excised from the day, I stood unaided in the boat and faced Mr Hardie one to one and saw nothing of humanity left in him.

Then the gears caught and time again ticked forward. I can't tell you what I was thinking or if I was thinking. I only know that whatever dangers we had faced had coalesced into something bigger and more menacing, and it seemed up to me to decide, not if Mr Hardie would live or die, but if the rest of us would live. Hannah's face was a terrible sight, bloodless except for the crimson gash where the knife had sliced into it, the colorless eyes, the black snakes of her hair. Hannah and Mrs Grant had each grabbed hold of one of Hardie's arms and Hannah shouted, 'Grace, grab the bloody bastard's neck.'

I did. I put my two hands around Hardie's thin neck. It was as cold as a fish, hard and stringy, like naked bones. In the instant before I tightened my grip, I felt the cloud of his breath on my face. The smell seemed evidence of what he contained within him: only death and decay. I squeezed as hard as I could; I felt the windpipe convulse beneath my fingers and the Adam's apple twitch like a grizzled heart.

'Squeeze harder, dear,' said Mrs Grant in an oddly soothing voice. She had none of Hannah's cold fury or the mad hysteria of the Italian woman who was again jabbing at Hardie's face with the bird's bony wing. There was a crazed look in Mr Hardie's eyes, and I was afraid to let go, for if I did, he would surely kill me.

Hannah was standing tall and straight beside me, and Hardie seemed to shrink in her presence. I felt a surge of strength infuse my limbs. To this day, I can summon up the feeling without the attendant power. Somehow, we were able to keep our balance in the wildly pitching boat. I don't know if it was the waves or the struggle that gave the boat such instability, but it seemed that the two things were only various aspects of the same life force that must play itself out as long as human beings draw breath. Mr Hardie's spectral face loomed closer as together Hannah and I pulled him to his feet. I could feel his beard scratching my face, smell his breath over the stench of the rotting birds, over my own putrid smell. The Italian women were still singing and shrieking behind us, and someone was bending over the prostrate form of Mary Ann, who had fainted, and was stroking her hair and kissing her cheek. I saw this, so I must have lost track of Hardie for a moment, and only when I heard Mrs Grant shout my name did I turn, just in time to ward off a blow that would surely have sent me flying into the sea. 'Kick his legs!' shouted Hannah, and as if we were one person, we kicked in unison. Hardie toppled forward onto us, his weight on our straining shoulders. He was surprisingly insubstantial, or I was stronger than I thought, though the source of my strength was discontinuous: it came in little bursts, it sputtered and caught, allowing me to reach inside his jacket for the box I thought he might be hiding, but, as I later swore to my attorneys, it wasn't there. Then, with a great concerted heave, we threw the only person among us who knew anything about boats and currents into the boiling sea.

We watched him for several minutes. He flailed around. He sank and rose again more than once, spewing water and invective each time he breached the surface. He cursed us. I think his words were 'Die like dogs,' and then he gurgled and went under, into the sucking sea. We stared at that hole in the ocean until a large wave rolled over it. Our little boat rose up onto the back of the same wave, up into the graying light of the premature dusk, but we kept staring, possessed of a common urge to know what it was we had done, or perhaps to justify or forget it; and we might have done so. We might have turned to check on Mary Ann, to join in with the Italian women, who were now singing some sort of aria or hymn, or we might have remarked to each other that the sky did seem to be getting a little brighter in the – was it east?

Could it still be morning? – where the clouds were now billowing up and out of the gray in sun-gilt shapes, if Mr Hardie had not reappeared, head and arms bobbing out of the water, close enough to the boat that we could see the water pouring from his mouth around the yellowing tombstones of his teeth. If he had long before stopped resembling anything human, he now resembled the hellish creatures depicted in ancient religious texts for the purpose of scaring children into being good.

Then, thank God, he was gone; and we did turn to face the others. As we did so, our personalities seemed to separate from the clot of our purpose. Mrs Grant emerged into a businesslike rationality; Hannah made a show of busy concern for the other occupants of the boat – after all, we had just killed someone for them, and wasn't that evidence of how much we cared? But I didn't wish to talk to anyone or even to think about what we had done. Instead, I started to pick up the mess of old bird pieces and throw them over the side of the boat.

There is one other moment that stands out in my mind. It occurred after Hardie went under and before he reappeared. I was standing by the railing, filled with the exhilaration and horror of what we had done, watching the empty space where Hardie had been and where he would be again an instant later. Hannah was close by, on my left, and gradually I became aware of the sturdy presence of Mrs Grant on my right, so that I was supported by those two staunch pillars in the same coveted position I had seen other women occupy over the preceding weeks but which I had never occupied myself. I dared to glance at Hannah, half-afraid that I was imagining her presence and that she would disappear when I looked at her and half-afraid I would be horrified by what I saw. But the cut side of her face was away from me. She had pushed her hair into a long and orderly twist, and the fire had gone out of her eyes, replaced by a cool and almost saintly glow. She gave me what I took to be a half-smile, but which was more a pressing together of her lips than a smile. It seemed to signify approval or acceptance, and in that moment I felt the way a man might feel when he vanquishes an enemy for the good of his town. My senses were in a heightened state – almost the opposite of the senselessness I had felt as I approached Mr Hardie only minutes before. Even as I was focused on Hannah, I was somehow also aware of Mrs Grant's matching nod of approval, but how I could have been looking to the right and left at the same time, I do not know. I felt their vibrant hands touch my shoulders and meet behind my back, and I knew I was about to be warmed and embraced the way most of the other women had at one time or another been warmed and embraced; and I understood then what it was that the others wanted from them, what Hannah and Mrs Grant had to give, for I finally had it for myself. A flood of relief washed over me as the slight pressure of their hands increased, almost to the point of causing me to lose my balance and frightening me a little, but then Hardie's head broke the surface for the last time and shocked us out of whatever shared state we were briefly in.

We set to our tasks in a sort of frenzied domesticity. We cleaned, we bailed, we straightened the chains of the oarlocks, we coiled the frayed ends of rope we had used with the sail and stowed the life ring as best we could. I don't know if we would have had the stomach to repeat the struggle with Mr Hoffman, but when it occurred to me to wonder where he was, he was gone. When I asked about it, pantomiming by pointing to the men and pretending to count, the Italian women wailed and looked fearfully at the water. Mr Preston and the Colonel sat silent and stupefied and had nothing to say about anything after that. And Mr Nilsson, who had been Hoffman's friend, looked like a hunter caught in a trap he had set himself and then forgotten about.

While we were imposing order on the boat, Mrs Grant set to work examining our provisions. Just as she was announcing that we had no water left, Hannah let out a happy cry and pulled a rolled oilskin from where it had been lodged behind the rear thwart, which is where Mr Hardie had been sitting. She handed it at once to Mrs Grant, who opened it to find several pieces of dried fish concealed in its folds. She sat in Hardie's place and passed a portion to all of us, starting at the back of the boat and working up and down the thwarts, clockwise around the boat. Greta said, 'He was hiding food after all!' and that was the prevailing opinion, but I wondered if he was hiding it for his personal use or if he was saving it for when we might need it most. Some of the women exhibited a weird hilarity, as if we had freed ourselves from a tyrant or come a step closer to being saved. I felt more quietly optimistic, but long before dark, our burst of inhuman strength had left us.

Hannah led us all in a little prayer, but without the deacon to make the words legitimate, the ritual seemed decidedly pagan, a prayer of appeasement to the sea to which we had just made a blood sacrifice. But the sleep of the saved is the same as the sleep of the damned. When dawn broke, the surface was calm, the horizon was clear, and after using the oilskin to patch the hole, we were able to get most of the remaining water out of the boat.

PART IV

PRISON

At this moment I am sitting on my prison cot, surrounded by three gray walls. The fourth wall is barred and through the bars I can see across a corridor and into the cell of a woman named Florence, who suffocated her children rather than let them live with a father who beat them. 'Why did you not simply take them to live with you?' I called out to her one day, by way of making conversation. 'They were living with me, but how was I to feed them?' Florence called back in an angry voice, adding, 'The judge was very happy to grant me custody, but not at all disposed to give me any of my husband's money. "It's the way the law is written," he declared in all his imperial majesty. "And who do you think writes the law?" I asked him, but he merely banged his gavel and asked if I wanted the children or not.' She was filled with anger but not regret, and when I asked her if the children had been boys or girls, she convulsed with a chilling laugh and said: 'Girls, of course! It's just my luck to have had only girls!' Every time I've talked to her since, she asks, 'And who do you think writes the law?' so I have begun to avoid her. Even when she stands at the bars and stares across at me, I pretend not to notice. My own mental state is fragile enough that I do not need to endanger it further by talking to the likes of her.

The encounter with Florence has disturbed me in another way. Her talk of money brought home to me certain realities of my own situation that will need to be solved if I succeed in proving my innocence before the magistrate. A week ago, my attorneys brought me a letter from my mother-in-law that has given me reason to hope, but has also given me no indication about how I would be received should I be acquitted of the charges before me. Neither did she explain her long delay in contacting me, and I can only surmise that she wanted to obtain independent proof of my marriage. I wondered again about the telegram Henry said he sent to her. Pre-trial evidence has shown that the wireless telegraph equipment on the *Empress Alexandra* was in fact broken at the time of the shipwreck, but whether that had happened before or after Henry tried to send his communication, I could not ascertain. I also found out that the operator of the wireless was not an employee of the ship, but had worked directly for the Marconi Company, which led me to believe that Mr Blake was not engaged in sending distress signals at the time of the explosion. I did not dwell on this. What I did think about was that if Henry had not been able to send the telegram, Mrs

Winter's first inkling of her son's marriage would have come when she read the list of survivors in the newspaper. In spite of the implications of the situation for me, I could only smile to think of the shock that must have disfigured what I imagined as her cold and haughty face.

My mother-in-law revealed little of her thinking in the letter, only suggesting that my attorneys might arrange for us to meet. I sent word to her through Mr Reichmann that I would not feel right about troubling her as long as this prosecution casts a shadow over me, for I did not want that shadow to fall upon her or anyone in her family. I must admit that I was also thinking of myself to a degree, for I do not want to enter the presence of anyone in Henry's family with my head bowed or with any expectation on their part that I should feel an ounce of guilt or shame. I feel neither, but I want our first meeting to be completely free of any doubt about my innocence. If she is paying for my defense, which I can only think she is, I am deeply grateful, but I do not want gratitude to be the sole foundation for any relationship we might develop. Of my own family, only Miranda seems aware of my circumstances. She wrote to say that due to our mother's fragile state, informing her of my predicament was out of the question. At some point I will write her back, but for now it is a relief to be free of family obligations.

Mr Reichmann came today and I gave him the notebooks containing my written account of our days in the lifeboat. He thanked me, and in exchange he handed me a new, blank notebook and a fresh supply of ink. I was surprised and pleased, for I find that I look forward to sitting and recollecting, as Aristotle would have called it. I don't remember everything right off, but one idea will lead to another, and in this way, I have remembered far more than I thought possible when I set out to fulfill Mr Reichmann's request. When he passed the new notebook across the table where we were obliged to sit, our hands touched, which seemed to startle him so much that he drew back suddenly and sought to divert attention from the incident by telling me something of what I could expect as my case makes its way through the courts. 'Justice can be slow,' he said, to which I replied, 'If it exists at all.' I made my voice sound very stern and certain, which seemed to startle him again. Then I laughed to dispel the impression my seriousness had imparted and was rewarded to see a fleeting shadow cross his brow, which indicated that this supremely confident man was not completely sure of himself in every regard. The laughter drew a disapproving look from the matron, who had stationed herself in a far corner of the room, and the look caused us both to laugh quite merrily, which restored Mr Reichmann's features to their usual state. No doubt it is frowned upon to show any sort of humor in prison, but I couldn't help but think how stupid it was to treat adults like children, to chastise and incarcerate them, and to try to construct a narrative that makes their actions fit neatly into either the virtuous column or the criminal one.

Of course, not a day goes by when I don't think about the lifeboat and ask myself if I would rather be there than here, but it is not a harping or morbid obsession of mind, as would suit Dr Cole's purposes. I enter that blue-vaulted chamber of memory rather the way one would enter a church: reverently, with awe in my soul. The church is filled with light, too – not the usual gaudy sort filtered through lurid images of Christ on the cross, but sea light, murky and green and as cold as Satan's heart.

Can you write about light without knowing what it is? Henry would have said no, and Mr Sinclair would have proceeded to educate me, so I have asked Mr Glover, Mr Reichmann's assistant, to bring me books on the subject. Does it help to know that light is only part of a continuous spectrum of wavelengths, as the scientists now say, or that light travels in both bullets and waves? Waves are something we knew about. They towered over us. We rode high on their crests and from there we could see, briefly, the majesty of the vast and desolate sea. We plunged into the troughs and immediately, great walls of water slammed up against the limits of our vision.

When I mentioned light in a letter I wrote to Greta Witkoppen, the German girl who had taken to Mrs Grant so early on and who had extended her stay in America in order to attend our trial, she wrote back:

> *Don't write to me about such things! In fact, the lawyers say I shouldn't write to you at all, for it might look as if we are conspiring. Tell Mrs Grant not to worry, though. We all know exactly what to do! As for the light, I'm trying to forget it, but I doubt I ever will. Spooky, it was. Everyone thought it was a sign from God, but I can't help thinking it was something conjured up by Hannah. Did it ever occur to you that she might be a witch?*

She was referring, I knew, to those odd bands of light that appeared on about the sixteenth day, moving across the water in the dead of night. I'll never forget it either, just as I'll never forget Hardie's head reappearing when we thought he had gone under for the last time. We were held spellbound, hardly trusting our eyes; but there was no disagreement among us. We all saw the bands of light, but we argued bitterly about what they meant. 'That's the sort of light you see before you die,' said Mary Ann.

'And how would you know that?' asked Isabelle, who had been the one to inform Mrs Fleming that a young girl had been hit in the head when our lifeboat was launched. Isabelle had moved next to Anya Robeson, who now admonished, 'Don't talk about such things! It's bad for the boy,' but we all ignored her, and Mary Ann went on to say, 'My mother nearly drowned once, and she said it wasn't at all like drowning in water; it was like drowning in light. If Mother wasn't rescued after the shipwreck, I hope that is really what it was like for her.'

'Well, we're not drowning,' said Mrs McCain, 'are we, Lisette?' And Lisette, who knew her duty, immediately agreed with her employer.

The waves of light were like puddles on the water – each self-contained, but moving in succession over the black emptiness. They swept over the water at high speeds, going eastward (according to Hannah); and then for no apparent reason, they swept back again, from east to west, moving very quickly so that they each illuminated the boat for only a blink of time. We had been amazed by manifestations of light before, but unlike the other occurrences, this one seemed completely inexplicable. The whole display lasted approximately thirty minutes. Then it abruptly stopped.

Mrs Grant was silent throughout the entire episode, but Hannah spoke of the light as a metaphor for understanding, which reminded me of the deacon, who had mistrusted the concept of understanding altogether. He had said that it was not for us to understand and likened all earthly things to icebergs in that we could never fully know them. He once told me that faith should be offered up without requesting an explanation in return, for explanations presumed understanding, and understanding was reserved for God.

But the deacon was gone, and we had only Hannah, who looked like a high priestess as she stood up in the boat and raised her hands into the stripes of light and asked whatever she believed in to rain down blessings upon us. I did not like to say so in front of the others, but my first thought on seeing the bands of light was that we were in the middle of a flock of angels, indeed that a flock of angels had come down to escort us up to heaven and that Mary Ann was right to think we were dying; so when she started crying out 'Over here! Over here!' I was sure she thought they were angels too, until someone said something about the sweeping floodlights of a search party. 'We're saved! We're saved!' Mary Ann shouted over and over, screaming frantically and nearly jumping into the water in her hurry to climb aboard the ship she knew to be steaming toward us through the night.

I had grown tired of Mary Ann's hysterics. No one could talk sense into her, and when she tore off her dress and threatened to dive headfirst into the sea and swim to the imaginary rescue boat herself, no one, not even Mrs Grant, tried to stop her. She must have thought better of it, but that night she rolled in the wet bottom of the boat and moaned dreadfully. Her hair clung to her face like seaweed, her lips were blue with cold, her cheeks red with fever. Her cries were unbearable, and at long last Hannah had the good sense to knock her cold. No one else moved. We lacked the strength to do even useful things – why bother about those things that wouldn't help at all?

A yellowish light filters into my cell from the hallway, and there is one tiny slit of a window set high up in the wall. It is too high for me to see out of, but I can tell it faces east, for in the morning I awaken to a bright and slanting shaft of silver light if it is sunny out and something more subdued if it is not. It is all predictable and reassuring, and at this point in my life, I am happy to be reassured. The light is fading now, and soon I will be unable to distinguish the letters on this page.

DR COLE

Dr Cole is the doctor of psychiatry who was hired by my lawyers to assess my mental state, and I have continued to see him every week, though to what end I am not entirely sure. I do not take him anywhere near as seriously as he takes himself, but our visits give me an opportunity to leave my cell, so I look forward to them. It has occurred to me that the things I say are not held in strict confidence, as Dr Cole would have me believe, and it has become a game with me to try to find the purpose behind his questions and to answer accordingly. Some of his stock replies seem to hold the response he is seeking within them. For instance, he likes to exclaim, 'That must have been terrifying!' so of course I always agree that it was. It took me several weeks of this before I began to think that he was making the game too easy, that even a man with such a round face and thick eyeglasses must have some experience of women. At first I suspected he was playing dumb to beguile me, and then I was back to thinking he wasn't particularly bright; but one day I hit on the answer. I realized he was trying to put me at my ease, hoping that at some point I would let a key detail slip and he would be able to use it to unlock the rest of my psyche. I told him what I thought, then added, 'My psyche is not a locked fortress, Dr Cole. It contains no buried treasure or deep, dark secrets. If you adopted a more traditional method of interview, I would do my best to answer your questions honestly, and I am sure you would find out everything you need to know.'

'An open book, are you!' he exclaimed. He seemed delighted by this idea and suggested we turn to the chapter on my parents. I told him about the family misfortune, hiding nothing at all. It took some time to give him the details of my father's fall from grace and my mother's slide into delusion. I had hardly started on my sister Miranda when he looked at his watch and said, 'I am sorry to say that our time is up,' but his tone of voice betrayed not the slightest regret. It seemed that this development was only another of the many delightful events that composed his day. I wondered where he was going next and whom he was interviewing, but then stopped myself, thinking that arousing my curiosity was part of the trap and that I should stick to my plan of methodically presenting the events of my life.

At our next meeting, he started in with a bold claim: 'So Mrs Grant represented to you the ideal mother.'

'I am a married woman, Dr Cole. I have no need of a mother.'

'But your own mother disappointed you.'

'I suppose she did, but life is full of disappointments, is it not? And by that time, I was perfectly capable of taking care of myself.'

'And how did you do that?'

I told him how I had found the rental house through our solicitor and how I had overseen the sale of our possessions and how eventually Henry had married me.

'Ah,' said Dr Cole, and I waited for him to go on, but he didn't. Was his great insight that women found themselves better off when married? I will never know, because when he spoke again, he said, 'Let's turn to the chapter on your sister,' and we both mentally turned the page. 'Did anyone in the boat remind you of her?'

I was amused by his attempt to identify the occupants of the lifeboat with family members, and I supposed that he was talking about Miranda, who seemed irrelevant, so that he could circle around to Mr Hardie and suggest that he had reminded me of my father. I laughed inwardly at the absurdity of this, but saw no reason not to play along. And, in fact, I had seen long before Dr Cole had suggested it that Miranda and Mary Ann were similar in many ways. Of course, Mary Ann was far more emotional than Miranda, but I had come to think that Mary Ann had the soul of a governess. I said, 'I suppose if I had to choose someone who reminded me of my sister, I would choose Mary Ann. I loved her, but she also made me angry, just the way Miranda did. I wanted more for my sister than she wanted for herself. As for Mary Ann, she was not marrying Robert to become something grand, but to firmly fix herself as something small, just the way Miranda would rather have the sure, small thing than gamble for a bigger prize.'

'And you are a gambler?' asked Dr Cole, which made me laugh outright.

We talked a little about Mary Ann and how, because she had reminded me of Miranda, I thought I knew how she would react to things. I thought I knew what she would say if I asked her if she liked children, if she liked them to sit on her lap and if she liked to read to them. I was not far off the mark: her eyes glowed with a distant, happy look, and she said, 'Robert and I plan to have children . . .' But then her voice trailed off as she realized this might never come to be. Of course I knew she was worrying that she would die at sea, but I chose to misunderstand her and to interpret her remark as a worry that Robert wouldn't wait for her or wouldn't want her for some reason after our ordeal. I replied, 'You could always be a governess. That way you could have lots of children, in a way,' and she looked at me oddly while a little tear made a track on her salty cheek. Later, she asked me if Henry and I didn't want children, and I replied that of course we did. But I wanted a child the way a queen wants one, as an heir rather than a plaything.

I told Dr Cole that I knew I was being unkind, but that Mary Ann provoked me and also that our nerves were frayed, which caused us to give voice to irritations that in normal circumstances we would have suppressed.

'What kind of irritations do you normally suppress?' he asked, which I, for some reason, found to be a highly irritating question.

'I suppose I am irritated right now,' I said, 'and if you hadn't asked, I would have suppressed the urge to say you remind me of my father, who was able to make a living for as long as his business partners supported him, but who was, ultimately, no match for their conniving schemes.'

I do not know what I was conveying by this banter, for half the things I said were motivated by the fact that I saw our encounters as a game, not as a means of delving into the mystery of the self. But my sessions with the doctor made the days go by more quickly, and I always returned to my cell refreshed, glad of the chance to talk to someone other than Florence, who had begun to think that the entire criminal justice system had been developed with the sole purpose of ensnaring her. She would whisper things like 'I'm sorry you got caught up in it, but you can see what's happening, can't you? They'll stop at nothing. You can see how they were after me from the start.'

Once she asked me if I had killed anyone, and I told her I supposed I had. Mostly I ignored her, but there were days when she pushed her face up against the bars of the cell for hours at a time, whispering things about her children or her husband or the judge in charge of her case; and occasionally something she said captured my interest. I had just returned to my cell from the bathhouse, and when the matron locked the door behind me, I thought I heard Florence say something about Dr Cole. She instantly had my attention, and I wondered for a moment if I should respond, and, if so, what I should say. Finally I called out, 'Excuse me? Did you say something?' but now she was on to something about an insanity defense and being transferred to an asylum, and I hesitated to ask anything more specific, which might have had the effect of telling her more about myself than I wanted her to know. A cold feeling came over me, and I began to suspect that Florence had been put in the cell across from mine to elicit information from me and pass it on to Dr Cole. I had assumed that Dr Cole had been hired solely for my benefit, but now I realized he might also be seeing others in the prison, and if he was seeing Florence, she might be telling him things about me.

This was a chilling thought, and I spent over an hour trying to think of anything I had said to Florence that might incriminate me, but I was not truly frightened until my mind progressed from the idea that Florence might be an informer to the corollary that Dr Cole might be telling Florence to plant ideas in my head that would throw me off-balance and make me reveal more in our sessions than I wanted to. This was the thought that kept me awake all night and left my nightdress soaked through with sweat. At the same time as I was thinking these things, I was also realizing that it was mad to think them. But if it was mad to think them, was my mind becoming unstable? It was the sort of circular track where one thought led to another and so on until I was back at the beginning and starting the thought loop all over again.

As I lay awake listening to the hollow echoings of the prison, I made an effort to think rationally, and it was that effort that led me to consider how being in prison works on the mind of a person just the way being in the lifeboat did. Up until then, I had not been unhappy to bide my time until the day I was released, for I had never really imagined that the charges against me might lead to some permanent change in my circumstances, that I might be executed or locked away until the day I died. I remembered telling Miranda once that life was a game, and I remembered how I had thought it amusing to banter back and forth with Dr Cole, but now I was severely shaken. Still, it is never a good idea to form any hard and fast opinions at night-time, which is a lesson I had learned during my family's ordeal and again on the lifeboat; and by the next morning much of my old equanimity had returned. After that, though, I had only to look at Florence to think about what might become of me if I didn't win my case. For the first time I thought seriously of my mother and wondered if somewhere in my psyche I harbored a lurking, susceptible gene.

I also became much more careful about what I said to Dr Cole. I decided I might find out more about Florence from him, and after telling him a little about her, I asked if such people had always been unbalanced or if they might be made that way by their circumstances.

'And what are this Florence person's circumstances?' he asked, betraying not the slightest evidence of whether he knew her or not.

'She has been locked in prison and accused of killing her children!' I cried, perhaps too forcefully, for I had already explained this to him and I didn't want to go over it all again.

'So they are much like yours,' he mused. His eyes were almost closed, giving the impression that he was pondering mightily and, really, talking to himself. While I didn't like to betray emotion in front of him, I threw up my hands in exasperation. But that is the way it is with Dr Cole. There is no subject that does not circle back to me.

THE LAW

I attended a hearing today in front of Judge Potter, during which the three sets of lawyers tried to get the charges against us dismissed. Mrs Grant, Hannah, and I had been charged with first-degree murder, which required not only that we had killed someone, but that the killing was the result of a deliberate design. Each side had already submitted a hefty brief that argued either for or against prosecution, and it was these to which the judge referred as he asked the lawyers his questions. I sat with Hannah and Mrs Grant on a pew-like bench from which we were allowed to observe the proceedings, but not to speak.

There followed a long discussion about whether or not it was murder for a man who clutched at a plank in order to keep his head above water to thrust away another who came after and would have taken it from him. Was it murder if the second man to arrive at the plank was successful in thrusting away the first? Does a charge of murder inevitably result from such a scenario, given that the men will naturally try to save themselves and that the plank can only support one man? Is the survivor doomed to spend the rest of his days in prison if he is caught and there are witnesses to his act?

'Surely not,' said Mr Reichmann. 'In this case no direct bodily harm has been done, and the loser has the chance of finding another plank.'

'I think prior claim is a relevant point,' said Hannah's lawyer, a gaunt and pallid man who looked like he never saw the sun.

'And what if bodily harm is done?' Mrs Grant's lawyer made a sharp contrast to Hannah's. He was robust to the point of severely straining the buttons on his coat. He had a cheerful face and ruddy complexion, but he smiled far too often, given the serious nature of the charges against us.

'But we are not talking about a mere plank, are we?' interjected the prosecutor, who was far too young to have had many life experiences and too brash to know it. 'A plank makes an entire boat look like a luxury. The two can hardly be equated. In the case of the plank, the men are in the water, making the life-and-death struggle far more immediate than it is for people in a boat. You say that the loser has the chance of finding another plank, but has the castaway from a lifeboat a chance of finding another boat? I think not.'

'In fact, there was another lifeboat in the area,' said Mr Reichmann. 'Lifeboat fourteen had nearly collided with it only hours before Mr Hardie was thrown overboard.' I had not thought of this myself, and I have to credit Mr Reichmann and his associates with the ability to dispassionately think through even the most oblique angle and most minute detail of the case. I tried to catch his eye to let him know the extent of my appreciation, but only succeeded in exchanging glances with Hannah's lawyer, who kept turning the bloodless oval of his face in my direction, craning his long neck at such a bizarre angle that it looked like his head was attached by a hinge. The extent of his interest caused me to wonder what Hannah might have told him about me.

'Besides,' Mr Reichmann continued, 'we know that at least ten lifeboats were successfully launched. Mr Hardie had a chance, albeit a small one, of finding his way into one of them. Is the chance of another plank in the first scenario any greater? And how are we to assess the chances of either scenario from this courtroom? What we are asking boils down to this question: Is the only way for a person who finds himself in an overcrowded lifeboat to avoid a guilty verdict to decide that all must sink or survive together? Is he permitted to make no move at all to save anyone, much less himself? And doesn't such passivity fly directly in the face of human nature and the instinct to survive?'

'I can imagine there might be some people who are noble enough to leave the lifeboat voluntarily,' said the prosecutor with an aggressive thrust of his pointed chin.

'Could they ask for volunteers?' asked Mrs Grant's lawyer.

'They can ask, I think, but they cannot require it,' said the prosecutor. 'There can be no pressure or coercion at all.'

The judge then asked if coercion arose merely in the asking and if there was a special duty assumed between a sailor and a passenger, and everybody agreed there was. 'However, no such duty exists on the side of the passengers toward each other,' put in the lawyer for Mrs Grant.

'Or on the part of the passengers toward the crew,' added Mr Reichmann gravely. 'But I keep coming back to the notion that the question is more properly asked "Shall some live?" rather than "Shall some die?" If you take for granted that some or all shall die if no action is taken, should an action be taken to save some? That, I think, is the proper question, and I don't see how you can fault my client for answering yes to that question, whether or not some other person might reasonably answer no.'

The prosecutor said, 'You assume there was some way of ascertaining whether the lives of some would actually be saved by any action the people in the boat might take. It was far more likely that life would only be prolonged rather than saved outright. Who could predict when the rescue might have occurred? Couldn't it as easily have occurred one hour after the taking of some irrevocable decision as after a day or a week?'

'You forget the storm,' said Mrs Grant's lawyer, who spoke glibly and seemed less prepared than the others. 'That brought the necessity down to a particular moment. For one thing, there was no likelihood of a rescue during the storm, for even if a ship were in the vicinity, there would have been no way for it to either see or approach the lifeboat in the violent weather. And for another, the storm itself made destruction of the over-crowded boat likely if not certain. The storm reduced the situation in the lifeboat to that of the men on the plank by making the life-and-death struggle as immediate as if the occupants were already flailing about in the water.'

'That may or may not be the case, but we are not now talking about the actions of Mr Hardie,' said the prosecutor, pointing out a failure in the man's logic that was obvious even to me. Until then, I had felt sorry for Hannah in her choice of the lawyer with the hinged neck, but now I felt sorry for Mrs Grant, for her lawyer had forgotten that the storm was over by the time we killed Mr Hardie, and indeed, the prosecutor went on to say, 'Mr Hardie was still in charge of things at the time of the storm. Whether or not his actions in arranging for the lottery were justifiable is open to question, but it is not a question this court has been convened to resolve.'

'Quite right,' said Hannah's lawyer. His too-long fingers fumbled through a sheaf of papers and extracted a particular one from the bottom of the stack. He held it up to the light, and a calculating look passed across his pale, oblong face. 'But if

Mr Hardie's actions can be condoned, then there might be grounds to condone the actions of the women, who were merely continuing a precedent set by someone else. Don't forget that the lifeboat had been damaged in the storm and that it was still taking on water at a rapid rate.'

'I don't think the rate can be established,' said the prosecutor.

'My point is that if emergency conditions existed in the case of the storm and in the case of the hypothetical plank, thereby allowing extreme courses of action, then such conditions also existed after the storm because of the damage sustained by the boat and the changed relationship between Mr Hardie and the rest of the group. By proving himself willing to sacrifice occupants of the boat, Mr Hardie had become an immediate threat.'

By this time I had completely revised my opinion of Hannah's lawyer, for he had taken the faulty logic of Mrs Grant's attorney and turned it to the advantage of us all. I could only admire his ability to see several steps ahead, when all I could do was to follow along behind the argument, hoping not to get lost in some byway of logic or law. Still, the man moved slowly and looked like he was made of putty, and I was glad that Mr Reichmann, with his staunch bearing, alert features, and retinue of assistants, was representing me. The pale man was gaining steam as he spoke, so that despite his wan and, really, sickly appearance, his delivery became more and more impassioned. His washed-out face began to glow and the black pupils and pinkish whites of his eyes resembled the coals and embers of an inner fire. He concluded by saying: 'And cannot the killing of Mr Hardie be seen as the overthrow of a malevolent ruler – a despot, if you will – in that little principality; a tyrannical autocrat who was endangering the lives of the people in his charge?'

The prosecutor replied, 'But didn't Mr Hardie express a reluctance, even an absolute unwillingness, to take the lives of women? If so, how did his actions regarding the lottery constitute an implied threat?' to which my very own Mr Reichmann responded, 'What about Mrs Cook? Didn't Mr Hardie, with his comments or suggestions, cause her to take her own life? And wasn't he slow to rescue Rebecca Frost? Didn't he, by those actions, include women in the list of people who were in immediate mortal danger due to his very presence in the boat?'

The prosecutor was a nimble man who rushed his words together as if the wheels of justice were turning very quickly and he had to hurry to keep up. He was nearly breathless as he said, 'We have contradictory statements regarding the events surrounding the death of Mrs Cook, and as for Rebecca Frost, it is reckless to conjecture that Mr Hardie purposely delayed in picking her up. In the telling of any story, it is possible to emphasize one particular aspect over another so that that aspect looms out of all proportion to the context.'

After perhaps an hour of such dialogue, Judge Potter said, 'In this discussion we, perhaps necessarily, keep straying from the general to the particular, and I must conclude that there is no general principle that can be derived to guide us in deciding whether or not it is generally permissible to jettison some passengers in order to save others. We must content ourselves with trying to decide whether it was permissible in this particular case, for the strange and anomalous facts of the situation are unlikely ever to be repeated. Each case must be decided upon its unique facts and merits and not by the application of some universal rule.' Thus the judge pronounced his jurisdiction over us. The majesty of the law was proclaimed, and we were cast upon its waters.

INNOCENCE

Perhaps it was the theoretical discussion about the plank and the other lifeboat that started the rumor that Mr Hardie was still alive. There was an item about it in the newspaper, which Mr Glover brought to the prison for me to read in contravention of a rule against giving anything to an inmate that hasn't been cleared in advance.

'If it were true,' he said, 'they couldn't charge you with murder.'

'Why not?' I asked, appalled by the idea that Mr Hardie might have clawed his way to the surface and found his way to shore.

'Because you wouldn't have killed anyone!' he said with some surprise, and only when I had thought it through did I realize that he was right, that it was only Mr Hardie's death for which we were being prosecuted, not for the deaths of anyone else in the boat, though I must admit it sometimes felt as if we were being blamed for the entire incident, shipwreck and all. When I understood what he was talking about, I was filled with irrational hope until I remembered how Hardie had repeatedly risen up in the water before he was finally lost to our sight. I could still see the black water dripping from his skeletal face. I could feel the wind sucking at my soul, and I didn't think I could bear any sort of resurrection where Mr Hardie was involved.

'It's a real possibility,' said Mr Glover. 'Some jewels that might be tied to the *Empress Alexandra* have surfaced in New York. Nothing at all is certain yet, but Mr Reichmann has assigned me the task of investigating the report.'

'If he is alive,' I said, 'I doubt he is filled with goodwill toward any of us. I don't imagine he'll show up at the trial and say, "I'm not dead after all, so no harm done. You can let these women go."'

'No, I don't suppose he will,' said Mr Glover, 'but he wouldn't have to. The very fact of his being alive would be enough.'

'I suppose we'd only be convicted of attempted murder, then,' I said. 'What is the penalty for that? And wouldn't Mr Hardie be subject to prosecution himself? The judge made it very clear that as a member of the ship's crew, he wasn't supposed to ask people to jump overboard the way he did.' I didn't say that Hardie was a wild man, perfectly useful in life-and-death situations, but unsuited to civilization. I didn't say that he would protect those who submitted to his care but would have no qualms at all about murdering anyone else, and that we had long since broken the bond that made us one of that protected class. I did suggest, however, that Hardie might have other stories to tell, even lies, about what had happened to some of the others. 'I wouldn't look for him too hard,' I said, shivering in spite of myself. 'After all, we did throw him out of the boat.'

'You have a point there,' said Mr Glover, looking at me with some concern. I realized that I was trembling uncontrollably and that Mr Glover was unsure of how to calm me, so I said, 'Even though I never want to lay eyes on Mr Hardie again, I suppose I hope he is alive.' I said it because that is what I thought Mr Glover wanted me to say. He would want me to say it because if Hardie were alive, it would mean I hadn't killed anyone, and I strongly sensed Mr Glover wanted to think of me without blood on my hands. Earlier that morning, I had considered asking him to look up Felicity Close and deliver a letter I had written to her, but I immediately thought better of it. I wanted to explain to her that I had loved Henry; that while his fortune is what had initially attracted me, I had loved him with all my heart. I wanted her to know this for Henry's sake, not for mine. But my instincts about what to say and when to hold back have always been keen, so I said nothing to Mr Glover about Felicity, and I later ripped up the letter and threw it away. Instead I repeated, 'I certainly hope Mr Hardie is alive!' as forcefully as I could, which freed Mr Glover to lay a comforting hand on my arm.

The next day, Mr Reichmann came to the prison to ask me two questions. First, he wanted to know if I had helped to push Mr Hardie out of the boat; and if the answer to that was yes, he wanted to know at what point I had decided to do it. 'I think I helped to push him out,' I answered tentatively. I asked him if he had read my journal, which I had given him over a week before, and he replied that he had; but now he asked me to go through the events that led to Mr Hardie's death one more time, for he was confused about whether I had made my way into the back of the boat with the intention of helping Hannah or with the intention of helping Mr Hardie. 'Perhaps you started out with the idea of helping the man you admired and whom you credited with saving your life. Perhaps Mr Hardie misread your intentions and started to struggle against you, and only then did your efforts shift to the support of Hannah.'

'You are right in thinking that as I moved through the boat I was not at all clear on what I hoped to accomplish.'

'So you moved almost automatically, as if you were following instructions?'

'I don't think it was automatic. I know I was thinking very hard at the time, wondering about the right thing to do.'

'So you wanted to do the right thing.'

'Yes! I wanted to help the person who . . .' I stopped myself, initially because I realized that I was going to sound very calculating if I said I wanted to help the person who had the most power in the boat. But I also became aware that Mr Reichmann was looking at me oddly, with a mixture of amusement and fascination on his face, and it occurred to me that he had given me the answer to his question and was wondering what was taking me so long to realize it. When I stopped talking so abruptly, his face clouded with a shadow of irritation. But I couldn't decide if it was irritation that I was slow to recognize the core of my defense or that I had caught myself before some truth escaped my lips. Or perhaps it was only irritation that the hour was getting late, for just then he took out his pocket watch, remarked on the time, and announced that he was late for a meeting with another client. 'We must make better use of our time together,' he said, sounding very much like Dr Cole, which in turn irritated me, for I did not like Dr Cole, whereas I was beginning to admire Mr Reichmann very much.

'Sleep on it,' he said. 'I think there is a very real possibility that you had no intention of participating in Mr Hardie's death and that you only decided to help Hannah at the last moment. If that is the case, it would be good to know before the hearing tomorrow. Tomorrow is when we have to enter our plea. Your co-defendants plan to plead self-defense, which means that they admit to the killing, but contend that they only killed because they saw Mr Hardie as a threat to their lives and to the lives of others. You must choose between not guilty by reason of self-defense and outright innocence. We will talk about it in the morning before we go to court.'

I spent a restless night going over and over the incident in my mind, searching for anything I might have forgotten or for new ways to interpret the events of that day. There was no question that Hannah and Mrs Grant intended to kill Mr Hardie. As for their claim that he had put us all in danger, I can only say that that argument was the only one they could make. Was it true? We were in grave danger, but had Mr Hardie's actions become a part of that danger? I think that once the two women had declared themselves against him, a dangerous situation existed in the boat, but was the blame for that really Hardie's or was it the fault of the two women for pushing an opposing point of view? And if it was the fault of the two women, did that mean that the only justifiable course of action for them would have been to sit passively in the boat and do what they were told, without anything to say about the best way to get ourselves rescued? But in the end, that was not the question I had to decide. I had only to decide what Mr Reichmann should tell the judge on my behalf.

At the courthouse the next morning, I was the one worried about the time. The hearing was set to begin at ten o'clock, but by quarter to ten, Mr Reichmann had yet to arrive. Hannah and Mrs Grant had gone off to conference rooms with their attorneys, and I was left to sit on a bench in a long hallway with the matron, alternately certain that Mr Reichmann would do nothing to jeopardize my case and filled with misgivings and doubt. 'Where is my attorney?' I asked the matron over and over again; and over and over she answered me in her kind Irish voice, 'He'll be here. I know Mr Reichmann, and he is as reliable as they come.' When he finally appeared, I swallowed my mounting anger and said, 'Are you all right? I worried that some accident had befallen you!'

He was all smiles, with none of the mixed signals of the day before. 'Don't worry, the hearing has been rescheduled for noon,' he told me as he placed his briefcase on the floor by his feet. It seemed that someone might have informed me of the change, but I was so filled with relief that I soon forgot the anguish his tardiness had caused me. The matron left us alone, and he sat next to me on the bench and said, 'Have you thought about what I asked you?' in such a way that I again sensed there was a correct answer to the question, and I was momentarily confused about what I was expected to say. I ended by telling him the truth, and I fervently hoped it coincided with what he wanted to hear. I looked into his eyes, which were no longer filled with amusement, but seemed to be deep, dark pools of concern, and said, 'When I went toward Mr Hardie and Hannah, I was not at all sure what I was going to do. I think I was seeking some course of action that would restore the atmosphere in the lifeboat to what it had been before Mrs Grant sought to prove that Mr Hardie was guilty of something. Of course that was folly on my part, for what could I, who was no match for any one of them, do to heal the rift that had opened and that threatened us all?'

'So we plead innocent!' cried Mr Reichmann, slapping his hand on his thigh. Seeing him so pleased with me made me happy in a strange way, but my happiness was clouded by a weird sensation that I was in the lifeboat again, that I was again choosing without really knowing the consequences of my choice; but the sensation was fleeting, and I walked calmly into the courtroom, glad that there was nothing more I needed to do, glad that I could now sit back and let Mr Reichmann do his work.

Throughout the fall and winter, Mr Glover continued to smuggle in articles about the wreck of the *Empress Alexandra*. Once, he brought me what was thought to be a complete list of the survivors, and while Hardie's name was absent, we agreed that there was no way of accounting for someone who didn't want to be found. Another time, he brought me an article that focused on the crew of the sunken ship. The article went on at some length about Captain Sutter, who had spent most of his forty-two years at sea and who had left behind a wife and two daughters. Just as my heart was clenching with sympathy on the daughters' behalf, the name Brian Blake jumped out at me from where it had been lying in wait a few sentences farther along. I asked Mr Glover to let me keep the paper and promised not to implicate him if the matron were to find it in my possession. When he had gone, I sat staring at the section I have transcribed here until it was time for supper.

> Captain Sutter was also a father figure to his crew. 'If you did the captain right, he'd do you right in return,' said William Smith, an officer on the *Empress Alexandra* and one of the few crewmembers to survive. 'Of course, you didn't want to cross him neither.'
>
> Smith recalled how another officer, named Brian Blake, had been arrested in London some years earlier on charges of receiving stolen property. 'The captain took it upon himself to clear Blake's name and prove that the evidence pointed to another man altogether. It shows the kind of man the captain was that when the other fellow was released from prison, Captain Sutter gave him a job,' he said.

It didn't seriously occur to me that the unnamed man was anyone other than John Hardie, and I lay awake that night trying to come up with explanations that accounted for William Smith's story and also for what I already knew about Hardie and Blake. Was there bad blood between the two men because of some incident where Hardie had been blamed for Blake's misdeeds, or had the men been partners in something underhanded for which Blake was lucky enough to be exonerated but Hardie wasn't? And if they had been partners at some point in the past, might they also have been partners when it came to removing a chest of gold from the safekeeping room of the *Empress Alexandra*? I knew firsthand that Blake had a key to the room, but he could never have carried the heavy chest alone. If the two men were busy with that enterprise, they would have been nowhere near the radio room and so would not have known that the wireless was broken and that no distress signals had been sent. This would explain their reluctance to leave the vicinity of the wreck. Finally, I asked myself if they were rescuing the gold on their own initiative or on orders from someone else, and I found I couldn't blame them for trying to steal the gold if that is in fact what they had done.

Just after dawn, I folded the newspaper clipping into a small square and tucked it under the edge of my mattress. I realized too late that Florence was awake and staring at me through the gloom. 'What's that?' she hissed. 'If you don't tell me, I'll call the matron.'

'What are you talking about, Florence?' I answered as calmly as I could. I didn't want the article to be taken from me. Perhaps I saw it as the key to something or perhaps I only felt about it the way all prisoners feel about their small store of possessions. In any case, trying to make sense of it gave me something to do.

'You put something under your mattress,' said Florence, poking her narrow face between the bars. 'I saw you do it. I saw it with my own two eyes.'

'Then you're seeing things again,' I replied, adding a note of concern to my voice. I knew that Florence desperately wanted to be believed, so I added: 'The matron will come to look and find nothing because nothing is there, and then she will have another reason to think you're insane.' Florence gave me her wounded look, but she became quiet, and just in time, for it wasn't two minutes later that the matron came through, ringing her bell.

Now and then I like to take the article out from where it is hidden and try to decipher it the way one would try to solve a riddle. It does serve to pass the time, but I haven't come to any firm conclusion about whether Hardie and Blake were co-conspirators or enemies. I think they were probably a little of both.

WITNESSES

Weeks passed while our lawyers collected evidence and prepared our case. During that time, I only saw Hannah and Mrs Grant when we were called in for a hearing, for they were confined in some other part of the prison; but now that the trial has started, I see them on the daily ride to and from the courthouse in the prison van. We say very little to one another, but several times during the ride and later in court, I have caught Mrs Grant eyeing me. At other times she seems to be whispering about me to Hannah, but there are long periods when her eyes are downcast or she stares off at nothing, and I wonder if she is still thinking the grand and powerful thoughts I imputed to her on the boat.

Every morning the route is the same: across a cobbled bridge, past a church with a tall steeple, then along a narrow street of brick buildings that glow blood-red when bathed in light from the rising sun. In the afternoon we travel the same route in reverse, but by then the houses have been drained of color and seem to be falling against their foundations more than their foundations seem to be holding them up. People hang listlessly about in doorways, waiting for fate. What are they thinking? Was it love or something else that made one brash young man pull the girl he was walking with into a doorway and kiss her on the lips?

Except for rare occasions, I do not talk to Hannah and Mrs Grant. My attorneys have instructed me to keep my own counsel, and for the most part I do. One exception to this was when we were being driven back to the jail after the first day of the trial. The two matrons who accompanied us were conversing with each other, and Hannah took the opportunity to say in what might have been a sarcastic tone, 'What do you think of the jury, Grace? Do you find them to your liking?'

Of course I had been curious to see the faces of the people who would be judging us, but apart from thinking that they looked a very usual lot, I had noticed nothing special about them. I replied that they seemed very fine and that I hoped they would listen to the facts with open minds and compassionate hearts.

'And how do they look so fine to you? Do you find them particularly handsome? Is that it?'

'By "fine", I meant alert and intelligent, I suppose. Just the sort of people one might expect.' Then I passed on to Hannah what Mr Reichmann had said to me about having been lucky that two of the jurors had relatives who had perished on the *Titanic*.

'Ah, yes! That is exceedingly lucky!' said Hannah. I was not at all sure what she meant, but I knew now that I was not the source of her anger; I only made a convenient target. Whenever I looked at Hannah I had trouble recognizing the woman from the lifeboat: what had seemed an independent and fierce spirit now seemed sullen and argumentative. Perhaps what I had admired had been suppressed by circumstance, or perhaps it had never existed except in my imagination. My thoughts on the matter changed from day to day, but I was concerned with much more pressing issues, and Hannah no longer seemed as important as she once had.

'Don't pay any attention to Hannah,' Mrs Grant said. 'She is merely upset that there are no female jurors.'

Foolishly, I exclaimed, 'But how could there be! Only voters are allowed to sit on juries, and women cannot vote!' It took me a moment to realize that I had made Hannah's point for her. I startled myself into silence, and for a while we trundled along without speaking. We were nearly at the place where I had seen the couple kissing when Hannah whispered, 'I am sure a jury of men suits you just fine, doesn't it?' But I only stared out the window and let her have the last word. It wasn't me she was angry at, and if the world needed changing before it would suit her, I could only wish her luck.

It was during another of these return trips that Hannah leaned toward me in order to be heard over the rattle of the van and whispered into my ear: 'You're not as weak as you pretend to be.'

Before the lifeboat, I had never had to consider

the notion of physical strength, at least in relation to myself; nevertheless, my stamina surprised me and was a great blessing. Of course, those who fell apart, either mentally or physically, were not prosecuted. Hannah and Mrs Grant pointed out that we were, if you looked at it a certain way, being punished for being strong, but I did not see it like that. When I had a chance to address the court at one of our hearings, I thanked the Lord for preserving me thus far and said I put my trust in Him and the jury to weigh the evidence and do what was right. The lawyers made the point that the three of us were hardly a threat to society – we had to be neither rehabilitated nor feared, for what was the likelihood that we would find ourselves in such a position again?

For those twenty-one days, I was surrounded by people losing their minds and expiring in the night, but this did not happen to me. I don't know why not. In his opening statement the prosecuting attorney asked, 'And why did you survive? Why did not the three of you succumb to the elements? Why didn't you become weak and sick like so many of the others? And wouldn't someone who was truly strong choose the nobler part and jump overboard in order to save others?'

'And who's truly noble?' asked Mrs Grant by way of reply. 'Are you?' Apparently she was not supposed to answer, and the judge tapped his gavel and told the jury her answer must be disregarded. When we exited the courthouse at the end of the day, a knot of reporters was waiting for us. 'Why did you survive?' they called out. 'Can you tell us the source of your strength?'

Later, Hannah stamped her foot against the floor of the prison van and cried, 'What is this, a witch trial? Is the only way we can prove our innocence by drowning?' I replied that perhaps there was a more profound point to be made about innocence, that perhaps a person could not be both alive and innocent, but Hannah gave me a cold look and went back to addressing Mrs Grant. Perhaps she was angry that I was the one who had answered the reporters' questions about why we had survived rather than perished. I could only reply – even though I had long since given up any semblance of traditional belief – 'The grace of God.' The next day the newspapers ran a headline in bold type: SAVING GRACE, it said, and underneath the headline was a short piece that conferred a sort of mystical meaning on my name.

From the beginning, the press and others were more sympathetic to me than they were to Mrs Grant and Hannah, who early on pointed this out, saying, 'Let's be honest, Grace. You're just innocent enough to get away with it.' Whenever anyone tells you a thing like that, you're bound to try to defend yourself, and I responded that she and Mrs Grant were the ones who were playing to an audience by insisting on going so far against the grain of the public's expectations. But eventually I had the realization that we all had to decide when to fight convention and when to accede to it, and in that, the three of us were not so different after all.

The chief witnesses against us were Mr Preston and Colonel Marsh. The Colonel's uniform was decorated with brightly colored ribbons and insignia of rank. He swore upon the Bible to tell the truth, then proceeded to relate a string of blatant lies. He testified that he had tried to protect Mr Hardie from us, but that he had been greatly outnumbered and was terrified the women would turn on him if he persisted in his opposition. I jumped to my feet, thinking the judge should know how Colonel Marsh had more than once argued with Mr Hardie about approaching the other lifeboats and how he had spoken out against him at the trial held by Mrs Grant; but Mr Glover pulled me back into my seat, where I sat in stunned silence as the Colonel informed the court that after we had pushed Mr Hardie out of the boat, we pushed out Mr Hoffman as well. The Colonel said, 'Mr Hardie presented a threat, all right, not to the women's safety, but to their status. It was clear from the beginning that Ursula Grant wanted to run things and that Mr Hardie and his staunch supporter Mr Hoffman were in the way.'

I fully expected Mr Preston to set the record straight as to the exact nature of our actions and the role the Colonel had played, but when he finally took the stand, his hands trembled as he put on his spectacles and he seemed unsure of himself. In any case, he was silent on that subject, and I suspect the prosecutor had cautioned him to leave out anything that the Colonel would not corroborate. After a while, he seemed to get his feet under him, and he was nearly his old sure self as he helped the prosecutor establish a timetable of events. He rattled off dates and quantities with great confidence, but without a coherent narrative connecting them, his testimony made little sense to me, and I could see the jury foreman shaking his head in confusion as he tried to keep all the facts and figures straight.

The prosecution's case against us took only a few days to present, after which it was the turn of the defense. The remaining Italian woman had gone back to Italy. No one knew if she was the one who had poked the bird wing into Mr Hardie's eyes or if that had been one of two who had died, but neither the prosecution nor the defense showed any interest in finding out. That left, besides the three of us, fourteen female survivors, twelve of whom either appeared in person to testify on our behalf or sent in sworn statements. All twelve said that if it weren't for Hannah and Mrs Grant they would be dead, even those who admitted that they could not reliably recount the events of that August day because of severe mental and physical exhaustion. Their statements were clearly rehearsed, for they all used the same words and phrases, such as 'Mr Hardie was undeniably insane and a danger to us all' and 'Mrs Grant was an island out there,' or 'a harbor,' and Hannah was 'the light that guided us to her.' They were unanimous in asserting that 'no one raised a hand against Mr Hoffman, who jumped out of the boat all by himself.'

Listening to them was like listening to the

members of a religious sect sing the praises of a beloved leader, and the newspapers dubbed them the 'Twelve Apostles' for their show of unwavering support. Throughout the repetitive testimony, Mrs Grant gazed at them with her characteristic concern, while Hannah shot them her serene high-priestess smile. This impressed even the judge, for I saw him staring at the two of them, amazed and maybe a little bit under their spell. I couldn't help thinking that the entire exhibition was an example of the kind of power Mrs Grant had over people and could only bolster my lawyer's claims that it was also the kind of power she had over me.

At first the prosecutor pestered the women with questions, trying to break the litany of 'I don't recall' and 'a harbor, a light,' but after the third one collapsed in tears, he stopped, realizing, I suppose, that he was the one who came out of it looking uncharitable and intent on causing pain to people who had already suffered enough. By then it must have been plain to everyone that the twelve women were banding together and coordinating their testimony because they thought we needed their protection, and why would we need their protection if we hadn't done anything wrong? This was an obvious point, and more than once, the members of the jury looked as if they were asking themselves that very question. Equally damning were the forceful lies of Colonel Marsh. Dressed in his full military regalia, the Colonel had made an impressive witness, and if

I hadn't known better, I would have believed him myself.

The only time one of the twelve women strayed from the script was when Mr Reichmann recalled Greta to the stand and asked her about my relationship with Hannah and Mrs Grant. He said, 'You all have been talking about Hannah West and Ursula Grant almost as if they were one person.'

'They thought alike on many things, and they worked closely together to see that the rest of the women were all right,' said Greta.

'What about the men? Did they tend to the men as well?'

'I think they assumed the men could take care of themselves.'

'But there are three defendants on trial here. Would you include Grace Winter as someone who also worked closely with the other two?'

'Quite the contrary. Grace was very aloof. She seemed to listen more to Mr Hardie than she did to Mrs Grant. We speculated that she was uneasy with the idea of a female leader. She was married to a powerful banker, you know, so maybe that explains it. I also thought she might have felt guilty about our predicament since she got into the boat after it was already full. If she was close to anybody, it was Mary Ann.'

Then he showed Greta the letter she had sent to me in which she had written, 'The lawyers say I shouldn't write to you at all, for it might look as if we are conspiring. Tell Mrs Grant not to worry, though. We all know exactly what to do!' and asked, 'Did you and the other women coordinate your testimony?'

'Of course not,' said Greta. Mr Reichmann's brilliance was such that it didn't matter what Greta said in answer to his question, and her denial allowed him to turn to the jury and say: 'You see the power Ursula Grant and Hannah West had over these women? Why wouldn't Grace be subject to the same influence?'

Who would have guessed that on the last day of the prosecution's rebuttal, Anya Robeson would appear and deliver the most damning testimony of all? She had taken part in nothing. She had not so much as lifted a finger to clear water out of the boat or care for the sick, but when she told this to the jury, it didn't sound reprehensible because she had the excuse of little Charles.

The prosecutor had provided a model of the lifeboat, complete with forty round holes drilled into it that allowed thirty-nine peg-like figures to be placed in the seats. The figures were labeled with the names of the survivors, and he handed several of them to Anya and asked her to place them in the seats they had occupied at the time of Mr Hardie's trial. Mr Reichmann objected to the entire exercise, saying that the forty drilled holes implied that the boat had been built for forty people, when he had established in prior testimony that the lifeboats had been built on a smaller scale than called for in the plans. After the objection was overruled, Anya placed the figure that represented Mary Ann next to the one that represented me. She found slots for Hannah, Mrs Grant, and Mr Hardie, then placed herself in the slot just astern of Mary Ann. 'They thought I wasn't aware of anything that was going on because of my preoccupation with my son,' she said, 'but I saw everything'; and she went on to damn the three of us. She described how, on orders from Mrs Grant, Hannah and I had fought with Mr Hardie, kicking him in the knees and legs until he collapsed in our arms. She told how Mary Ann had fallen away in a dead faint, but that the two of us were more than a match for Mr Hardie, who had a badly injured arm. One thing she was right about: we had hardly noticed her out there in the boat, but if you think about it, she had managed to save her son, which was the one thing she had set out to do.

Mr Reichmann then got her to testify that I had not voted to convict Mr Hardie the way most of the women had. In response to further questioning, she said that I had returned to my seat next to Mary Ann after Mr Hardie's death and had had very little to do with Hannah and Mrs Grant after that. She said she had been able to see both of us clearly and hear something of what we said to each other.

'And what did they say?'

'They had an argument, I think, for Mary Ann seemed very upset. But they must have made up their differences, for they were huddled together during most of the last few days except when Grace went to help Mr Nilsson with the steering.

In fact, Mary Ann was lying with her head in Grace's lap when she died. Mary Ann must have told Grace to take her engagement ring as a keepsake for Robert – Robert was Mary Ann's fiancé – for Grace slipped it onto her own finger before Mary Ann's body was disposed of.'

I listened to this part of the testimony with great interest, for I remembered very little about the days between Mr Hardie's death and our rescue nearly a week later, and I sometimes wondered what exactly had happened to Mary Ann. I vaguely remember thinking Robert would like to have Mary Ann's ring, but if I took it off her finger, I must have lost it, for I certainly don't have it now. After court had adjourned for the day, the full weight of the day's developments descended, and I said to Mr Reichmann, 'We're doomed. There's no chance of an acquittal after that!' His eyes were glittering with unreasonable glee as he pulled me into a recess in the corridor and said, 'What do you mean? That testimony about the voting was an incredible stroke of luck! And both Mrs Robeson and Greta did an admirable job in distinguishing you from the other two defendants. But why didn't you tell me about Mary Ann?'

'What about her?' I asked.

'That she was lying in your lap when she died!'

'Perhaps she was. That day is completely lost to me. You have my diary. It contains everything I can remember. If I could remember more, I would write it down, but I remember almost nothing at all about those last few days.'

'It's time you stopped acting so passive,' said Mr Reichmann, pulling on his coat and preparing to go off to wherever he went at the end of the day.

I drew myself up in a way I hadn't done in a long time, and when he had finished with his coat buttons, I looked him in the eye as an equal might do. 'Do you think I'm acting, Mr Reichmann?' He looked at me sharply for a moment, but then he winked and said, 'No, no, it couldn't have gone better today.' He hadn't answered my question, but his words filled me with irrational hope, so I wished him a warm good evening before I remembered that even if I had reason for optimism, I was not yet free. 'I suppose you're going home to a nice wife and a good dinner,' I said, trying to keep a tinge of bitterness out of my voice as I thought of all that Henry and I had lost.

'Oh, heavens no!' he exclaimed. 'A wife would merely get in my way.'

'Then you haven't yet met the right person. Everyone knows that behind every successful man is a woman. It's one of the reasons my Henry married me.'

'Never mind about me, you just worry about yourself. It's time you made some serious decisions regarding your future.'

Despite the grave nature of the charges against me, I had to laugh. Mr Reichmann was brilliant and very good at what he did, but he was still a man, and men rarely knew what decisions a woman had or hadn't made.

DECISIONS

I didn't mind that throughout the trial I was characterized as indecisive. It is true that I did not come out strongly either for or against the plan to kill Hardie. For this, I have been criticized by both sides; but whether it was the toll taken by those days in the lifeboat or whether it is not in my nature to feel strongly about such things, I can't really say. Even my marriage to Henry, which greatly pleased me for a variety of reasons, failed to provoke in me the continuous raptures of emotion that Mary Ann described whenever she spoke of Robert. Occasionally I felt something similar, but it wasn't a pleasant feeling – I likened it to hysteria, and I considered it something to be suppressed or controlled. Besides, look what happened to those who felt strongly and expressed it: the deacon threw himself overboard; Hardie and Mary Ann are dead; and Mrs Grant and Hannah are in jail. Of course, I am too, but I don't group myself with them now and never did.

Besides, when it appeared that Mrs Grant would get her way, I easily decided to throw my lot in with her and the rest of them, and in the end, only Mr Hoffman remained steadfast in his support of Hardie. Once I had decided, I did not waffle back and forth or regret my decision. I was not forced to do this, and despite the urgings of my lawyer, I could not testify to being compelled to join the women through explicit or implicit threat of bodily harm. He had to content himself with saying, 'Imagine yourself in Grace's predicament, confined with these powerful women in a twenty-three-foot boat, surrounded by nothing but open sea. You had just seen a man condemned to death by these very women. Wouldn't you too, in fear for your life, do whatever it was they asked of you?'

I would not testify that this is what went through my mind when I pushed Mr Hardie out of the boat. I even contradicted Mr Reichmann when it eventually came my turn to take the stand, but he turned to the jury box and said, 'It's obvious that she is still afraid of them.'

This line of questioning came up several times during the trial. At one point the prosecutor asked me if any of the women were ever directly threatened by Mr Hardie, and I had to reply in the negative. My own attorney then turned the question around and asked me if I had ever been threatened by Hannah or Mrs Grant, clearly implying that if I had refused to go along with them, I might have suffered the same fate as Mr Hardie. 'Not directly threatened, no,' I answered. 'Did you, at any time, fear for your life?' he then asked me. 'Yes' was my answer, for of course I was filled with fear from the moment of the explosion on board the *Empress Alexandra*. Even after I had answered, Mr Reichmann kept asking related questions in an increasingly hostile tone. 'Mrs Winter, I think you're lying. Did you feel threatened?' he demanded again and again, startling me with his vehemence.

'Yes!' I finally cried out, 'I felt threatened every day!' and only later did I realize that the genius of Mr Reichmann's technique was to induce the jury to wrongly infer from the juxtaposition of the answers that I was afraid of Hannah and Mrs Grant.

During the next recess, Mr Reichmann took me aside and told me, 'You survived out there in the boat, now you have to survive in here. And don't make the mistake of thinking the situation is any different now.'

'What do you mean?' I asked. He gave me a very knowing look, the kind of look the lawyers gave each other during questionable testimony and the kind that continually passed between Hannah and Mrs Grant, both in the courtroom and in the boat. He said, 'If you have to sacrifice someone to save yourself, I guarantee you won't be prosecuted for it this time.'

In preparing me for my testimony, Mr Reichmann had spent several days asking me a series of questions that Mr Ligget and Mr Glover had prepared. The two junior lawyers hovered in the background; then one or the other of them would play the role of the prosecutor and ask a different, more aggressive, sort of question. Throughout this process, even the wan Mr Ligget would be transformed: his pale features would twist and his red lips would curl into a terrifying sneer. I sent an injured look toward Mr Glover, who had always been kind and gone out of his way to reassure me, but he merely avoided my eyes, as if he did not notice me at all. When it came his turn to play the part of the prosecutor and ask me questions, I detected a barely suppressed delight that he was now the master in some way, as if our roles had undergone a reversal and he was punishing me for some perceived slight of which I had been entirely unaware. I could not help feeling that he was not as mild of personality as I had supposed, and it was a relief when Mr Reichmann took over the questioning again, for he was unfailingly respectful and kind in all of the practice sessions, always playing himself, always my unwavering advocate in the face of the prosecution, so ably represented by his associates. On several occasions he complimented me on my 'diary,' saying it had been helpful in preparing our case; but it was everyone's opinion that it should not be entered into evidence.

Because of these rehearsals, I knew to expect that the prosecutors would ask me difficult questions, that they would try to get me to incriminate myself by blurting out some detail of my actions that I had not yet admitted to. But of course, there was nothing new to admit, and while I found the process upsetting, I came out of it fairly well. What I was not prepared for was to have Mr Reichmann, who had been so unemotional and even placid during our rehearsals, turn on me with a vehemence that shook me to my core. His booming voice rattled the light fixtures, and at one point he slammed a book against the table so hard that the judge had to bang his gavel and remind him that I was not a hostile witness and that he should calm down.

By the end of the day, I was limp with fatigue, and when Mr Reichmann smiled exultantly at me and mouthed the words 'I'm sorry,' I wasn't sure what to think.

I was the first of the defendants to testify, and I felt a vast relief when it was finished. If I had made a positive impact on the jury, it was impossible to tell from their faces. Exhausted and perilously close to tears, I lowered my eyes. My hands shook, and I realized that my strength, so depleted by the weeks in the lifeboat, had not fully returned and that, in comparison to my co-defendants, I must seem miserable and weak.

When I look back on it, I see that Mr Reichmann had sought from the very beginning to distinguish me from the other two women, and it is true that Mrs Grant presents a fearful sight. She dresses in nothing but black. Her hair, which in the boat had been pulled back into a tight knot, is now nearly shorn, and though the ordeal left her twenty pounds lighter, she is still robust, and it is easy to see why the others clung to her as if she were the earth itself. There was no talk of Mr Grant or any little Grants – she existed alone. She alone did not cry for what was lost. Neither did she cry at the trial, and, of course, this went against her. Hannah is tall and gaunt and has an angry, dangerous look about her. She confided in me that her attorneys tried to get her to soften her appearance for the trial and wear the sort of dresses I wear to court, but she would hear none of it and continues to wear trousers. I was only too happy to listen to advice on this score: I alternate between a dove-gray suit and a dark blue dress with a high collar and lace at the cuffs that were purchased for me by my attorneys, with what money I do not know. Hannah told me she possesses several dresses in gray and green that her husband had brought to her all the way from Chicago, but she wouldn't wear them. It was a shock to me to find out she is married, for never once had she mentioned it. There was a rumor that she wouldn't meet with her husband and intended to divorce him, but she never said this to me. Neither did she try to disguise the scar that makes a red line down her cheek. Instead of inspiring sympathy, it makes her look like a pirate, but when I suggested this to her, she replied, 'A pirate, am I? Then the way I look on the outside matches the sentiments of my heart.'

Before I entered the lifeboat, I never thought much about the sea, not even when I was crossing it on the *Empress Alexandra*. Then it was merely a picturesque backdrop for my life with Henry, at most a wash of changing blue or a choppy inconvenience, the cause of nausea, perhaps, but not real sickness; and I sometimes believe I was forced – or chosen – to endure twenty-one days in a lifeboat so that I would never again think of nature as a garden for man and so that I would never again think of power as the thing Henry possessed when he pocketed the keys to the vault or the authority wielded by Judge Potter, who was the magistrate in charge of our case.

As the event recedes in time, and as theories, stories, rumors and testimony accrete to it, it becomes less clear, less a matter of any objective reality – ocean or sky or hunger or cold – and more a stew of armchair commentary by newspapermen and moralists. There is no one who has not had his say about it, which causes Hannah to wonder why the casual observations of others carry any weight at all. I don't know. I can't help but wonder what Henry would have thought. Henry was as decisive as they come. We could have used him in the boat, and I often think about how things would have turned out if he had been with me. Surely, with my husband at my side, I would not have been accused of anything, certainly not of being, in the words of the newspapers, 'anti-man.'

I miss Henry. With him, I felt that character was less of a requirement in me, as his character was so well defined and unyielding. Above all, with Henry I felt safe, which is ironic because if we had not met, I would never have had occasion to board the *Empress Alexandra*. Without him I feel exposed and completely subject to the judgments of others. There has probably been much written about this – I wouldn't know, for it is not the kind of reading I do – but I can't help but think that people were meant to pair off, to face things together, to be married. The benefits can even be seen in the example of Hannah and Mrs Grant, in the strength they have found in each other, though of course they aren't married and never could be. In any case, of all of us, they formed the strongest bond, and it is they who were hurt least by the experience. Of course, they are in jail, which is bound to make up for any hurt they failed to suffer at sea, but I mean they seemed the ones least hurt by the ordeal in the lifeboat itself. Sometimes I wonder if they would have been incarcerated if Mrs Grant had been a man.

One night, while I was looking out over the black water under the endless canopy of stars and admiring the tiny luminescences of marine life, too tiny to describe accurately except in the cumulative effect large masses of them had, I stopped being terrified. I had always envisioned God as hovering somewhere above us, smiling or frowning down from above the clouds depending on His mood and whether He was pleased with us or not, perhaps inhabiting the sun or blowing storms violently out of His cheeks to wake us up from our torpor and deter us from deceit. Now, however, I knew He was in the sea, lurking there, hand in hand with Hardie, rising up in those big waves and splashing down random pieces of Himself on our boat.

I planned to say nothing of this at the trial, for I have witnessed enough to know that personal revelation is alternately seen as heretical and insane, but I mentioned it during one of my conversations with Mr Reichmann, who said belief in God was a good strategy, that I should go ahead and use it if I liked as long as I kept out some of the specifics, for faith was something the jury understood. 'They understand nothing,' I started to say, but instead I held my tongue.

Without the deacon to point out the spiritual way – if somewhat somberly for my taste – I was constrained to try to see it for myself. I tried to remember snippets of the Bible, of sermons that made an impression on me, but hardly any had as I was not a particularly attentive listener, being more of a visual person or, really, more of a person who does things than one who endlessly contemplates them. I remembered the light streaming through the stained glass, the shiny, just-washed hair of the girls in the choir, the children fidgeting in their seats until they were finally released to the Sunday Bible class, the sudden hush when they were gone and how I longed to be gone with them even after I was grown. I remembered the purple and white costume worn by the minister and the fancy hats worn by the ladies of the parish more than I remember anything that was said.

After three weeks in the lifeboat and two more in a courtroom on trial for my life, I listen more attentively now. I heard, for instance, when Mrs Grant told Hannah to make her way forward to look inside the barrel for a wooden box, even though I pretended not to hear. I heard it when the judge refused to allow Hannah to testify about what Mary Ann had told her about some jewels she thought to be in Mr Hardie's possession, calling it hearsay and uncorroborated evidence. I heard Dr Cole call me weak of will and suggestible, and I heard Mr Reichmann when he said he supposed not all wives were alike. And when the jury pronounced me not guilty, I heard it as clearly as I had heard the foghorn on the seventh day.

Hannah and Mrs Grant were found guilty of premeditated murder, and it wasn't until they were being led away by the matron that I felt as if some last chain were being stretched until it could no longer stand the strain and finally snapped. I watched after them, but only Hannah looked back. There was something in her eyes of the old fire, and I was sorry to think I was probably seeing her for the last time. The judge said, 'Mrs Winter, you are free to go,' but I stood fixed to a spot near the defense table, watching the court stenographer pack up his things while the benches of the court emptied around me. This took some time, for the court was bursting with people who had gathered to hear the verdict. Eventually, only my lawyers and I were left in the cavernous and echoing room. Mr Glover seemed eager to take me to a celebratory lunch. I started to turn toward Mr Reichmann, wondering if he would accompany us, but his solid presence was no longer by my elbow, and I had a strange and unsettling intuition of what my new freedom might really mean.

Some of my emotions must have shown on my face, for Mr Glover was just reaching out his arm to support me – and I was on the verge of taking it – when Mr Reichmann materialized in a dim corner of the room, talking to an elegant woman who was rising from her seat. For all that I had tried to picture her face, I had never imagined her to be smiling, but she was smiling now. 'Thank you, Mr Glover,' I said, withdrawing my arm and rewarding his worried look with a smile. 'I am quite all right now.' I drew myself up and did my best to ignore the beating of my heart. While I had always imagined a different sort of entrance into society, I reminded myself that I was Mrs Henry Winter and that this was not the time or place to let my husband down.

RESCUE

The day after Hardie's death dawned bright and clear. Mrs Grant pulled a comb out of her bag and had Hannah fix our hair into braids and knots so it didn't stream into our faces. The sun shone for two days running, which allowed us to dry the blankets, but made us lose moisture very rapidly through our skin.

There were now twenty-eight occupants in the boat. Mrs Grant chose new seats for us in order to redistribute our weight, then asked the men to put up the sail, and we steered for England or maybe France. The wind was steady in the west, and soon we were making brisk headway through the water. I was ordered aft, where I was supposed to spell Mr Nilsson at the rudder, a task at which I proved to be highly ineffective. This was the first time I had occasion to observe Mr Nilsson close up, and I saw that he was a young man who had only appeared older by virtue of his air of knowledge and authority, which he had now entirely lost. When I asked him to show me how to work the tiller, he looked at me like a frightened rabbit and said only, 'You must hold it in the opposite direction from where you want to go,' and he demonstrated by pushing the tiller so that the rudder moved and stirred up a frothy wake. When I told him he was bleeding and offered to wipe away the blood, he drew away from my touch, again with that frightened-rabbit look.

I spent most of my energy merely trying to keep hold of the tiller, but I can't say I was truly steering; and once, perhaps because of something I did, the rudder popped loose from its fastening pins and we almost lost it to the sea. On several occasions I suffered from a vertigo that might have taken me overboard if Mr Nilsson had not grabbed my shoulder and pulled me back. This task took all of my physical and mental resolve, so I was mostly unaware of what others in the boat were doing. After some time had passed, Greta switched places with me, and some time later, we switched back.

Amazingly, very little water came into the boat. We kept the hole in the hull patched as best we could, and, of course, the boat was much lighter now with fewer people in it and those people mere shadows of their former selves. When the wind died, our forward progress stalled, and we lay about the boat without the strength or will to do the first thing to look out for ourselves. Only Mrs Grant sat upright, glaring out over the horizon for signs of ships or peering over the rail in hopes of seeing a fish in the now dead-calm and translucent water.

Once, we spotted a whale in the distance. 'Oh,'

said Hannah with a skeletal little laugh, 'a whale would last us a good long time.' She closed her eyes and stretched her hands out over the water as she murmured some kind of whale-catching incantation, but of course a whale would have knocked the lot of us into the ocean once and for all. Colonel Marsh called it a leviathan and went on to tell a disjointed story about a book of that name and someone called Thomas Hobbes who believed that people are moved primarily by desire for power and fear of others. He said, 'Hobbes believed that everything that happens can be predicted by exact scientific laws and that such laws govern human nature and force people to act selfishly to preserve themselves.'

'I don't see how that helps us,' Mrs McCain replied. Then she and everyone else re-entered the separate and silent chambers where we spent most of our time. I don't think anyone thought past the lifeboat. We finally accepted it. It was where we lived.

I alternated between sitting next to Mr Nilsson, where I clutched at the tiller, and sitting in my usual place next to Mary Ann. There are still gaps in my memory, but while I was waiting for the jury to return its verdict, I tried to fill them in. I think it was two or three days after Hardie's death that Mary Ann became ill. I must have been ill too, for I remember shivering with her, huddling in against her bony shoulder, falling against her exactly as she fell against me. Every once in a while, someone would be pronounced dead, and those who could summon the strength helped to heave their bodies over the rail. I can't remember who realized that Mary Ann hadn't moved in a long time, and later that morning she joined the others who had been consigned to the sea.

At one point, Mr Nilsson suggested that the bodies of the dead could be used for food, but Mrs Grant put a stop to such discussions, and no one mentioned it again. I remembered what Mr Preston had said about survival and the will to live, and I wondered if any of us still possessed it. We spoke very little, and as I think back, I suspect any words I remember saying were mere hallucinations. My tongue was swollen, and without enough moisture, my saliva had gone from being thick and foul-tasting to non-existent, so that my tongue sat in my mouth like a dead animal, no longer supple and quick, but parched and cracking, like a dried and hairless mouse. My eyes, too, felt sticky and dry, and when I stood in the boat to make my way to the forward blankets or back to the rudder, I seemed to have lost the ability to tell up from down. Bursts of light and inky blots of darkness obscured my vision, as if I were floating in a dark and starry sky. I was often faint, and I fell once into Mrs McCain's arms and knocked her over. We lay together in an awkward embrace, too depleted to right ourselves, and we might have stayed that way if Mrs Grant hadn't shouted at us to come to our senses.

The boundary between sleep and consciousness had become blurred, and I was never entirely sure what constituted a dream and what reality. The most frightening example of this was when I was struck with the realization that Henry had been in the lifeboat with us for the entire time, but we had all been mistaken about his identity. He had, I realized with mounting horror, put on a ship's uniform and taken the name of Mr Hardie in order to get into the lifeboat with me. This meant that the person I had helped to kill was Henry! I pulled myself along the railing until I was sitting next to Hannah. I was trembling with a panic I had never before known as I said, 'I don't think Mr Hardie was one of the ship's crew after all.'

'Who was he, then?' she asked me.

'Henry!' I whispered, trying to form the words with my uncooperative tongue. 'I think we killed Henry!' I would have cried, but my body had no moisture for tears.

'No, no,' she crooned, putting her rough hand to the side of my face. 'We didn't kill Henry. Henry wasn't in our boat.' That was when I woke up, if I had been asleep, or when I came to my senses if I had been awake already. I found myself sitting beside Hannah, who had her eyes closed and was slumped against my shoulder, as I was slumped against hers. For the rest of the day, I wandered the halls of my Winter Palace, more like a ghost than an architect.

Later that evening, or maybe the next, the

heavens opened up and water poured forth in glassy sheets. It took us several minutes to realize what was happening and nearly half an hour of bumbling to lower the sail enough to divert the water that fell on it into the empty casks the way Hardie had shown us. Our severely weakened state made this all but impossible, but at the end of the downpour, we had drunk our fill to the point of retching and we had a good amount of water in reserve for whatever future remained to us.

During those last days in the lifeboat, the rigid structure of our existence disintegrated entirely. Mrs Grant did not enforce Mr Hardie's roster of duties, and if something needed doing, she did it herself, or Hannah did it, for if she did ask something of one of the rest of us, we were mostly too weak and dispirited to comply. We made no more attempts to sail – it was almost as if Mrs Grant's resolve had depended upon Hardie's opposition for its force.

Either that day or the next one or the one after that, an Icelandic fishing boat appeared on the horizon and picked us up. This point was belabored at the trial: How long after Hardie went overboard were we rescued? How many days did we go without water? I don't know precisely, but the exercise of creating this journal convinces me that the fishing boat appeared one week after Hardie died. Hannah also claimed to know: 'Nine days,' she said under oath. In its summation, the prosecution said it was significant that we disagreed among ourselves and made the case that the time period was shorter, a mere day or two perhaps, which would have made Hardie's death 'unnecessary, frivolous, and undeniably a criminal act.'

We did not notice until the Icelandic fishermen tried to lift them that two of the Italian women were dead. The third clung to her companions as if they were part of herself, but Mrs Grant said something to her and she finally let the fishermen drop the stinking corpses over the side. I remember strong hands pulling at me, and I remember my unwillingness to let go of the tiller that had been put in my charge. I remember the overpowering smell of fish from the hold of the fishing boat and the respectful demeanor of the captain and his crew, who, rough and unshaven as they were, seemed to represent the height of chivalry and civilization.

The fishermen were solicitous of our health and gave us the best of their food. We were on the fishing boat for two days, which were spent looking for other lifeboats while we waited for a mail packet that was to take us to Boston. Mr Nilsson stayed with the fishing boat, saying he would go to Iceland with them and from there make his way to Stockholm. The rest of us were on the second boat for another five days, so by the time we reached Boston, some of our strength had returned to us. I think it hurt our case, because the first impression we made on the authorities was not one of near-starvation. By the time of the trial, the fishermen were back in Iceland, and we had only the written statement of the captain, who had never envisioned that we would be arrested and charged.

When Dr Cole asked me to tell him about the rescue, it was hard to find words for my feelings on seeing the fishing boat emerge from the mist like a dream. I told him that I would keep the memory in a treasure box for times when life seems bleak, for I experienced a mixture of joy and amazement that I have never felt before or since. He then asked, 'Are you hoping for an Icelandic fishing boat to appear on the horizon now that you are facing trial?' and I replied that of course one already had – didn't he fancy himself its captain?

Isabelle, who was very serious and devout, insisted that we touch not a morsel of our food before giving thanks, so at mealtimes, we spent long minutes bowed over our cooling plates and listening to her enumerate the many things we had to be thankful for. While she thanked the sea, which had buoyed and sustained us even as it threatened us, and then the fish and the birds, which had offered themselves for our use, and finally the people who had died so that we might live, I said my own inward prayer that some miracle might still bring Henry to safety. Others would interrupt to voice their own prayers, and I understood that they, too, were superstitiously making last-ditch bargains on behalf of loved ones while trying not to sound as if they had not been given enough already.

I wondered how long their newfound piety would last, which reminded me of something Mr Sinclair had once said. 'Those who create a deity must also destroy him,' he told me before going on to say that man's relationship with God replays the life cycle. 'When we are babies,' he said, 'we need an authoritative figure to guide and take care of us. We ask no questions about that authority and imagine that the small circumference of our family life is the limit of the universe and that what we see before us is what exists everywhere and also that it is all as it should be. As we mature, our horizon expands and we begin to question. This continues until we either throw over our creators – our parents – for good and take their place as the creative force in our own lives or find replacements for them because the terror and responsibility are too great. People go one way or the other, and this accounts for all of the great personal and political divides throughout history.'

I admired the sweeping nature of his statement, how it included all people in every era and admitted no tiresome nuances or exceptions. After our rescue, I saw how all of us had been reduced to helpless children by our ordeal, but at the time of my conversation with Mr Sinclair, I found myself considering what he said more as it pertained to Miranda and me in the family of our birth than to anything grander or more encompassing.

Miranda sought to replace our parents with an external authority, while I was happy to be free of them. When I said this to Mr Sinclair, he replied: 'You have an unusual strength,' and whether I did or not, just hearing him suggest it made me feel stronger than I was, which is a testament to the power of words.

A day later, Mr Sinclair took up the subject again as if no time at all had passed, even though much had happened in between, including the entire drama of Rebecca Frost's rescue. 'But Grace,' he said, 'if you are so much more independent than your sister, how do you explain Henry?' I had always thought of Mr Sinclair with the highest regard, and up until then, I had also thought of him as my friend and mentor, for everything he had said to me before that point indicated that he harbored only warm feelings for me. Now he seemed to be questioning something, although I wasn't quite sure what it was.

'I love Henry,' I said. 'I am sure that on both sides of your personality divide there is room for love and companionship.' I wanted to emphasize the point, but I am not always quick with words, so it took me a minute before I added: 'I do not think that the only way to show courage is to face the world alone.'

'Nor do I. But you must admit that it is only in lonely and challenging circumstances that our true natures show through.'

'And are we being challenged enough for you

yet?' I asked somewhat archly, and he replied that indeed we were. I bowed my head to hide my confusion, and when I looked up again, I was startled to see that Hannah was staring directly at me. My skin ran hot and then cold, and I nearly forgot all about Mr Sinclair, who was looking at me too – not unkindly, I think – but it was Hannah's gaze that held me; and I stammered some reply about not being as glib with language as he was, but that I appreciated his attempts to bring rigor to my thinking. 'We are all being tested, Mr Sinclair, and I hope that my underlying nature, which I am sure has been completely bared by now, meets with your approval,' but it was not his approval I sought that day.

Hannah kept looking at me throughout that afternoon, and one time she said, 'Grace.' Only that one word – my name – with no message attached to it, simply 'Grace.'

But on the mail packet, I joined the others in thanking God and credited him with the ability to save Henry just the way he had saved me. Gradually, we gained strength, and on our last evening before reaching Boston, instead of her usual prayer, Isabelle insisted that we remember the deacon and Mr Sinclair, who had willingly sacrificed themselves for us. In the deacon's memory, she led us in a recitation of the 'Song of the Sea', which he had taught us what seemed a lifetime before so that we might recite it when we were rescued. The only part I remember now is this: *And with the blast of Thy nostrils the waters were piled up. The floods stood upright as a heap; the deeps were congealed in the heart of the sea.* It seems a fair description of what we experienced, and I was glad Isabelle thought of it, for the rest of us would certainly have forgotten. The ship we were on was carrying ten other passengers, and now they gathered around as we recited what must have seemed to them a bloody and partisan account where God saves Moses and the Israelites and drowns everybody else. But I suppose it is in man's nature to feel special, and we were no different than the Israelites in that regard.

The land rose from the water almost magically, and while the others flocked to the railing of the boat, I hung back, wondering if anyone had come to meet me. The captain of the mail steamer had been in constant communication with the authorities, and by that time we had a good idea of who had survived the shipwreck and who had not. Mary Ann's mother had been rescued nearly two weeks before, but there was no mention of Henry Winter or Brian Blake. Even though I knew that Henry's name was not on the list of survivors, part of my mind was obsessed with the idea that he would be waiting for me when I got to shore.

The land was blue-green, obscured at first by a thin haze. Then the blue-green resolved into colors that included the red of a lighthouse and the bright hulls of anchored boats. All around me were exclamations: 'Lord have mercy!' shouted someone, and

Mrs McCain, who had brushed past me in her haste to stand at the rail, shouted, 'At last, civilization!' But what I saw before me were not social structures and cultural achievements. I saw something more natural and inexplicable, not some opposite of the sea, the way solids and voids are opposites or the way life is the opposite of death, but some extension of it. Perhaps I had a premonition about what was to come, or perhaps my perceptions were merely colored with worry about what might await me: Was I to be accepted by Henry's family or rejected outright? If I were to be rejected, where would I stay? I imagined I could go back to the house where I had lived with my mother, and while I could hardly think of that without a profound feeling of dejection, I steeled myself with the thought that at least I wasn't dead, and that with life came hope. But hope had always seemed to me like a weak emotion, a kind of pleading passivity or entrenched denial; and as the tree-lined beach neared and spread before us like Moses's promised land, I determined not to become victim of it. We had been told that rooms had been reserved for us at a hotel and that doctors were available to examine us, so I knew I had a day or two to plan where I would go and what I would do, never imagining the turn events would take.

I was the last of the survivors to make my way down the gangway to stand on the wharf in Boston Harbor. The first step onto the graying and weathered timbers was like stepping onto a rocking boat, so unused were we to walking on a firm surface. The sight of my fellow passengers trying to keep their balance was comical, and our laughter was as much an expression of our joy at being on land as of our awareness of how unsuited we had become to walk on it. I stopped once, halfway down the long incline, to look back at the glimmering lagoon of the harbor. Above me, the captain of the mail packet was standing at the railing before turning his attention to his crew and to whatever preparations needed to be made for wherever he was going next. He stood with his hands on his hips, squinting into the morning sun that streamed in golden bursts from between the clouds, and gazed after us – after me, I liked to think. We looked at each other for a long moment, and in him I saw Mr Hardie, though the two men were nothing alike. Where Hardie had been dark and slight, the captain of the mail steamer was tall and had an air of substance and refinement that Mr Hardie lacked. Our eyes met. I lifted my hand partway and he, in return, lifted his and gave me a kind of salute. It was exactly the gesture Mr Hardie had given Henry the day the *Empress Alexandra* sank and Henry had approached him on the deck and he and Hardie had exchanged words, which I didn't hear except to ascertain that some kind of transaction had taken place, for Henry had that look of fixed concentration he had adopted in the London shops where he had bought me the jewels and dresses that were now lost. Then Henry had backed off and raised his hand the way I was raising mine now, and Mr Hardie had saluted with one hand while he tucked the other inside his jacket. The gold buttons of his uniform glinted in the sunlight. His seaman's cap sat firmly on his head. His cheeks, clean-shaven at the time, were hollow even then, and his deep-set eyes were dark and inscrutable.

I nodded. The captain of the mail packet tipped his chin in return, and that is the last I saw of him. I turned from him just as he turned from me; then I walked with the same uncertain steps as the others down the rest of the gangway. By the time I had traversed the wharf and put my foot on firm soil, my steps no longer faltered, and even when I realized that no one had come to meet me, I walked steadily toward whatever the future might hold.

EPILOGUE

Acquittal has not solved everything, though I suppose the situation is worse for Mrs Grant and Hannah, whose sentences were commuted to life in prison. Dr Cole has suggested I expand the notes I made for my defense, saying that what I need now is psychological acquittal. 'How many times do I have to tell you I don't feel guilty!' I exclaimed, heartily sick of the good doctor. Of course there are things I want to forget, but I wonder if it is wise to continue to dwell on them. If only I could forget, for instance, the deafening roar of the wind and waves, the puny *slap slap slap* of the wooden boat against the boundless majesty of the sea, those sticks of oars that got us nowhere, the black-green immensity that ever threatened to engulf us. Forget the sight of Rebecca's hair spread out over the water before she went under and the relief I felt when at first she failed to reappear. Forget, most of all, my own temptation to interfere with fate and the sick, dead weight of Mrs Fleming on my lap and later of Mary Ann. Hannah and Mrs Grant, at least, were capable of making a plan and seeing it through, but I could make no hard and fast decisions. More than once I wished Anya Robeson would hide me under her coat with little Charles.

As I write this, there is word that a transatlantic steamship called the *Lusitania* was sunk by German submarines that were sliding darkly beneath the waters of the Irish Sea. The news made me wonder if our ship had been an early victim of the war, but the authorities were quick to say it wasn't, for both the timing and location were wrong; and even if it had been, would that have changed anything? I smile to myself to think how Mr Sinclair would have answered with a resounding 'No!' but I am not sure I agree with him. The authorities aren't right about everything, and it still gives me a sense of importance to think my life was shattered because I was caught in the crossfire between powerful nations rather than because of carelessness or greed.

After I had wrestled Hardie out of the boat, it was my turn to lie, exhausted, with my head in Mary Ann's lap. I slept fitfully and awoke with a start, thinking that Mary Ann was talking to me. 'I only pretended to faint,' I heard her say. 'I could never kill anyone, but of course Mrs Grant never had any doubts about you.' Later in the night she said, 'I'll tell them who did it if we're ever rescued. I'll tell them it was you, and I'll tell them about the jewelry and how you bought your way onto the boat.'

'There was no jewelry, Mary Ann,' I said or

didn't say, for such was the erratic nature of my thoughts that it was as likely to have been a nightmare as something that had actually taken place.

For nearly a year now Dr Cole has been harping on the events of the lifeboat. He is beginning to sound exactly like the prosecuting attorney. I have told him I won't talk about the lifeboat any more. Of course it affected me, but not in the way he thinks! This he refuses to accept. I don't see how reliving every day again in detail will reveal the source of my anxiety, which stems far more from the trial and worry about my future than from anything that happened out there. It was not the sea that was cruel, but the people. Why should any of us be surprised by that? Why did the jury sit there with their jaws hanging open and their eyes popping out? Why did the reporters follow us like hungry dogs? Children! I thought. I would never be a child again.

I have lost patience with the idea of an insignificant human being standing up above the rest of us – whether he is called Reverend or Doctor or Judge – and shouting at us all about this thing or that. As soon as someone starts to pontificate in this way, I am apt to cut him off or leave the room, or, if this can't be done gracefully, I simply arrange that sweet vapid smile on my face that was so useful during the trial but that so infuriates Dr Cole. After all, I have already taken the measure of my own insignificance, and I survived.

When I said something to this effect, Dr Cole

began lecturing me about guilt and saying that people are not responsible for the good or ill fortune that befalls them. I keep telling him I do not wonder 'Why me?' any more than I wonder about the accident of my birth. Rather, I feel both lucky and unlucky about it, suffused with a sort of happiness as it has opened up a whole new world to me, one quite devoid of dependencies on other people, devoid even of the fear of death and belief in God, though this could be exactly what baffles him; and it occurs to me that Dr Cole is as interested in curing himself as he is in curing me.

Today I told Dr Cole I am going away, though I am not yet entirely sure where I will go. 'But our work is not finished!' he cried. I said I was about to embark on a grand new adventure now that this one was done. 'You're getting married!' he exclaimed.

'How unimaginative you are! There are endless possibilities. There's no telling what I might do,' I said, and I felt very free and relieved as I said it, but I fear that the world is as unimaginative as he and that I will have to accept Mr Reichmann's proposal of marriage for want of a better plan. Henry's mother has been asking me to come to New York, and at some point I will visit her, but I keep putting it off. Is it strange that what had seemed a crucial element of my future no longer seems to figure into it at all?

'You'll never find inner peace if you don't resolve

your ambivalence toward the lifeboat . . . towards me,' Dr Cole started to say, but I replied that I had already found inner peace. Life at that moment again seemed like a game to me, a game I might even win, mainly because I had been acquitted and I hadn't made any other irrevocable choices yet. No doubt I soon would. One couldn't inhabit the knife-edge cusp of possibility for long without stepping off on one side or the other, as my experiences in the lifeboat had unambiguously shown. Did I get butterflies of happiness in William's presence? No, but he professed to get them in mine, and it made me happy that he did.

I had heard from Greta again, who wrote that the women from the lifeboat were collecting money for Hannah's and Mrs Grant's appeals. Did I want to contribute? Furthermore, they wanted me to use my influence to persuade Mr Reichmann not only to take their cases, but also to reduce his fee. The previous day I had sat for a long while over my notebook, drafting a reply – several replies, in fact. In one, I offered them any assistance within my power and in another I asked how people who had not only implicated me in their crime but later turned against me could ask for my help. In yet a third, I politely and distantly wished them well and promised nothing. I told Dr Cole about the three letters and asked his opinion about which to send. 'Which one do you want to send?' he asked, as I had known he would.

'Of course, I have no money to give them,' I

said. I honestly wished them well, but I did not want William spending the first year of our marriage immersed in the events of a time that was now behind me.

Unlike the dank prison room where we had met, Dr Cole's office was large and airy and had a bank of windows that overlooked the harbor. I spent the last minutes of our time together gazing out at the water, which was frothy with white caps. In the distance, a fleet of small sailing vessels scudded like graceful birds before the wind. 'You're smiling,' said Dr Cole. 'Yes,' I replied. 'I suppose I am.'

I was wearing a new silk dress and it rustled magnificently when I stood up to go before the allotted hour was up. I said, 'You will have to find your answers without me,' which made him tap his fountain pen so hard in frustration that it left a large blot of ink on his compulsive little page of notes. If I had not felt so sorry for him, I would have laughed out loud at his desire to pin everything down, at his naiveté, at his childish desire to know.